Praise for *Made of Honor,* the first title in The Sassy Sistahood series by Marilynn Griffith

"Griffith's debut is engaging, and Dana's relationship with God follows a refreshing course."
—*Romantic Times BOOKreviews*

"With honesty and humor, Marilynn Griffith takes you on a poignant journey through the pages of life— yours or someone you know. *Made of Honor* is a spellbinding tale about the power of love between family and friends, with one's romantic soul mate, and from the Lover of our souls."
—Stacy Hawkins Adams, bestselling author of *Speak to M' Heart* and *Nothing but the Right Thing*

"Marilynn Griffith digs deep inside to write a novel abou' yday people who love the Lord."
haunda C. Hoffman, editor, *Shades of Romance* magazine

"With a voice that begs you to relax, sit down and put your feet up, Marilynn Griffith writes of the complexities of love, family, friendship and what it means to be the bride of Christ, and does so with honesty, humor, and grace."
—Lisa Samson, Christy® Award-winning author of *The Church Ladies, Songbird* and *Club Sandwich*

For my husband, Fill.
You are a grace to me.

How beautiful are the feet of those who bring good news!
—*Romans* 10:15

MARILYNN GRIFFITH

If the Shoe Fits

Steeple
Hill
Café

Published by Steeple Hill Books™

STEEPLE HILL BOOKS

ISBN-13: 978-0-373-78576-6
ISBN-10:   0-373-78576-3

IF THE SHOE FITS

This edition published by arrangement with Steeple Hill Books.

® and TM are trademarks of Steeple Hill Books, used under license. Trademarks indicated with ® are registered in the United States Patent and Trademark Office, the Canadian Trade Marks Office and in other countries.

www.SteepleHill.com

Printed in U.S.A.

Acknowledgments:

Love, patience, prayer and a lot of good people's time go into making a book a reality. This one is no different. For anyone that I neglect to name, please know that I do thank you and I thank God for bringing you into my life.

Special thanks to:

Christ, thank You for seeking me when I hide, for covering my bumpy life with Your shoes of peace. Thank You for loving me.

Fill, for your quiet strength and unwavering love. Without your support, I couldn't do any of this. You're the best.

Ashlie, Michelle, Fill, Jr., Ben, James, John and Isaiah, thanks for putting up with me working on this through the holidays and for praying for me. I love you all.

My mother, Donna McElrath, thank you for working so hard to take care of me, for sacrificing your own desires so I could make it. May God continue to bless you.

Kent and Debbie Nottingham and the women's Bible study of Calvary Chapel Tallahassee, for always giving me a fresh understanding of God's Word.

My editor, Diane Dietz, for loving my work enough to make it the best it can be; and the Steeple Hill team, for working so hard on my behalf.

Claudia Griffith, my mother-in-law, whose diligent faith inspires me.

Claudia Burney, for pushing me when I wanted to give up. Thanks for loving this book and for writing books that inspire me.

Jessica Ferguson, for being my best critic and my cheerleader in hard times. I never could have done this without you.

My friends, Joy, Melissa and Gail, thanks for tolerating my silences and disappearances. Each of you is a gift to me.

The ladies of The Threshing Floor: Amy, Jennifer and Staci, thanks for your great feedback and support.

To Heather, Angie, Lisa, Claudia, Bobbie, Paula and all my friends in the blogosphere. Thanks for the encouragement.

Chapter one

I kicked him before I knew it.

Right on the chin.

"Lord have mercy, Rochelle done knocked the boy's teeth out, ain't she?" Deacon Rivers made the declaration in earnest, but he didn't take his feet out of his own basin to get up and help the victim. Getting his feet washed seemed to suit the deacon just fine.

Mother Holloway, the head of the Seniors Bible Study and grandmother to my son's pregnant girlfriend, tightened her grip around the deacon's ankle, probably to get him to stop staring at my toes—the Rochelle Gardner secret feet I'd been pretty much hiding all these years. He ignored the old woman's grip and made a sour face. "I see why you make shoes, honey. Them's some tore-up feet. You earned those the hard way."

If anyone else had said that to me, I would have been totally humiliated, but coming from Deacon Rivers, I knew it was a compliment. Hard work ranked high with him. (Right up there with beauty.)

Tad McGovern, my partner in this surprise foot washing, rubbed his face where I'd kicked him. He smiled at me, which made me feel even more embarrassed.

Mother Holloway pushed her plastic bowl away from us, jerking the deacon's legs a little as she went.

"Hey! Don't be all rough now, Mother. My feet ain't that dirty. I soaked them in Epsom salts last night." He looked at me hopefully. "You should try that, Chelle. It might help some of those corns. And Tad, I'm sorry she kicked you, but you should have warned the girl that a foot washing would be a part of the lesson this morning. Everybody knows how she is about them feet." He grasped at his pants leg before it rolled down into the water.

Mother Holloway, probably the one who'd suggested this madness, winked at me. She'd do anything to get some Biblically justifiable physical contact with Deacon Rivers. (I'd spent the past two years trying to convince him that the seniors study would probably minister to him better. His response? "Isn't that for old people?")

Anyway, like Deacon Rivers said, somebody could have warned me. Everybody at Broken Bread Fellowship *knows* how I am about my feet.

Everybody it seems…except Tad, who despite sitting next to me in church for ten years and co-leading the singles group with me for five, had somehow missed my foot phobia.

That roundhouse kick I'd laid on his chin would help him remember in the future. How awful. I'd actually kicked a man down in the Sunday school room. And I still wasn't sure why. By the time my toes met his jaw, Tad had already seen my feet. It must have been reflex from so many years of trying to keep my feet under wraps. He'd pulled off my shoe and my foot had shot out like lightning. If only I could move that fast in my workouts.

From the way Tad was wiggling his jaw, he seemed okay but was definitely thinking about something. Probably having me committed. Everyone else in the room, all married couples who headed up various ministries, save Mother Holloway and the deacon, hadn't given Tad's exclamation of pain more than a glance. Those folks were having foot-washing church and couldn't be bothered with us other than to glance over and check for blood.

I, on the other hand, was having a meltdown, something I'd grown used to since hearing the news that my handsome Christian son had a child on the way. First a grandmother before forty and now my crazy toes had been seen by Tad the Harvard Grad and the leaders of all the church ministries. And Tad seemed very happy about it, despite me almost decapitating him with my foot. If he knew how dangerous these feet really were, he wouldn't be smiling.

Tad steepled his fingers under his chin. "Ready to try this again? Minus the kick, of course."

My hand slipped from my mouth, allowing another apology to escape. "I am so sorry."

Tad stood easily. The towel he'd borrowed from the baptismal font remained girded around his waist though a little crooked from his fall. That towel, the truth in his eyes and six days a week of Tae Bo had put my trigger foot on notice. There was too much Jesus in this foot-washing business, too much intimacy—one of Tad's favorite subjects in the single's group was finding intimacy with God, not a girl or guy.

"It's okay, Rochelle," Tad said, kneeling in front of me again. He grabbed my heel and tugged, sweeping off my other shoe this time with a sure but gentle grip. I wiggled my ankle, but he held on, dragging the bowl of water toward us with his other hand. This time, he was smart enough not to look up at me. Despite my kung fu moves, this man was determined to make his point—real leaders got their hands dirty, real servants wash feet.

My breath tangled into a knot in my throat as he emptied a familiar envelope into the tub. Eucalyptus and rose petals fluttered in a shower of chamomile tea. Lemon zest stuck to the tops of my ankles, sifted between my toes. It was Shoes of Peace, the foot soak that my friend Dana Rose named after my shop.

I'd been flattered when my best friend gave me my own scent among the goodies in her bath and body store, so much so that I included it in my care kits for first-time customers at my shoe boutique. People raved about how soft the blend made their feet, but I'd never thought to buy any. Not that I didn't trust my girl or anything—these feet just require some industrial-strength stuff. Now, as the brisk sweetness flooded my mind, I made a mental note to buy a box of it.

Evidently, Thaddeus McGovern, the local weather anchor, adult Sunday school teacher and the most handsome and most annoying bachelor in our church, had already made a note to buy some, marking his first kindness that didn't in some way benefit him in a long time. (Let's plan a singles trip…to the meteorology center. I'd like to meet with some other weather people there. Not.)

Tad was acting different and it scared me. His arrogance had always kept me safe from him. Now he wanted to go and get all deep? Ever since our talk a few months before about the unexpected return of my son's father and my definitely unexpected grandchild on the way, Tad seemed to treat me different, shouldering my load of the work with the singles group and covering for me at meetings, all the things I'd done for him over the past years.

All that was nice, but a foot washing? Come on. If I hadn't been daydreaming about having my bunions removed when he passed out the bowls and towels, I would have run for my life. It still sounded like a good plan. Running, I mean. When he squeezed the sponge over my ankles, it was definitely time to go.

"You know what, Tad? I can't do this. If I'd known ahead of time, I would have—"

"What? Washed your feet at home? Cleaned up before you came? No. This quarter's theme is about leadership, service, being last to become first. It's about washing souls—and soles. Please, let me serve you. You do so much for the church."

A rose petal snagged on the hump on my big toe. I dunked my foot to set it free. Perhaps to set me free, too. The pleading that rushed beneath Tad's usually condescending tone scared me more than the sight of my toes. What did Dana keep telling me? *Stop trying to control everything, just roll with it sometimes.*

Roll with it.

Whatever wheels I was supposed to be using felt like squares instead of circles, but I was determined to see this through. Sunday school ended in thirty minutes anyway. The worst part was over. They'd all seen my feet now. My heart groped for words, but there was nothing sensible, suitable to say. Another apology spilled out as his chin began to swell. How would he mask that on the news tonight? "I'm sorry. About kicking you, I mean. Do you need some ice?"

How many times are you going to apologize?

He grinned wide, revealing his dimples. "I'm okay, but you kicked me pretty good. Thankfully, you missed all the good stuff." He motioned toward his head.

From here, it all looked like good stuff. Though usually a total jerk, Tad was ridiculously fine. From his spidery lashes to his cleft chin and square jaw, he was born for the camera. Usually though, his performances—on- and off-screen—were sadly lacking. Today, his acting was a little too convincing.

He touched my second toe, the Little Piggy Who Stayed Home, the digit most responsible for the knuckled imprints in all my shoes. I concentrated on the kindness in his hands, nicer than the firm rap of the pedicure lady at the mall. Still… I flirted with the thought of running to the parking lot screaming like a lunatic.

My foot slipped from his hands as I turned the thought over in my mind, deleting the screaming and concentrating on the running. A bit of pinkish water sloshed over the side of the bowl—which I now realized was a kitty litter container—and onto the floor. My head turned real slow, as if it weighed five hundred pounds. I was doing it again, thinking crazy things. "I'm so sorry. It was a reflex. I have a thing about my feet—"

"Me, too." He paused, smiled at me. His news-at-eleven smile, only better. Special. "I have a thing about my *own* feet, I mean. Don't worry, I won't kick you when you wash mine." A chuckle whistled through his lips.

I didn't find it funny. Wash his? Why hadn't that occurred to me? Service definitely meant doing for others, but in this case, I'd have to pass. Seeing my own feet was bad enough. The Little Piggy That Ate Roast Beef curled back as reality dawned on me. My whole left foot drew up like a fist. "You know what? No offense, but I'd rather not wash your feet. Or have you wash mine."

Tad kept scrubbing, all while staring at my bumpy toes. "That's okay. I understand. But I'd appreciate it if you'd let me finish."

I grimaced, doubting I'd ever be able to look him in the face again.

The others around us, except Deacon Rivers and Mother Holloway, of course, worked quietly, ushering in the wings of morning, the edges of heaven, in muffled prayers and quiet sobs. Deacon Rivers's surprise at Mother Holloway's "pretty dogs" punctuated the harmony of soft sobs, whispered prayers and the sound of water lapping in the plastic bowls.

A woman who'd confided in me weeks earlier of her plans to leave her husband wept as she held on to his ankles. We'd gone through the Scriptures, she and I, but this touch, this tenderness, preached a much better sermon. He pulled her up beside him and they held each other, staring with eyes as wet as their bare feet. The music minister's wife grunted in approval as her husband scrubbed her heels gently, praying as he went. They too had recently come close to parting.

My heart leaped, both at Tad's touch and the kiss of Christ on this place, affection I wasn't prepared for, an exchange I wasn't ready to accept. Still, tears threatened. I'd come to church today determined to resign from the singles group, the choir, everything. I'd come sure I had nothing left to give, that there was no point in even trying. And after many years of debating about what to do with my feet (it's a little nutty to own a shoe boutique and have Frankenstein toes), I'd decided to take my podiatrist's advice and have my toes broken, using the time I usually spent on everyone else to recover.

A year ago, I never would have considered doing something like this. Service to my church, family, friends and customers was the call of my life. Then my son's father came back into our lives and my best friend had a stroke and almost died. My son moved out of my house and into his dad's apartment with his pregnant girlfriend. Everything that I'd hung my heart on, my faith on, seemed turned inside out, leaving me to wonder if I'd been trying to work for God instead of walk with Him.

Who knew? Perhaps the podiatrist could not only fix my feet but redeem something from the gnarled mess that had become my life. I certainly couldn't. All I could do was try and protect myself, create a little safe space. That was all I'd come to church for today, to redeem the time, to set some boundaries in my life.

Tad came for something else entirely.

To wash my feet.

And to take my turn teaching Sunday school. This quarter, the pastor had implemented a new program for the lay leaders. Each ministry in the church, deacons and deaconesses, women's auxiliary, singles group, seniors fellowship, married enrichment group, music ministers, children's department and everybody in between, would take a turn teaching Sunday school to a class made up of peer leaders. Tad had surprised me last week by calling to say that he'd take today's entire lesson.

I was relieved then, calculating the extra minutes I'd have to run through my choir solo and check with my ministry volunteers. For a moment, I was a little miffed that Tad responded to the pastor's edict but never called to help with any of the programs *I* put together. Why can't I just be thankful? It never dawned on me that Tad had something like this planned. It wasn't as if we communicated verbally enough for me to read him. Though we interacted often, today was the most words we'd shared at one time since that talk earlier in the summer about my son.

Instead we spoke in actions, a language of Secret Santa gifts and assigned seats in the choir stand. We shared a silent and frustrating loyalty, both to each other and to the church. Ours was a bottomless desire to outserve, outgive and outsuffer everyone else, including each other. A need that I wanted to eliminate from my life, starting today.

I'd probably never stop serving in church completely but with a grandchild on the way and my son's father in the congregation every Sunday with his diamond-dipped girlfriend, the unending well of my Christian love seemed to be running dry. I needed to take Dana's advice and let God be good to me for a while, maybe even be good to myself. It didn't seem likely than anyone else was planning to take on the job. At least not until this morning. Now I wasn't so sure I wanted anyone to. This was just weird.

Though we were president (me) and vice president (him) of Brothers and Sisters in Christ (BASIC), Tad usually looked past me, as if too busy to give me his full attention. Today though, another man lived in his skin—a towel-brandishing, knee-bending, foot-washing man.

His towel hung from one side of his waistband now, like a child's napkin at a barbecue. He tugged it free and tossed it to the floor before tapping my ankle for me to lift my foot out of the tub. How he knew to do that I didn't know. Did he get pedicures too?

Too embarrassed to look at him any longer, I stared at my sunshine shoes, the yellow peekaboo pumps I'd made for Dana's wedding but had only been brave enough to wear today, three months later. Now, I longed for a pair of fuzzy slippers. They'd be easier to escape with. I'd tried to roll with it, but this was ridiculous. "I appreciate what you're trying to do, but I have to go."

I struggled to get up, but Tad held my foot, massaged my heel. He took a deep breath. "Wait… Listen."

The rhythm of Mother Holloway's humming my favorite hymn, the music minister praying under his breath, someone's wife crying behind me, and the splashes of simple service moved me, moved through me. It started as a shiver at first, then a stream and finally a flood. The room faded as I shut my eyes, letting the sacred sounds close in on me. Who knew that feet could bring such peace to a place?

Warmth poured over my ankles, flowed between my toes. That Tad. Sneaky. I sat in my chair, head buried in my hands. If he'd only stopped there, I could have endured it, pretended none of it had happened. But as always, Tad went too far.

"You have beautiful feet, Rochelle, the Gospel-spreading, life-giving kind, the kind that make it to the finish line." He said it loud, in his tornado-warning voice.

Mother Holloway stopped humming. I stopped sitting, dropping my unopened Bible from my lap as I stood. The book splashed Tad's face as it thudded into the water. The black cover peeled back and released the gold-edged pages, billowing at first, then bloating.

Tad grabbed the book and squeezed as though saving a life. And he *was* saving a life. Mine. From the cover, bought by my son as a boy, to the notes scribbled in the margin on almost every page, that book contained the past ten years of my life and all God's promises for my future. Still, I went for my shoes, to run, to save my heart. To save my mind.

"Wait." He held out the damp Bible. When I took it, he held it with me, knowing I wouldn't stay. Everyone was looking at us, listening, but he didn't seem to care. "Really, Rochelle, your feet are beautiful. So are you." He released his grip on my Bible, but tightened the grip on my heart. Why had he waited until today, when I was giving up on everything, to get all brave? I held the wet stack of pages in front of me like a shield and headed for the door.

"If that boy thinks those feet are pretty, Chelle, you'd better marry him. No offense, sugar." Mother Holloway's voice followed me to the door.

None taken, I thought, unable to speak. As for marrying Tad or anyone else, the thought that had always been laughable before became painful now. Why was Tad saying stuff like this now, when it was too late? When whatever shred of womanhood had that survived seventeen years of single parenting, entrepreneurship, church service and a really bad attempt at having a boyfriend last year lay dead on the bottom of my heart. It was best to leave it there. Sometimes it's been too long for a resurrection.

On his arrival, Jesus found that Lazarus had already been in the tomb for four days.

Now at the door, I looked back at Tad, still kneeling and reaching out with those long copper fingers. He was looking at me, his lips curved into a waning moon full of starbright teeth. "Thanks for coming. You have so much to offer." He whispered it, but again, everyone heard.

I stabbed my feet farther into my shoes, grinding my toes into place. Water dotted the canary leather like tears. My own tears refused to fall. After months of crying for everyone else, I had no tears left for myself.

Tad's smile, a small one, was like a boy with a secret, a man with a plan. I stepped into the hall, reminding myself of how other women in the church had been sucked into a web of mixed messages and ended up with broken hearts and, in some cases, broken faith.

A thousands Sundays of hide-and-seek with Tad had taught me never to put my trust in him. Or my hope. Our game stayed the same each week. ("It's good to see you, Sister Rochelle." "And you.") Stolen glances that would have rendered lesser souls legally blind would follow, but never anything more, unless you counted that February eight years ago when he held my hand for four Sundays in a row. He'd made up for his slip by ignoring me for months, like he'd probably do after today.

On my way to the car, I reminded myself of that, as well as how cruel he'd been to say those things in front of some of the main grinders of the church rumor mill. I'd spend the rest of the year explaining that we weren't dating, but things like that never occurred to him. I stepped painfully toward the car, trying not to think about the Bible leaking through my dress. How could I start over without my notes? My thoughts? Tad's thoughts came to me instead.

Gospel-spreading feet.

Yeah, these tootsies could spread cement from here to Mexico. In fact, they'd tried to do just that. When pregnant with my son, the doctor had advised cutting back at work as my feet swelled and my not-so-sensible shoes cramped. Determined to show my teenage heartthrob (who I was sure would marry me at any moment) that I wasn't a lazy woman,

I ignored the doctor's advice and worked *more,* not less. If my son's father was impressed, he had a sorry way of show-ing it, going to the bathroom during my labor and never re-turning.

The next time I saw him was on a TV screen as he drank and fought his way through a few stormy years in professional basketball. Though it'd hurt to see him in magazines with pretty women on his arm, the money he sent (a couple hun-dred thousand, which I invested in design school, my home, my shoe boutique and Dana's shop) was helpful. One day the money stopped and the only man I'd ever loved or made love to disappeared from the face of the earth. I realized quickly that he might not ever come back. Might not save me.

It was then that Jesus revealed Himself to me, a God more than willing to be my husband, my son's father and my clos-est friend. For years, I gave myself freely to Christ without regret, except for my secret, that somewhere in a nursing home in Mexico my son's father slumbered in a coma like a male version of Sleeping Beauty. From the returns on my well-invested funds, I paid for his monthly care, each night secretly praying the same prayer, *Let today be the day, Lord. Let Jordan wake up and come home.*

Instead, Jordan's sister Dana, who'd shared parenting chores with me since her teen years, and Tracey, another friend and former neighbor, filled much of my void for companionship. Though we'd spent time together online as the Sassy Sista-hood, we became something more, sisters in Christ. When Dana found out last year about her brother and, worse yet, about me knowing about her brother's condition and whereabouts, our relationship was a little strained. Okay, so a *lot* strained. We're close still but in a different, more distant way. For one thing, she's married now. Talk about changing relationship dynamics…

Anyway, about Jordan. Though I continued to pay for his care, Jordan coming home drifted away from me with all my other happily-ever-after dreams. Many times, I almost told Dana that I knew where her brother was and what had happened to him, but I never could find the right words. Last year, Jordan woke up and found the words himself, coming home to turn my son's head and break my heart all over again.

Working too hard to keep a man had broken these feet in the first place, broken my heart. I couldn't let that happen again. Not for anyone. Not even intelligent, handsome, aggravating Tad.

And He will be called Wonderful Counselor, Mighty God, Everlasting Father, Prince of Peace.

The Scripture leaked from my mind into one of the puddles I passed on the way to my car. I paused at the trash can near my trunk and slipped off my shoes.

Afraid that some thrifty deaconess would rescue the yellow pumps and put them in the clothes bank, forcing me to see the stain of this morning on the feet of a stranger, I gripped the shoes to my chest along with my soggy Bible. Tomorrow's trash pickup at home was a safer option, one that ensured I'd never see those sunshine shoes again.

Chapter two

My son, his father, my son's girlfriend—the whole crew of fools—awaited me at home. I didn't even get to squish the rest of the water out of my Bible before facing them.

"Hi-eeee," Shemika said, waving with one hand and covering her watermelon-size belly with the other. She bowed her head quickly, nibbling one of the emergency croissants from my freezer.

I dumped my wet shoes beside the door next to the others. I took in the scene in disbelief. Not only had these folks invaded my home—with the help of my son's key, no doubt—they'd kicked off their shoes and cooked themselves some breakfast, too.

The nerve.

Still armed with my wet Bible, I grabbed the empty plastic bag my croissants had come in and wrapped the Bible in it. It was a total loss, but I was too afraid to throw it away. I have a thing about Bibles, too. As ink blurred in the margins and bled across the pages, I bled inside too. I'd meant to get a new Bible sometime, but not now. Not yet. Everything was changing without my permission. Sort of like my unexpected guests.

I turned to my son's father, eating eggs at my kitchen table as though he belonged there. As many times as I'd envisioned him in that seat, the sight bothered me now.

"How did you get in here, Jordan?" I knew already, of course, but I wanted to let all of them know that keying into my home and waiting for me was unacceptable.

"Well, we—"

"Leave Dad out of it, Mom. It's my fault. I used my key." My son, Jericho, stood, hands shoved into his jeans.

"Dad? It's like that now? That's rich." About as rich as his father, whose gifts seemed to have worn away any of my son's remaining brain cells. Sure it was great that Jordan was here today, but what about when he disappeared again?

"Can we not start with that? What's with you anyway? Are those the sunshine shoes?" He pointed to my wet pumps by the door.

"That's them. It's a long story. Sunday school was, well, interesting. I had to come home." I looked over at Shemika. "Your grandmother had a good time, though."

"I'm sure." Shemika shrugged and gave me the same guilty smile she'd worn since her pregnancy started showing. Today though, something different played around her eyes. Maybe the reality I'd been trying to describe to them was finally sinking in.

My son didn't look as amused. "Church? Is that really it?

You seem really out of it. And is that your Bible wrapped up over there? The one that you write in?"

Jordan stopped pushing his eggs around on his plate and looked at me with a concern that shook me a little. I must have looked like a fool in this wet blouse and rumpled skirt, but he looked at me as if I was wearing an evening gown. Tad was one thing, but Jordan was going to have to get out of here. They were all giving me puppy-dog looks now.

"We had an exercise in Sunday school and I got a little wet, okay? The question isn't about me. The question is, what are you people doing here!" Whoa. Had that come out of my mouth? I was definitely going to have to check with the doctor about those perimenopause supplements. Kicking folks and screaming all before noon? And on a Sunday too? I needed a nap and some sugar-free chocolate.

Shemika piped up this time. "Well, coming here was my idea, actually. I'm not feeling so well, Mrs. Rose—"

"That's *Miss*—*Miss* Gardner, same as Jericho." I didn't scream this time, but my meaning was clear. What had they been telling this girl? As long as she'd known us, hadn't somebody clued her in on the whole horrible story.

"She was never my wife, Shemika," Jordan said. "Though she should have been. I wasn't as brave as Jericho, but she was as brave as you. And hardworking, too. She worked double shifts in the supermarket and picked up hours at the hospital until the day she went into labor." He paused and stared at the floor. "Even messed up her feet to do it. I'm sorry about everything, but I'm sorry about that."

I braced myself against the chair at the sound of Jordan's

voice. For years, I'd thought that marrying Jordan would have saved me, taken the shame of my teen pregnancy away. All these years later, listening to him, looking at him, I realized things could have been worse if he'd stayed. I couldn't think of anything he could add to my life. Nothing I needed to think about, anyway.

Shemika tugged my son's sleeve. "I thought they were divorced—"

"Shh." Jericho squeezed her hand and gave me a look, one that I deflected. Sure it wasn't the best way to explain, but since my son was so bent on marrying this girl, he should have told her himself. Suddenly wishing there was another croissant, but glad at the same time that there wasn't, I backed up against the wall. My bare feet squeaked against the floor.

Even Jordan's cold eggs called to me as images of the morning—kicking Tad, him washing my lumpy toes, opening the door to find everyone in my kitchen—melted across my mind. This had been a crazy *year* all around, with Tracey and Dana getting married and Jordan coming home, but this was a bit much. A bit too much.

"Shemika, if you don't feel well, come into my room and lie down. I need to change my clothes anyway." All eyes in the room had been focused on my feet since Jordan's little speech and my words didn't break the spell. I jetted through the dining room to my bedroom, daring even one tear to fall and hoping reality TV cameramen weren't waiting behind my drapes.

Shemika followed and stretched out on my favorite comforter—the key-lime pie set I'd gotten from Austin, our newest member in the Sassy Sistahood, during our Christmas-in-July gift swap. The plump comforter plus my queen-size waterbed brought a smile to Shemika's face.

"Nice," she said, as I changed into a periwinkle sundress. Not my color exactly, but I wasn't feeling myself.

I sat down on the edge of the bed. "I'm sorry for all the commotion this morning. You're welcome here anytime, you know that. I just had a bad morning. Now, tell me what's wrong."

She fluffed the pillow under her head. "I just don't feel so good. My back hurts, but it's not time yet and the doctor says to just come in tomorrow. We even went to the hospital, but they said it's Brackstum Lips—"

"Braxton Hicks." During the months of my son's relationship with this girl, I had actually started to warm up to her. Her quietness had given the illusion of wisdom. She should have stuck to that plan. I tried to remind myself that she was only sixteen, no matter how old she looked.

Lord, help this child. And mine, too.

"Yeah, those. But now it's really hurting. Every now and then. Grandma doesn't remember all this stuff and my mother, well, she changed her number when she put me out. Maybe I can rest here for a while and go home—"

"Stay as long as you want." I stroked her head to check for fever and thought about what she'd just said. Home. Jericho had brought the mother of his child to my house because she had nowhere to go. And his shacking-up baby's daddy had done the right thing and taken Shemika in, given her something to call home.

True enough, my son hadn't explained the situation to me, but as always, I jumped to the wrong conclusion. And as Jericho loved to remind me, if I'd just have signed the papers to allow him to get married while he was still legally a minor, this wouldn't be an issue. But I couldn't. Raising a baby was hard enough. Building a marriage was something else all together. Grown folks with steady jobs struggled at it. How could two teens with a new baby make it work? And what about his basketball? College? No, they needed an education. I'd help with the baby... somehow.

"Shemika, I'm sorry about what happened in June with the big fight about you being here with Jericho alone. If he'd told me the situation—"

She tried to sit up, but I shook my head and she eased back down. "I asked him not to tell you. I was embarrassed. I didn't want you to think bad of my mother. She has her own problems and a baby is more than she can deal with right now."

That stunned me for some reason. Sure, Shemika had made a big mistake, but her mother was an adult who should have done better than toss her child into the street. But here Shemika was defending her. More than I could say for myself about my own mother. I tried not to speak against her, but the way she'd abandoned me when I was pregnant with Jericho still hurt all these years later. I hadn't realized it until now.

Kids. Who needs therapy with them around?

"Embarrassed? You didn't need to worry about what I think. And you told Mr. Rose, right? Why weren't you embarrassed for Jordan's dad to know?"

She shrugged. "He's different, you know? More like us. You're like Grandma. All holy and everything."

I laid down on the bed beside her and stared at the ceiling. "Shemika, I try to live by God's Word, but I'm far from perfect. A long way from holy. I don't know what I've done to give you the idea that I couldn't or wouldn't deal with your problems, but I'll do better. Try harder."

She smiled and closed her eyes. "It's okay. Like I said, I just want to go home."

My eyes closed, too, with images of Jordan's glamorous town house scrolling behind them. Sure I was glad that he'd snagged a job as a consultant to the NBA, but sometimes it didn't seem fair. Though Jordan's "I've been in Mexico in a coma for the last decade" story fell hard on most people's ears, the NBA had heard stranger tales.

And so came his new job, a fresh start, a fraction of what Jordan might have had if he'd kept playing, but so much more than he'd hoped for. I tried to be happy for him, even if the way my son had come to depend on him made me feel a little lost.

Hadn't that been what I prayed for all those years when it was just me? That one day Jericho would have a dad he could depend on? Believe in? I hadn't realized then that prayers seldom have an expiration date and sometimes they're answered when you least expect it. So I went on, working hard and praying hard and trying to embrace this new life alone—no husband, no son, no single friends. The people in BASIC didn't really count. I couldn't really talk with any of them. They'd be shocked enough to know that

I'd kicked Tad, let alone the things I thought about sometimes.

And most of them had little sympathy for my up-and-
down feelings for Jordan. So what that I'd worked my fingers to the bone building a business? He'd given me the
start-up money. Really, there wasn't much I could say if he
hadn't. He was still my son's father no matter how I turned
the plate.

Shemika's chest moved up and down, her round belly rising as if it was breathing, too. Jericho had done that in my
stomach, too, even danced when I ate lasagna or Adrian
Norrell's mother played Sting full blast next door. Adrian
married Dana, Jordan's sister—but I digress. Watching Shemika sleep, I prayed for all of us, even for the guys around
the league that Jordan was helping. I prayed that he'd keep
them from turning out regretful, like us. Well, like him. I'd
stuck around, done my duty….

I covered my eyes. Yuck. There it was, that holier-than-
thou thing Shemika was talking about. Why was I like this?
Why did I always have to be right? It wasn't that I didn't have
regrets, too. I had plenty. Jordan was here now and trying to
do what was right. I had to find my way out of the past and
make peace with that. Somehow.

With Jordan convinced that a shotgun wedding would
solve this new problem, the Jericho-and-Shemika problem,
it was difficult to deal with him, especially when Jordan
hadn't married his own live-in girlfriend yet.

I reached out and touched Shemika's stomach gently,
thinking about the many women from our church I'd helped

through labor. Shemika didn't really have the look of a woman in labor, but with the young ones it was hard to tell. I once had a girl laugh and talk with me all the way to the hospital and deliver as soon as we got her into a room. This time would probably be a typical first baby, hard and long. Just like mine.

The door creaked open and Jordan entered, taking a few steps and peeking at us. When he leaned over far enough to see my open-eyed stare, he jumped back. "Girl! I thought you were sleeping, too."

I wish.

"Nope. Just thinking." I squirmed a little as he looked around my room. I could tell he liked it by the way he narrowed his eyes at the picture on the wall. Some things never changed.

He moved closer to the bed, then settled on a chair in the corner. "Thinking about what?"

"Nothing." Frustration whistled through my lips. Why did just the sight of him make me angry? Maybe because hard as I'd worked to get these two kids to finish high school, he'd pressed just as hard for them to get married, something I still wouldn't agree to. Most likely it was because of Shemika's words earlier, that Jordan's place was her home. The other thing that bothered me, the thing I wasn't ready to deal with, was that the grandchild that I'd refused to deal with might be coming.

Soon.

Careful not to wake her, I reached for Shemika's hand, praying as I touched her fingers. I wasn't ready for this. I might never be ready. But God was ready. God was here. As I prayed, the soft flesh under her shirt stiffened into a tight ball. Her back arched, but she continued sleeping.

Jordan saw it, too. "Hey, what was that?" he whispered.

I checked the clock next to my bed—11:02 a.m. "That is the beginning of labor. Looks like our granddaughter wants to meet us a little early."

"So what did the doctor say?" Jordan's voice went with his feet, pacing up and down my front hall.

"They said to let her rest as long as she can. That if it's the real thing, it'll wake her up and we should time the contractions when it does. When they're five minutes apart, we should bring her in."

I nodded and started again, puttering around the kitchen, trying to make something to bring along for Shemika to eat. Every doctor was different, but some still believed in nothing but ice cubes and for a long labor that could be torture.

Somehow I sort of felt like that now, pulled by my anger one moment and my happiness the next. Angry yet happy that they'd come here, put me in the middle of it all.

I should have been happy to come home and find my son and people I hadn't invited inside my kitchen. Throughout Jericho's childhood, I'd turned the key in my front door every day knowing there'd probably be some child with a problem on the other side. Only this time, it was my child. My problem. And I had no solution. Only hurt and a strange hope, a joy at the thought my grandchild's arrival remained. The feeling was stronger than I'd expected, but overshadowed by my pain.

Still, it hurt to see my son, so much a kid, trying to be a father, doing what a husband should. It made me want to go upside his head for doing this in the first place. "So you were just going to hang out and hope it stopped hurting, huh son? Sounds like a very well thought-out plan."

My words came out sharper than I'd liked, but the question rang true. I should have been honored that my son had thought of me first (well, second—he went to his dad first) after all we'd been through this summer, but I wasn't. I was disappointed. I tried hard not to be, but I was. This just wasn't how it was supposed to go. God had only given me one child. There wasn't any room for black sheep and mess-ups. This wasn't on the program.

I wiped my eyes and kept at the cupboards until I un-earthed a can of Chunky soup my son had left behind. I zipped it open with my electric opener and dumped the goo into a pot, wondering if this was how my mother had felt when she'd happened upon my growing belly? Though my mother had split town, leaving me in my aunt's care long be-fore my first contraction, my current emotions explained a lot. Not enough, but a lot. Maybe one day I'd be as spiritual as Shemika and even be able to defend her. For now, my feel-ings peaked and dipped all over the chart, resting on *happily disappointed*.

Jordan joined me at the stove and gathered my free hand into his. My heart did a free fall, like an eaglet tossed out of its nest. In all these months since he'd come back, he hadn't touched me. I'd made sure of that. Even with all he'd done to me, the physical connection between the two of us hadn't diminished. From the first time he'd held my hand at one of his father's Sunday evening fish-fry dinners, Jordan and I were physically drawn together like two magnets on a refrigerator. Spiritually though, our poles had always been opposite. (Now he professed Christ, but loved someone else.) I tried to pull away, knowing better than to let his touch linger.

He held my hand with that loving grip of his and snaked his other hand around my waist, the way he had when I was pregnant. Though my belly was flat now, he rested his hand at my waist, barely touching my dress.

Jordan cleared his throat. "Father God, we haven't done everything right, but let us get this right. May this baby be a grace to us, a healing. Help me to be to this girl what I wasn't to Chelle, to Jericho. Help me to be as a grandfather everything that I wasn't as a father. Help us all to hold together. To be a family. In Jesus' name, Amen." As he released me, his mouth brushed my ear.

"Amen." My knees felt like rubber bands. Jordan's Halston Z-14 cologne, the same scent I'd bought him for Valentine's Day our senior year, whispered along my neck, mocking me. I felt God holding me now instead of Jordan, extending an invitation for me to walk with Him, to fly with Him on the wings of the morning, to walk into this grace, this second chance. Instead, I backed away from the pain that was Jordan, who had never been there for me, for us.

Until now.

Before I could melt down again, Jericho tiptoed into the kitchen. "Mom? She's still sleeping, but I can see the contractions. Should I wake her? What do you think?"

I sighed, again calling upon my birth-coach training for many of the mothers of our church. First labors were always the longest and the worst and Shemika seemed calm so far. "Let her sleep. I think she's in early labor—"

"Ohhhh." Shemika's voice thundered down the hall, sounding more like a moo than anything.

My eyes met with my son's first and then with his father's. That sound was one I'd heard before…from my own lips. I bit the inside of my cheek as the memory, the terrible pain, came flooding back. Fifty-six hours of anguish and all of it paled to the hurt of realizing that Jordan hadn't just gone for a drink of water, that he'd run for his life and would never come back.

"Perhaps I spoke too soon. Put her things in the car," I said, checking the kitchen clock—11:13 a.m. "We'll watch the next few for a pattern." My mind locked as I tried to sound calm instead of screaming like I wanted to. Why had helping strangers have their babies been so much easier than helping bring a piece of me into the world?

"We'll stay here as long as she's comfortable. Keep her moving, Jericho. Walking, squatting. I've got something for her to eat before we go."

My son looked scared but strong. "Thanks Mom. I know this has to be hard."

You have no idea.

Were those pink onesies and blankets still in my trunk? I hadn't touched them in months. "I've got some clothes and things in the car. It'll be fine."

"I knew you'd know what to do. I love you, Mom." My son pecked my cheek, leaving a wet spot on my face.

As he turned away, I blinked back a tear of my own. In all the fighting, I'd forgotten how much I missed hearing that I was loved, being called the name that had defined my very being for so many years.

Mom.

Jordan stood in the kitchen doorway with admiration and confidence in his eyes, the look that had made me fall for him in the first place. A look that said, *You amaze me. You can do anything.* Nobody had ever talked to me like that back then. Nobody but him. And he really must have believed it, because he left me with everything to do. I turned from him now.

His long legs covered the distance to me with ease. "I know I've said sorry a million times, but I have to say it again. I'm sorry." He choked up a little. "Seeing that girl like this. Remembering—"

"Fuhgetaboutit," I said, adding a fake laugh for decoration. He would, or course, forget about it, so he might as well do it now. I, on the other hand, wouldn't have such a luxury. Someday soon, he'd disappear and I'd be stuck again, this time with a grandbaby to take care of. They all assured me otherwise, but I'd been around long enough to know how the story would end. He'd get his fairy tale like everyone else. Everybody but me.

Jordan leaned in closer. "I can't forget about it. Ever. Even now, marrying Terri… I told her that I don't know if I want to have children with her. I don't think it'd be right. Or fair."

My foot lifted off the floor, but I caught myself before I kicked him.

I've really got to try a new workout.

The pan slammed against the burner, a redirection of my anger. I wished I could escape this room, this conversation. One reason I hadn't been able to deal with this baby, to go to Jordan's house and even discuss it was because of her—Terri, his girlfriend. I had no reason to care, no claim to him. In truth, he'd tried to get back with me again, but too much had passed between us to make things right. Still, seeing the two of them together was hard. At least he hadn't brought her along today.

"Have all the babies you want. It doesn't matter to me." I jerked away from him, ransacking the cupboards.

Another moan, this time followed by a shriek, sounded in the living room. I checked the kitchen clock—11:22 a.m. The contractions were consistent and getting closer. So much for the soup. A box of my precious Zone bars would have to do.

"You care about me, Chelle. I know you do. Sometimes I even think about calling off the wedding until you can forgive me—"

"I have forgiven you." Another box of low-carb bars, the ones I'd bought off of a cable shopping network during a bout of insomnia, tumbled down out of the cabinet. I forced the box back into the cabinet and when it refused to stay, I wedged a box of low-carb pancake mix in front of it, wishing I had something to prop myself up with. Why hadn't I stayed at church and let Tad give me a full pedicure? Someday I'd learn to take my blessings where I could get them.

Jordan continued. "Your head may have forgiven me, but not your heart. If so, you wouldn't retract whenever I come near you, or look away when I enter a room. The sight of me brings you pain. I know that. If not for Jericho, I wouldn't have stayed in this town. But I have to stay. You of all people should understand that. I have to make things better for him if I can. You did well with him. Better than I ever could have."

"But still not good enough, or we wouldn't be here hoping a baby won't be born in the next room. I did everything to keep him from turning into you—into us—but it wasn't enough. He messed up anyway."

Shocked that I'd actually said that, I grabbed the three Coke cans they'd left on the counter and rinsed them before crushing them in my new Can Killer (another insomnia-induced purchase) and tossing them into the recycle bin. It wasn't as gratifying as kicking people, but much safer.

"So that was your parenting goal? Keeping Jericho from becoming me? From becoming us?"

I scrubbed the counters as if my life depended on their cleanliness. "Us? That was a bad choice of words. There is no us. There never was. I don't have your name. I only have your child. That was the only blessing that came out of my sin."

Jordan's face sobered. "You make it sound so horrible, like my leaving was God's punishment to you for being with me."

I shrugged. What difference did it make? I'd sowed a lot of bad seeds with Jordan and reaped every one. In the midst of it, God had given me more than I could ask for: His love, friends, family, a handsome, intelligent son, a business I loved.

The questions didn't matter anymore. The answer remained the same—Jesus Christ.

"We were young, Chelle. We didn't know. We didn't get it."

"Didn't we?" I stirred the soup like a madwoman, trying to hide my trembling hands. "It doesn't matter whether we knew or not, Jordan. God knew. He's loving, but He's holy. He couldn't change that for us." I leaned forward to listen for Shemika. Nothing. "He can't change it for them, either. It is what it is—"

Jordan kissed the back of my neck.

Even after so many years, my body melted at his butterfly kiss, reserved for times when words wouldn't suffice. My womanhood leaped to her feet and sighed in satisfaction. I pushed her back. And him, too.

My heel crunched down on his toes. I was embarrassed and sorry for doing it, but he wasn't going to toy with me like this. I'd come too far, been through too much. I was past angry now. I was "salty," as his sister Dana would say.

"Ow!"

We both turned. Shemika's voice carried over Jordan's grumbling. I stared at the clock—11:26 a.m. This one was closer. Too close.

Jordan gave me a puzzled look and let his hurt foot drop to the floor. He took my shoulders into his big, brown hands.

"It's time, isn't it?" he asked in a steady tone.

I nodded and pulled away, turning off the stove and grabbing my protein bars plus the extra pack I'd so carefully put back. I tossed the soup pot into the dishwater to soak. Jordan looked at me as if I was insane. I sucked my teeth. "Nobody else has to think about later, but I do. When I come back home, I'll be alone."

Jordan ignored my words. "Just tell me what to do. I'm here for you. For us. Whatever you need."

How I'd love to believe that, but I just can't.

"Thanks."

It took us a lot of stopping and starting between contractions to make it to the living room. When we made it there, the doorbell rang.

No one moved at first.

"I'll get that if you'd like," Jordan said.

I nodded. There was no way I could untangle myself from Shemika now if I tried. Her arms were around my neck, her hair in my face…and my son was holding up the both of us.

As entwined as I was, I heard the woman's voice at the door. Terri, Jordan's girlfriend.

"I never thought it'd be this bad," Shemika whispered as we struggled forward after the next contraction.

"It's not bad, even though it feels bad," I said. "It's good. It's bringing your daughter to you. To us. Now hold my hand. We're all here for you."

Terri fluttered toward us like a bird made of pink silk. I tried to ignore her, but that was a tall order.

"That's right, darling. I'm here. Breathe just like we did in the class. Puff! Puff! Puff!" Jordan's girlfriend pushed around me to reach for Shemika's hand, but I couldn't get out of the way. Nor did I want to. Puffing was good if you were trying to smoke a cigarette, but it wouldn't help now. Reading books about having babies and actually having them were two different things. I was about to tell Miss Thing so, but Jordan beat me to it.

"Terri, thanks for being so supportive, honey, but I'm going to need for you to go."

One of her rings, a starburst diamond, almost gouged out my eye as she whirled around. "What?"

"You heard me, hon. We're going to the hospital now. My family needs me."

Her bottom lip quivered. I looked away. Terri wasn't my favorite person, but this was a private thing.

"But…but…aren't I your family too, Jordan?"

He took a deep breath. "If we were married, you could come. We're not. This is Rochelle's home, sweetheart. You shouldn't have come here. We talked about that, remember? Now, relax and go home. I'll be back soon." He smiled. "Hopefully with baby pictures."

With that, he took Shemika's hand and pulled her to the door. Jericho and I helped her outside, one of her arms over each of our shoulders. Jordan joined us again as we paused for two more contractions then finally got Shemika into the car. It wasn't until the hospital floor chilled my bare soles that I realized that I'd never put on any shoes.

Chapter three

Shemika made it to the trash can. Then she went down just where I did, in the lobby of Saint Elizabeth Hospital, by the west entrance. The security guard took one look at us and shook his head.

"Oh no. I'm not delivering any more babies out here this week. Had one looking just like her the other night. I had to do the whole thing." He wiped his forehead. "Don't think I ever will get over it." He jogged to a wheelchair and pushed it toward us.

Shemika doubled over before he reached us. She let out a low rumbling noise, letting the earthquake inside her fill the room.

The security guard's eyes widened. "The other one, she made that sound, too! Right before she fell out and…" He pinched his eyes shut and grabbed Jordan's sleeve. "Help me get her in the chair, man. I'm going to have to run for it!"

Jordan looked at me and then back at the man, who

looked to weigh about a hundred pounds—well, maybe if he was under water holding dumbbells he'd be that heavy. There was no chance of him running Shemika anywhere in a wheelchair.

"I've got it, man," Jordan said as, to my amazement and shock, he did for Shemika just what he'd done for me seventeen years before—picked her up and made for the elevator like only a former basketball star can.

The security guard followed in a limping run. "The second elevator," he shouted before a fit of coughing overtook him. Before I realized it, I was running too, along with Jericho, who was less than thrilled with his gray-headed father's show of athleticism. Shemika was a big girl and Jordan was about fifty pounds lighter than he'd been back in the day. His gait showed the strain. My son's face showed it, too. "Dad, slow down!"

"Triage elevator. Right there." The security guard pointed us in the right direction and explained to the approaching nurse what was going on.

The last in line for the elevator, I ended up taking the nurse's questions as we waited for the elevator to arrive.

"Who's her doctor? I can call that up for you at least."

I smiled, embarrassed to have no response to a question any grandmother should be able to answer. "Um…Jericho?"

My son punched the button with one hand, with his other hand he tried to comfort his girlfriend, now standing on her own but making faces. "It's Dr. Wallace."

Shemika shook her head. "No, it's his midwife, Chris," she managed to say as the elevator arrived.

The nurse smiled. "Great. I'll call it up." She patted my hand. "Good luck, Grandma."

I filed my new title in the back of my head as we all squeezed into the elevator. Once the door slammed shut, a manly quiet, the kind of silence that only males at an impending birth can muster, filled the elevator as Shemika turned into a brown spider, legs and arms everywhere, trying to climb away from the pain.

Though Jordan had helped usher her to the elevator, it was my son who held Shemika now, rubbing her back, trying to get her to calm down.

"Breathe, babe," he said in a voice I'd never heard.

Shemika tried to suck in a breath, but screamed instead, her arms swimming against a wave of contractions.

After several blows to his back and shoulders, Jordan moved into the front corner of the elevator. I fought against the urge to be happy that she'd landed a few blows. The image of his girlfriend in my living room would be forever stained on my mind. I flattened myself to the front, too, leaving my son to endure the kicks. During first births, I tried to stay out of the way and not take anything personally. I did hope she'd calm down upstairs, though, before she wore herself out.

Moments later, as we spilled from the elevator, I touched Shemika's hand, hoping a soft touch would help her relax. We made it to triage quickly. Jordan opened the door, while my son and I helped Shemika inside.

I tried to encourage her. "Remember our deal? You relax, your body works and your baby comes."

Shemika didn't look convinced. Evidently my birth-speak was a little rusty. It'd been a full year since I'd attended a laboring mom, but it was all coming back. Good thing, since my friend Tracey would be delivering soon. She lived out of town, but I hoped to be there somehow. "I know I'm making it sound easy, but really—"

Shemika grunted in response.

"Are you okay? Just a few more steps…"

Shemika didn't even try to answer. She just started sliding to the floor. Jericho and I grabbed her, but Shemika's weight, combined with her flailing arms and legs, proved too much for both of us. We were all still standing, but heading for the floor. Where was Jordan?

"Let me help you." The voice stung like hail.

Tad.

One look at him and I lost my grip. The whole wild, pregnant mess that was the three of us landed in his arms, including my supersize son. Jericho jumped as though he'd touched a hot stove. Must be a man thing.

As we untangled, Jericho helped Shemika up. I looked into Tad's kind eyes and at his bruised chin. Bless his heart, now here I was about to beat up the rest of him. "You poor thing. What are you doing here?"

He smiled. "I got a call from someone on the Men's Fellowship prayer chain."

I shrugged. Who'd made the call I didn't know, but I was thankful. For all Tad's annoying traits, he was calm in a crisis.

Jordan's face glistened with sweat. His eyes looked bloodshot. Maybe this whole birth thing was weighing on him harder than I'd thought. He shook Tad's hand. "Thanks for coming. Sorry for calling you out of service, but you said—"

Tad nodded. "I said call anytime. And I meant it." He spoke to Jordan, but his eyes were locked on me.

And my bare feet.

Shemika managed to get herself into a tan gown and we were guided behind a series of curtains and asked to wait for a nurse. Shemika latched on to Jericho's hand with a death grip. Or maybe a life grip.

My son gave her a smile, then leaned down to me with wide eyes I'd seen only a few times, one of them on the day he'd met his father for the first time. "I have a bad feeling, Mom."

A snort escaped my lips. "Me, too, but my bad feeling was about nine months ago."

"No, really," he said, trying to whisper but forgetting to do so. "And she's grabbed my hand so hard. It was almost like she was…pushing?"

"Pushing?"

My voice must have really carried, because a nurse emerged from what seemed a thousand layers of curtains. "Who's pushing?"

Cringing from the way his girlfriend was squeezing his hand, my son nodded slightly. "I'm not sure, but she's doing something."

The nurse's eyes narrowed. "Okay. I'll check her. Could you all step outside? And Grandma, can you stop at the desk and answer some questions?"

Grandma.

"Sure," I said.

As Tad led the way, a woman behind one of the curtains let out a scream worthy of a horror movie. Jordan cringed. "Whoa..."

I snickered. "You ain't seen nothing yet." I wanted to say that he'd have seen worse if he'd stuck around with me, but that water was under the bridge. And over it.

Conscious again of my bare feet and lack of preparedness, I fumbled in the suitcase-size bag that serves as my purse as we approached the front desk. I immediately stumbled on my wet, ruined shoes. Who'd slipped those in for me? It didn't matter. This time, I was much happier to see them.

Jordan's voice creaked as he spoke to the nurse. "Yes, ma'am. She's thirty-six weeks, six days according to the wheel. Thirty-seven by the ultrasound..."

I felt jealous for a moment and suddenly wished I'd been the one to let the kids stay with me, the one who'd taken Shemika to her doctor's appointments. At least they'd listened to me and preregistered for the hospital.

"Her medical card?" the nurse said coolly. "The number wasn't filled out on the form that was mailed in. We'll need to copy that card."

Jordan and Tad looked blankly at me.

Known to be quick on my feet, even when they're cold and wet, I started mumbling. "In our haste, we—they—don't have the cards handy, but I'll stop home and get them once she's in a room. Until then, perhaps the doctor's office could provide the number by phone?"

The woman tried but failed to smile. "They will, but we'll still need the cards. I'll be back shortly."

Jordan's arm brushed mine as I ransacked my purse for my emergency copy of the big, gold card that signified my son's inability to take care of his child.

Though covered by my self-employed insurance, there was no policy clause for the offspring of unmarried dependents. It turned out that Shemika already had a state medical card anyway. I dug for my copy of it now, knowing it probably wasn't there. Didn't my mother used to go through her pocketbook like this? Yes. And it had freaked me out. Totally. I was officially turning into her.

"That's fine. Perhaps you want to go to the waiting room for a while? They're probably going to get her a room."

We went quietly, dividing in the waiting room. I dropped into a chair to continue attacking my purse. Tad went to the window. Jordan approached the TV. Suddenly, he looked more interested in the game show prizes than the birth of his first grandchild. For once, I wasn't sure if I blamed him. This was a wonderful, horrible day.

I rifled through the contents of my life, dumped on the next chair: cell phone, nail files, Bible memory cards, old church bulletins, Franklin planner, Montblanc pen, a key to Dana's store and a handful of low-carb bars I'd stupidly brought along for Shemika.

She needs carbs. She's in labor, not a beauty pageant.

Still, I hoped her hairweave was tight enough to endure labor. In my post-birth pictures, I'd looked as if my hair had been rotated ninety degrees—without bringing my head along. Shemika would look much better, so much better than I did. She had to. I'd make sure of it.

Shemika rolled by on a gurney and Tad and Jordan shot out of the room like toothpaste from a new tube. I shoved my things into my purse, jabbed my feet into my shoes and ran to catch up. I guessed that chivalry was dead during emergencies.

Without my consent, the memory of my son's birth came to me—a blur of helplessness. I forced it back. This wasn't my birth. And my son wasn't going to run out on this girl. Thoughts of today replaced my memories—images of me with Shemika's head cradled to my chest on the ride over, the sound of my voice saying, "You are strong, Shemika. And beautiful." My heart ached as I walked down the long hall, realizing that I'd shown Shemika more kindness today than in all the time I'd known her.

Though still far-off, I could make out Shemika's birth soundtrack—a ballad of moans and wide, wonderful sounds. Sounds that make men very, very afraid.

"It hurts…" she said in a low wail, not a scream anymore but a moan of discovery, a beach that seemed lifetimes away.

I was running now, purse banging against my shins. On the right, I passed a room where a woman was shouting at her husband. He waved at me and munched ice chips. He'd done this before, too.

Jordan took my hand and I reached the room, where I heard a different cry, the birth call of my grandchild. It played in my ears like a symphony.

In my nightmares, there is a monster with a pink cell phone. In real life, she has a matching Prada bag, the messenger model that I admire but would never pay that much for, and the love of my high-school sweetheart. No doubt Terri bought it for use as a diaper bag. Dealing with Jordan is one thing, but this chick? She's going to make me go Tae Bo all over again.

"I kept calling the hospital for news. Imagine when I heard the baby had been born! I sped right over, love."

Jordan deflected my eyes. "Oh. Yeah. I was going to call once we saw the baby. We're waiting." He tried to slither out of Terri's grip, but she wound him up like my son would soon be winding a baby swing.

I held my breath for a moment, fighting the urge to pull Tad toward me, inferring a relationship that didn't exist. Being the gentleman he was, Tad took a step toward me… and away from the nauseating couple. He brushed the bruise on his chin, then extended his hand to Terri. "I'm Thaddeus, Jordan's prayer partner in the Men's Fellowship. And Rochelle and I run the singles group at the church as well. We'd love to have both of you—"

The inference that she was single and the thought of Jordan praying with anybody didn't seem to go over well. "I know who you are. I've seen you at church. Thanks anyway, but we're getting married, the singles group isn't the place for us. We already live together—"

"I'm going to go get a drink. Anybody want something?" Jordan's voice was even. Detached.

Tad pursed his lips. "Sure. Get me some coffee."

Terri smiled, pulling Jordan closer. "Sugar? They probably make it stiff here."

I silently prayed that the coffee would be strong enough to shock some sense into her or wake Jordan up from the fog of stupidity he was living in.

Tad shrugged. "Sure. Two sugars."

"Got it. Anything for you, Chelle?" Jordan looked at a spot just above my head.

I stared right into his eyes, trying to see something better, something different than what I'd seen seventeen years before. Looked the same to me.

"I don't think so, J." Why was I calling him "J" again? All I wanted was to get back into that room with my grandbaby, not all this drama. The hospital staff had shooed us out like flies. Needed to check a few more things, they'd said, but I didn't feel right out here.

Jordan nodded. "Right."

My stomach turned as Jordan and Terri walked away, taking the stairs instead of the elevator, probably going straight to her car. I closed my eyes, wondering if I shouldn't be thankful. At least Tad would pray with me if I came down to it. Jordan seemed to put his faith and his family on layaway, investing a little bit at a time. I liked to live debt-free myself.

"Sorry about all that," Tad said. "I meant what I said to Jordan. I know this can't be easy. But I do believe God is working on him."

I didn't know what God was doing to Jordan and I wasn't sure that I cared. "It meant a lot for you to be here today. I know it may have been difficult." In truth, it probably wasn't difficult at all. Answering Jordan's call as a member of the

Men's Fellowship would have been much easier than responding to my call as a friend. I didn't dare think past friendship—it made my head hurt. Either way, he'd come.

I squared my shoulders and turned to Tad. "Two sugars you said?" As much as I wanted to be with my grandbaby, getting Tad a cup of coffee was the least I could do. Hadn't there been a coffeepot back in triage? Maybe they'd be kind enough to let me get a cup. Jordan had left me with the bag again. Everything was on me now. As usual.

Tad stared toward the stairway Jordan had left by a short time before. His eyes narrowed. "They went for coffee. You don't need to—" Slowly understanding spread across Tad's face. He shook his head. "I don't know Jordan as well as you do, but I don't think he'd make the same mistake again. I don't think he'd leave."

I didn't need to think. I knew. "Two sugars?"

Tad stared at the floor. "Make it black."

Ten minutes later, I drank the black coffee. I'm a tea girl, and burnt hospital coffee is a hot, slow way to die, but I had to play it off somehow.

Jordan wasn't buying it.

"Here, take this tea," he said, opening a cup with a milky streak running through it. I took creamer in my tea. Everyone but Jordan had always thought that strange. He'd always laughed at my old habit. He held out the cup and produced two packets of Equal from his pocket, another trend of mine he'd obviously picked up on.

Somehow I turned down the perfect cup of tea. "You have it. I'm fine, thanks." If drinking black glue was fine, then fine I was. In my anger, I turned down even that small peace offering.

Tad sipped his just-right coffee with a smile, obviously grateful that Jordan had returned to prove him right. Something else—pity or understanding, I wasn't sure—tinged his eyes.

Jordan took a pack of sugar from his pocket and emptied it into the tea. One stir with his finger and he took a gulp even though it was still steaming. He'd always been crazy like that.

Terri, who'd almost tricked me into thinking she had one sensible brain cell, refused to stay silent. "You didn't think we were coming back, did you?"

I sighed, surveying the duck wallpaper. What did she want me to say? "No, I didn't."

Terri's face clouded with anger. Her pink exterior shifted black. "You see, J? You see? She'll never believe anything you say. I don't know why you try so hard. Your son forgives you. Why don't you move on so we can move on? It's like she holds you captive or something." She reached for Jordan, but he pulled away, taking a sip of my once-perfect tea.

He shook his head at Terri, then took my hand. "I don't blame you. I haven't given you any reason to believe in me. But I just thought—I thought that maybe you could."

Why was I always the villain? "I have forgiven you, Jordan. Some things are just hard to forget." I looked around the waiting room. Were those ducks the same ones from when my family had waited in this room? Surely not. Maybe they'd bought the stuff in bulk.

Jordan smiled weakly at Tad. "I guess some things don't

change no matter how much you pray." His wide palm smacked Tad's shoulder, before Jordan took a few steps and plopped down in front of the television. The NBA finals, of course.

Tad passed Jordan's weak smile on to me with his own mouth. He scanned my face as if looking for something. Whatever it was, he didn't find it. I pitied him. I knew the feeling. I wish I could say that Jordan's pain or Tad's frustration moved me, but I'd be lying. And Terri? Well, she was doing good to still be standing.

Lord, what does he expect me to say? What do You expect?

Tad walked over to Jordan, ignoring Terri as he sat down. "Give Rochelle more time. And yourself, too. None of this is easy."

Wow. Tad sounded like some counselor assigned by family court. All he was missing was a comb-over hairdo and a bad suit. It was nice of him to be here, but right now, I needed my friends from my Sassy Sistahood—Jordan's sister Dana, who was off at a trade show with her new husband and my other dear friend, newly married, quite pregnant and two hours away. How dare my friends have lives of their own? Right now, I'd even take Austin, one of our newest members and someone I hadn't quite clicked with yet.

I wanted anybody who'd understand how bad I wanted to see my granddaughter, but how scared I was to see her, too. I'd failed at being a parent, made a mess of my own life and now had a pink-clad monster, the local weatherman and a washed-out NBA player to deal with, none of whom had a clue how I really felt. And vice versa. No, for times like these, a girl needs God…and her girlfriends.

"Let's go back and see about the baby. They said twenty minutes." It was all I could think of to say. This was supposed to be about the kids, wasn't it? And the baby? How it turned into some grown folks' version of baby's mama drama, I had no clue.

Jordan and Terri walked ahead of us to Shemika's room, with the former giving Tad the look of an apprentice hoping for his master to fix the situation.

Tad had sense enough not to signal any hope. Instead, he picked up my purse from where I'd almost left it. "Here. You might need this, Grandma." His smile and his tone were comforting.

I pushed my purse up on my shoulder and stared down at my now war-beaten shoes, shocked at how good they looked despite the stains.

"Thanks." This let me know that I was totally out of control. My purse was like an extension of my body, always attached.

His gaze rested around my ankles as we started back to the room. "I'm glad you found your shoes. Gotta take care of those—"

"Don't say it." I sucked up half the oxygen in Illinois. Didn't he know not to go there while my illegitimate grandchild was being born? Goodness. My feet had been through enough. My mind, too.

He smiled, the little-boy-with-a-secret grin again. "I won't say it. I don't have to."

★ ★ ★

The baby, whose cry had filled the room not long before, now rested in a nurse's arms, swaddled by enough baby blankets to almost double her size. We'd only been allowed a peek at her before, but this time, the nurse motioned for Jordan and me to approach. The little face, cocoa with a splash of milk, looked beautiful to me. A bed of thick curls framed the baby's face.

Her face.

"A girl, right?" Jordan asked.

"Yes," my son said, pointing to the card attached to the bed. "Girl. Seven pounds, eight ounces."

Tad patted my hand as I moved closer to my grandchild and then to my son.

Jericho smiled but didn't say anything more. Instead, he mopped Shemika's brow. The furrows in his forehead worried me. Terri chattered on, pulling designer baby clothes from her bag in more shades of pink than I knew existed. I paused, listening to the deadly quiet that had rushed into the room.

"Should she still be bleeding?" my son whispered to me.

"No." I tried not to get anxious, turning to the midwife for the look of reassurance. Instead, concerned eyes met mine. My toes balled up in my shoes. This couldn't happen. Not again.

The midwife pushed her glasses up on her nose with a gloved wrist. "Shemika's blood pressure rose significantly during the birth, almost to stroke levels. Her pressure is coming down, but not as quickly as I'd like. There's also a blood-loss concern. My backup doctor will take over from here."

Jordan, who'd somehow managed to hear over his girlfriend's loud talking, gripped my arm. We'd never talked about what had happened to me after the birth of our son, but someone must have told him. Or perhaps he figured something must have happened for me to only have one child. That the woman he'd known back then could have been celibate all these years was probably his last guess.

As I started running through all the scenarios and how my son and I could split the care for Shemika and the baby, something told me to be still. I was.

The nurse took the sweet bundle from my arms. Terri reached out her hands, but the woman ignored her. "The baby is going to the nursery now to get cleaned up—"

"Can I come too?" Jordan interrupted the nurse. "I'd just like to make sure that she's okay." Terri gave me a contented look of victory, but the voice in my head remained.

What was that Scripture in Ephesians that Tracey liked to quote?

Having done all to stand...stand. Stay here.

"You can come on with us, Tad. I know all this can be a little overwhelming, especially for a single cat like you." Jordan nodded for Tad to follow.

Tad shook his head. "I'll stay here." None of that "if it's all the same to you," or "if you don't mind" stuff, just, "I'll stay here."

Already walking behind the bassinet, Jordan waved. "Suit yourself, man." He turned to Shemika. "Don't worry, sweetheart. Grandpa's on the job."

It was a sorry attempt to lighten the mood, but it was much

needed, even if it only lasted a few seconds. As soon as the baby was out of the door, things went downhill quickly.

"Prep the O.R. She's bleeding out."

"Lord, we ask that You stop this blood, in Jesus' name…"

Those voices, first the doctor's and then Tad's were the last I remembered hearing. From there, I was back in an icy recovery room, waking to the sensation of my insides on fire. No one was in the room but a nurse who looked as if she'd rather be somewhere, anywhere else. Her voice, though, was much kinder than her appearance when I asked about the baby.

"He's fine," she'd said in a soft tone. "There won't be any more, though. Babies, I mean. You had some problems. The doctor will come and talk to you about it later. Just be thankful that you got one."

She wasn't the last person to tell me that and the doctor never came to explain. But now, here in Shemika's hospital room, all the pain and regret came back to me. I gripped my waist and doubled over.

"Are you all right, Grandma?" one of the nurses asked as they moved Shemika from the bed to a stretcher.

I could hear Tad still praying under his breath. "I'm fine, just a little shaken."

Jericho, who had said nothing in the past few minutes, squeezed my hand. "I'm sorry, Mom. I never knew it was like this."

My fingers trembled. I didn't know if he was sorry for what was happening to Shemika or for what had happened to me. Either way, I wasn't the one he needed to be concerned about. "Go with her, son. Go on."

He nodded and disappeared down the hall. I fumbled for my purse as the room emptied, leaving Tad and I alone. I grabbed for my phone but dropped it.

Tad picked it up. "Who do you need to call—Mother Holloway?"

I nodded. Shemika's grandmother hadn't wanted to come to the birth, but now I needed to let her know what was going on. Most likely she wouldn't take the news any better than I was.

As he pressed the buttons from memory, Tad moved his lips silently.

I was too tired to make out the words. "What are you saying?"

"Still praying. There's always a chance— Hello? Mother Holloway—"

The stretcher crashed back through the door on the way to the operating room, with the whole cast following. Tad and I scurried out of the way. Shemika looked sedated or seriously asleep. Jericho was crying.

"She's stable, Mom. They were prepping her for surgery and…" He buried his face in his hands.

Tad grabbed him around the neck and hugged. "Mother Holloway? It's me, Thaddeus from the church. This morning's lesson? I enjoyed that, too. Yes, ma'am. Look, I just wanted to tell you that your great-grandbaby has arrived. A girl."

He covered the phone with his mouth and leaned in to my son. "What's the baby's name?" he asked.

I shook my head. "Just tell her we don't know—"

"Moriah." Shemika's voice was barely more than a breath, but we all heard it.

"Moriah," Tad repeated into the phone. He laughed, then nodded. "Yes, it is a good name. I pray she'll live a mountain life."

"Me, too," I whispered into the folds of Tad's shirtsleeve as he held me up, too. "Live tall, little one. Live tall."

Chapter four

Shalomsistah: You okay, Rochelle? I haven't seen you on the list for a few days. Dana told me to check if you disappeared for too long.

I stared at my computer monitor with tired eyes. It was Austin, one of the newer members on the devotional list and Dana's new best friend, on the other side of the computer. Usually, the list was a lifeline, both to the Lord and to my friends. Lately though, I'd come unplugged, both from the Internet and from my relationship with God.

After this memorable day—Moriah's birth, Terri's presence and Tad's chin—I definitely needed to talk, but I wasn't sure if Austin was the person to sing my blues to. I'd prayed about my attitude toward her and tried to figure it out, but still something about her just didn't sit right. Perhaps the fact that, without trying, she'd taken my place in Dana's life was the cause for my misgivings.

Sassysistah1: Shemika had the baby.

Shalomsistah: CONGRATULATIONS!

I stiffened. This was one of the things about her that got on my nerves. Austin had always been too perky, even when she'd just been the evening anchorwoman, a stranger on the news. At least Tad knew how to turn off his TV persona…most of the time anyway.

Sassysistah1: Thanks. I guess. ☺ There's a lot going on.

Shalomsistah: Want to talk about it? I know you don't eat sugar, but I've got lots of chicken soup. My mother-in-law thinks it can bring world peace.

I had to smile at that. Mrs. Shapiro, so meticulous when she came in to select her shoes each season, certainly believed in the power of chicken soup. In truth, her matzo-ball variety had put the whammy on more than one of my colds and her words always warmed my heart. These days, I showcased the designs of other people's shoes more than I made my own—except for Mrs. Shapiro.

"Shoes of peace," she'd say. "Just like the name on the door, just like you. You make them with your own hands, with your heart." Those words and the baskets filled with chicken soup, tea and vitamins always made me feel better. Stronger. Sometimes I forgot that Austin had married Mrs. Shapiro's son. The girl couldn't be all bad.

Sassysistah1: It's hot outside, but soup sounds good. I'd come over there, but I'm too tired to drive.

Shalomsistah: Not a problem. I'm there.

Sassysistah1: Knock hard. I'll probably be asleep.

Shalomsistah: Got it.

Sassysistah1: Wait! Do you remember where I live?

Shalomsistah is not signed on.

Hmm…Austin must have remembered the directions or she would have asked. I couldn't muster the strength to get up and look for her number. I needed to go and dig my Bible out of the trash in the other room. Someone had actually dared to throw it away. Jordan maybe? I needed to fall on my face in prayer, but I didn't. I pulled away from the computer to the creak of my bones.

The plan had been to come home from the hospital, change my clothes and rush right back, even though everyone advised against it. Especially Terri. I'm convinced she was stalking outside the hospital or something, but what did I know? Not much or I wouldn't be trying to figure out how to be a single grandmother. As if being a single mother wasn't job enough.

Shooting off a round of tangled prayers, I stretched my hands upward. Weariness poured down my legs, past my ankles and straight into my toes. With a thump, I dropped to the couch, the one that was just for decoration. It was time for that thing to earn its keep. As I sank back into it, my feet arched as if by their own will. I wiggled my toes, but it didn't help. What I needed now was the foot washing I'd run from this morning.

Life is funny like that. What I try to outrun one minute, I needed the next. In truth, I could use a lot more from Tad than a soak in his kitty-litter container—a generous look or one of his steady prayers would do me just fine about now. Even when things had got bad after Shemika's birth, the man hadn't even flinched. He just stood there tall and strong, speaking loud and clear—

"We ask Lord, that this blood would stop, in the name of Jesus…"

When the room blurred into a rush of nurses and the smell of fear, there Tad was, rooted to the floor like a tree, his pecan skin glowing with sweat. The blood didn't stop then, but the atmosphere did, and so did my attitude. This wasn't my life all over again. No matter what happened, God was in control. Too bad Tad hadn't been there the day I delivered Jericho. The outcome might have been the same, but maybe my heart wouldn't have…

The doorbell sliced through my musings. I took a deep breath and hobbled for the door.

Behind it was Austin's smiling face and two armfuls of low-carb goodies—almonds, teriyaki steak jerky, a veggie tray, some of Mrs. Shapiro's chicken soup minus the matzo balls and a jug of diet V8 Splash. The tropical kind.

I hugged her inside. "Dana's been telling you all my secrets, I see."

She shook her head. "Nope. I'm just observant. It's the reporter in me."

We both laughed and put the spread on the table. She pulled two cold Diet Cokes from her purse and plopped onto the couch beside me. "We'll get to that stuff later. Tell me about the birth."

"It was something," I said, sounding more like Jordan than I was comfortable with. My fingers gripped the cold drink while my lips refused to recount Moriah's story. At least not yet. I looked back at the table, wondering which item would loosen my lips. Being on the receiving end of a girlfriend gift pack seemed strange. I'd been doing similar things for Dana and Tracey for years. I was used to it, being the one who gave, who smoothed things over. Having someone do it for me? Well, I didn't know how to take it exactly. I sipped my pop anyway. Mine was vanilla, hers was lime.

It tasted wonderful. Much better than that bitter coffee, better than the story I had to tell. "This is good. And you got lime. Is it your favorite?"

Austin shook her head. "I don't usually drink diet. This wasn't about me though, so I just went along." Her smile lit up the room like a candle.

"Sounds like a practice I should try." I put my can on a coaster, suddenly deciding against my usual speech about being careful not to spill anything. If we made a mess, I could have it cleaned later. For once, I just didn't care.

Austin took a coaster without being reminded and rested her can on it. She smiled at me, but made none of the usual chitchat or self-deprecating jokes that Dana provided. Not even any of Tracey's goofy music and movie trivia that had nothing to do with anything. She just sat there sipping, ready to listen. This was a lot to get used to.

"Well, I'll try and make this short," I said.

"That's your call. I've got four hours. The husband is fed, kissed and napping in front of ESPN. Pre-season games. He even has snackage. I left a note, but he'll realize I've been gone after I walk back in the door."

I made what must have been a horrible face. "Four hours? Please. I don't talk to anybody that long. Not even God."

Austin took another sip of her pop and curled her feet beneath her. "You'd be surprised."

Five hours later, I was surprised…and full. I talked about everything from Jordan to the foot washing to the birth. I'd cried and eaten and cried some more. With Austin past due to be home, we were getting to the good part.

I stared at the clock in horror. "Oh my goodness. You need to go. I'm so sorry—"

She waved me off. "Double overtime. I called him in the bathroom. He thought I was in the other room on the computer. I will go soon, but we're okay. What I need to know is, are *you* okay? You keep talking about everybody else and your concerns for them, but what about you? It's okay to feel something just for yourself, you know."

Was it okay? The thought stunned me. "Haven't I been talking about me all this time?"

"No. You've been talking about your son, your granddaughter, your son's father, Tad, the church… Before I go, I need to hear what's really going on. With you." She paused. "If you want to go there, that is."

My defenses sprang up. My walls. How dare this little skinny blond girl come here and try to tell me to get real about something! What did she know about it?

A lot, from the look in her eyes. From the patient quietness she'd blessed me with the past few hours. No wonder Dana rambled on about her so much. She had a deep, just-what-you-need faith.

Sistah faith.

My true feelings quaked inside me, shook my shoulders. Before I knew it I was crying again and half shouting. "How could my baby have a baby now? What did I do wrong? I prayed, took him to church, went without a man. How could God let this happen?"

I was up off the couch now, pacing the room. Austin didn't say a word. She just got up and walked beside me. Poor thing. She'd opened the floodgates now.

"And Tad. Talking about some beautiful feet. All these years I've been standing here dying, trying to serve God only to have people look down on me because I didn't have a husband, and now this fool wants to try and be good to me?"

She took my hand, laced my fingers. I didn't pull away.

"There was so much more I wanted, but I was trying to do the right things. But it didn't work, none of it. Jordan is back and instead of fixing everything, he's messed it all up. Him and his silly girlfriend. I don't even know that I want him anymore, but he should have tried harder, done more than just propose to some heifer he barely knows—"

"Yeah." Austin finally spoke.

We stopped walking and I tried to breathe. I guess it was time for her to rein me in. "I'm sorry. I didn't mean to say all of that," I said.

She shrugged. "It's okay. You needed to. Everybody needs to bleed. That's what friends are for. The thing is making sure the wound is clean after. It's the infection that can kill you."

This time I took her hand. We walked to the couch, the one unused until today and knelt there together. I bowed my head.

"Let's pray," Austin whispered.

"Mom, I didn't think it would be this hard."

I stared at my son through bleary eyes, spotting his face across his daughter's crib. Moriah, my sweet pea of a grand-daughter, had been crying nonstop for thirty minutes. It was four in the morning. "Actually, this is the easy part. They sleep a lot at the beginning." My arms extended to take her from him.

Jericho swiped at his chin. "This is a lot of sleep?"

Moriah snuggled into my robe, no doubt looking for milk I didn't have. "This baby does well. You kept me up most of the night until you were five years old. If it wasn't for Dana, I don't know how—"

"I'm sorry." He dropped into the rocking chair I'd brought down from the attic, the one I'd rocked him in. It was still functional, but as creaky as his voice.

"Don't be. This is what it's all about. There were great moments, too. Being a parent is the most difficult and the most rewarding job I've ever had. The shop, my faith, most of who I am—it's all somehow tied to making a better life for you."

He scrubbed his eyes. "But it could have been easier if Dad had been there, huh?"

I paced to the door and back again. "I try not to think in could-haves, honey, but yes, I suppose it might have been easier with your father around, but then again, maybe not."

With a final wail, Moriah went limp against me.

"Finally," I whispered, starting toward the crib.

My son held out his hand, shook his head. "I'll walk her a little more. Until she's asleep for real."

Asleep for real? I stared down at her closed angel eyes, tiny chest rising and falling. What was this, fake sleep? I didn't dare ask. I wanted to tell him that even if she woke up she'd go back down again, just like he always had, but that would be parenting advice, which I'd promised myself not to give. Though I still think parents who live with their parents need all the advice they can get.

In spite of Jericho's warning, I placed Moriah in her crib. If she was going to spend half of her time here, she was going to have to learn how to sleep sometime. Besides, I had a feeling I might not want to be holding a newborn for whatever my son was trying to say.

Jericho paced my route, to the door and back. "I think things could have been much better if Dad had stayed—I don't think this babysitting switch-off stuff is enough—"

"Look, I can't let Shemika move in here, you know that."

Especially not with her breastfeeding. It gave me the willies just thinking about her popping out the goods every few hours. Warming up the milk and keeping that electronic pump maintained was a nightmare, though. Whatever happened to good old boiling water and formula? If something happened to Shemika, that baby would probably starve. She didn't even take a pacifier.

"Okay Mom, I get that. I wouldn't feel right about that anyway. If I just wanted to live with her, I'd be at Dad's right now."

I froze. "Why does it always have to come back to this tug-of-war between your father and me?" Moriah started to fuss in the crib. Maybe there was something to this fake-sleep theory after all.

Jericho reached in and rubbed the baby's back. "No, Mom, it isn't about you and Dad. It's about Shemika and me. I want her to be my wife."

This again?

"What?" I took a cleansing breath, the kind recommended on my new exercise video. No help. Jericho's plan to marry Shemika wasn't a new concept or a smart one. "I thought we'd permanently tabled that one for now."

He gathered the now-screaming child into his arms. "You tabled it, Mom. Not me. I'm going to do it anyway, but it'd be nice if you'd just support us—"

"I can't. You don't have a job or an education. What about college? We've been over this a hundred times. If you really love your child, you'll think of your future. And hers."

He rolled his eyes. "I do have a job lined up. As soon as

Moriah is a little older, I'll start college. Plenty of ball play-ers have wives and kids."

Here we go with that again.

"Plenty of ball players beat those wives and ignore those kids, too. You're nothing more than a child yourself. I don't know how I'll do it, but Mother Holloway and I will find a way to look after Moriah so that you and Shemika can fin-ish school. What happened to you, Jericho? What happened to wanting to be the best?"

He tapped the baby's back. A sour burp exploded from her little body. "I still want to be the best, Mom—the best dad."

I sighed. "Did your aunt Dana put you up to this?"

Jericho shook his head.

"Your Dad's father? I know you've spent a lot of time down at his restaurant lately."

"Nope. You changed his mind. He's against it now, actu-ally. Says I should go into the army, *then* get married."

Great. The idea had possibilities actually, but with all the turmoil in the world, I wasn't sure about that one, either. Best to ignore it completely. "Your father then?"

He looked away.

"I knew it!" I started across the room toward the phone.

He cut me off as I picked up the cordless from the base. "Don't. *I* brought it up to Dad. He just said that maybe if he'd married you, things wouldn't be so hard for me right now. He said that he'd wanted to marry you, but people talked him out of it, told him that it'd hurt his basketball ca-reer and that he was too young to handle it."

"Looks like they were right." I tried not to wonder who

these "people" were and why they would have said such a thing. It didn't matter now. I pushed Jericho aside and clicked the phone on.

Jericho unplugged the phone from the base, preventing me from calling out. "Maybe they were right. Maybe not. Maybe Dad just believed what people said more than what his heart said. I know this won't be easy, but I think it will be better, better than this." He stared down at the baby, sagging against him in a fitful sleep.

"Better than this? Better than this, would have been for you to have listened to me in the first place! Shemika could keep the baby all week and take her to the nursery at her school. You are the one making things 'like this.' It's a little too late to try and be the Cleavers, don't you think?"

"I didn't want to only see my daughter on the weekends or every once in a while like all the guys I know. I don't want to be some fool at the mall getting yelled at by his child's mother because he didn't bring diapers over. I know you don't believe this, Mom, but this has really changed me. I don't want to just be another baby's daddy. I want to be a husband. I want to be a man."

The conviction in his voice blew through me like one of the fall winds soon to arrive.

A man. Wasn't that what I raised him to be? Why had he waited until now to come to this conclusion? Why couldn't he have been a man last year and not gotten the girl pregnant in the first place? "So now you want to be a man, huh? That's convenient. You act totally irresponsible, risk everything I've given you, everything God has given you and all of the sudden I'm supposed to believe you're grown-up?"

He took the phone from where I'd curled it to my chest and hung it back in place on the wall. "You don't have to believe it, Mom, but it's true. Everything that's going on—with Dad coming back, Aunt Dana getting married to Adrian, Grandpa cooking again, even Aunt Dahlia and Trevor being around—it's all I ever wanted. Family. And now I have one of my own. I want to make it work, make it last."

I turned away so that my son wouldn't see me cry. Dahlia was Dana and Jordan's younger sister. She'd dedicated herself to the Lord during Dana's wedding ceremony and was going through marriage counseling with the father of her child, who was also Dana's ex-boyfriend. As much as Jericho drove me crazy, he and Shemika were probably easily as mature as that couple. And I supported their marriage wholeheartedly. Still, it wasn't *who* Jericho had mentioned that bothered me, but *what*.

Family. The thing he'd always wanted.

Hadn't I been his family? It was hard enough to be put aside in the church, in business, in the world, but I'd always thought that what we'd had as mother and son had been enough. Evidently, I'd been wrong. What hurt more than his words was the fact that somewhere inside me, a part of me nodded in agreement. I wanted a family, too.

"I know that your baby needs you, but you are my baby. My family. I just can't let you ruin your life."

He put the baby down again, lowering her an inch at a

time. He started for the door, then looked back. "Ruin my life? Like you ruined yours?"

We stepped into the hall together, trying to keep our voices down. I didn't do so well with that. "That's not what I meant and you know it. You may be turning eighteen in a few months and have some mystery job lined up, but you're not grown yet. I love the both of you, but we can't even discuss this again until you've graduated. I just can't take the chance that you won't. Moriah needs a father with an education as much as she needs this perfect dad you want to become."

My son's shoulders sagged. "Don't make this difficult, Mom."

I straightened, tightened the belt on my robe. I knew a threat when I heard one. "What's that supposed to mean?"

"Just what I said. There are ways to get what I want. I'd rather not go around you, but if I have to, I will." Jericho disappeared down the hall, but his words hung in the air.

As August eased into autumn, the vise of tension between my son and I tightened more and more. I arrived early at my shop and had a special prayer time followed by working some new leather samples and playing around with some shoe designs. By seven-thirty, I'd made my decision to call Jordan to get to the root of our little parenting problem.

I still feel strange using "parenting" and "Jordan" in the same sentence after his seventeen-year absence, but men seem to be able to pull off tricks like that—reappear and become the hero. If I'd left my kid, then come back almost twenty years later and tried to be a mom, I'd have been laughed out of town. Oh, well. Such is life.

Though we'd gotten along well in the weeks following Moriah's birth, a divide had developed between Jordan and me, no doubt facilitated by Terri, his future bride. She answered the phone when I called.

"Good morning!"

I pulled the cell away from my ear. How Jordan could ever have been interested in me and her in the same lifetime defied my best logic. "Hello, Terri. It's Rochelle. It's Jordan available?"

Her cheeriness took a quick vacation, replaced by her "Oh, it's you" voice. "He's a little tied up. Maybe I can take a—"

"Who is that on the phone?" Jordan's voice echoed in the background. Probably still asleep. "Hello?"

"It's Rochelle. Sorry to wake you. I'm calling to set up a time when we can talk about Jericho and this getting-married business. I think it best to come at this from a united front."

He sniffed away all that remained of his night's rest and cleared his throat. "I'm not sure if I can do that, Chelle. To be honest, I'm pulling for them. And I'll do anything I can to help them."

"We both will!" Terri's enthusiastic cheer from the background set my teeth on edge.

Jordan muffled the receiver, but I could hear him say, "Sweetheart? Why don't you go and start us some breakfast, huh?"

I held my stomach, hoping its contents wouldn't end up

on the Persian rug I'd recently purchased for the shop, or worse, a pair of the shoes on the display table. Was everyone losing their minds?

"Help them? Are you insane?" Oops. I hadn't meant to sound so shrill.

"When I left you, I was insane, but not now." He lowered his voice.

I raised mine. "Don't go there, J! This is about the kids." So it was about us, too, but I couldn't deal with that now.

"Hold on."

The sound of Jordan's size-sixteen feet padding down the hall came scuffling through the line. A door slammed. "Look, I'm trying to build a relationship with our son—with you or without you. If the boy wants to be a man and try to do the right thing, I'm going to support him."

A dull ringing sound filled my ears. I stared around the shop, my eyes resting on a bright fucshia pair of designer pumps that arrived last week to fill a special order. This was real. I was awake. "All right, thanks for letting me know where things stand. I'll be in touch—"

"Wait, Chelle, I—"

I jabbed the button on my phone and pasted a smile on my face as the bell jingled over the door.

My first customer of the day.

Chapter five

"These are banging."

My lips forced themselves into a smile as I watched Dahlia, sister of my best friend and aunt to my son, maul my display shoes and jangle my nerves. With a gentle hand and a swift movement, I took the pumps from her and replaced them on their perch in the front window. "Those certainly make a statement. A five-thousand-dollar statement to be exact. Perhaps you'd like to see something more…"

"Quiet?" She adjusted the brim on her cap. It was green plaid with a pom-pom on top. There was a jacket to match and *knickers*. She looked like an extra from *Caddyshack*.

"Exactly. Something that speaks a little more softly." As if that were possible. Everything about Dahlia was loud and larger than life. Her new gift shop, Urban Interiors, was setting the town on fire. Thankfully, my store was far enough away from hers—three blocks—to endure the blaze. Though I carried shoes that many a diva would die for, trendy was not one of the attributes of my business brand. Classic, innovative, exclusive, loyal and warm—those were the things my customers came for. Except for friends and family like Dahlia who could easily mess up my brand—and my life—if I let them.

I chose not to let them.

Regaining my rhythm, I walked farther into the store, bringing Dahlia along with my other hand. I stopped on one of the lower shelves, where the lower-end-yet-still-special styles were kept. "Here is a nice silk mule. Available in pink and gold. Perfect for this late-summer early-fall period—"

"Don't you have a sale rack?" She'd obviously spied the price tag, $179.99. I started to tell her that these had been discounted for the incoming winter styles, but I knew better than to try and explain anything to Miss Ghetto Fabulous.

"I don't. Sales sections don't work well with my customer base. The one time I tried it almost wrecked my business."

Dahlia nodded. "Okay. I'll take one of each of those in an eight a half. And those hot pink ones in the window."

Fuchsia. Not hot pink. Fuchsia. I paused, remembering that my special order still hadn't paid. Naomi, Dana's former boss, was one of my best clients, but even she knew the rules. I'd gone out on a limb to hold them. But was Dahlia serious? "Do you want to try them on? The mules, I mean? The pair in the window are, well, a little expensive."

She nodded. "I know. I saw them in a video last week. Just ring me up."

Never one to miss a sale, I obeyed, confused as I could be. I knew her boyfriend made money with his little rap records and all, but *this* kind of money? Maybe I was as out of touch as everyone said. I boxed the shoes and scribbled the total on the pad and turned it to her, not wanting to have to void a purchase on my register.

"Sure." She flipped out a credit card and a red, glossy smile.

I shrugged and rang it up, wondering if my call with Jordan had played into how I'd treated Dahlia. All of a sudden, she seemed to look so much like him. Moriah even looked a little like Dahlia, I realized as I studied her face. I smiled at the thought of my little grandbaby.

Her hand warmed mine. "I know you've never really liked me, Rochelle. And I can understand why. But I've changed. Things have changed. And you're going to have to give everybody another chance. I know that's hard."

My vision blurred. This was the longest conversation I'd had with this child—that's how I still thought of her—since she'd turned wild and stopped listening to me so many years ago. "Things have changed to be sure. We're all going through some things."

The register spit out a receipt, which I stared at in amazement. The purchase had cleared. I layered the boxes with my signature paper, lavender with pumps embossed onto the tissue. Good paper, like good shoes, spoke volumes. I reached under the counter for something else, a silk scarf painted in purple, teal and fuchsia. "This is a gift for all customers with purchases over one thousand dollars. Made it myself."

Dahlia whisked it from my fingers and around her throat. "Ooh, one of your bad scarves? If I'd known this was the gift, I'd have come in here a long time ago. Forget the shoes, girl, you need to be selling *these*. Where's yours today? You're looking tired, Grandma. Don't let the kiddies get you down." She winked and headed for the door.

I know she didn't call me Grandma.

"Yep, I said it. And while I'm at it, get out of here and meet some people. I did."

Of course she had, at Dana's expense. I'd been front and center when Miss Thing had run off with the leather-clad rapper I'd once despised. Now he was one of our best ushers at church. "Right. When is your wedding anyway?"

She held the door open, shook her head. "Trevor and I? Our wedding? I have no clue. We're still talking, of course. Going to church together. Raising our child together. But I'm not convinced anymore that I'm even ready for that. I'm just going on some group dates, meeting some nice people."

I leaned over the counter. "Group dates?" I wasn't sure why but this spiked my curiosity.

"Check out A Match Made in Seven dot-com. Seven the word, not the number. They guarantee a connection—friendship, relationship, whatever—within seven group outings. It's Christian and legit. Who knows? You might make a love connection. At worst, you'll make some new friends—which you look like you could use."

She let the door slam without looking back to see what must have been my stunned face.

I needed a change, more specifically, one of the male variety. For what purpose exactly I still wasn't sure. Someone to talk to on the phone about the Lord or even e-mail with occasionally would be nice. I think. Or maybe it would be torture. Either way, I was ready to find out.

After a volatile few days with my son and a blunt conversation with my lawyer, I admitted to myself—and to God— that I wasn't crazy about the idea of being alone for the rest of my life. I'm guessing I'm not the only one who was surprised. For all my teaching on the gift of singleness, I didn't have it after all.

The phone call was what really got things going. I'd spent most of last Wednesday's lunch hour on the phone with my lawyer, who'd painfully informed me that my son was old enough to live with his father if he wanted and probably old enough to get married in a few states. In other states, one parent's signature would suffice.

"One parent?" I'd said. "He doesn't even have custody."

"He signed the birth certificate and the two of you never had a court order for support. Though he abandoned you and your son, let's face it, back in the eighties, Jordan was a household name. He did leave you several thousand dollars for the boy—and I do mean several…"

"But-but that was one time. He never paid child support until now, never visited—"

"I know, Rochelle, but it will still be considered. Then there's that sob story about him being in a coma for ten years. You pay for his care and then he wakes up and comes home to pick up where he left off? It's too good. I'm surprised you guys don't have a reality show already. If he wanted to help the kid get married, most likely it'd go his way. It's not necessarily fair, but true."

Wasn't that the story of my life? "Is there nothing I can do?"

In his honest but annoying way, my lawyer had laughed. "Are you dating?"

I cleared my throat. "I don't see what this has to do with—"

"Any prospects?"

The directness I'd always valued in this man got to me now. "Not really."

"Well, friend to friend, I suggest you get on with your life, Ms. Gardner. You're a good-looking woman with a strong faith. This thing with Mr. Rose has controlled your life from the day I met you. When you get married, and not to that guy, invite me. I've gotta run."

Good-looking? Strong faith? Why did these compliments feel like a series of slaps in the face?

"Okay. Bye," I'd said, sifting through his comments. When I got married? Was this what things always came back to, my fate in the hands of some unknown Prince Charming?

The sad thing was, this time he had a point. Or did he? I'd spent the past few days pondering that one and only one thing was clear—the idea of being alone for the rest of my life didn't appeal to me anymore.

While debating with myself about having sent in the Match Made in Seven questionnaire, I'd listed my prospects. It was a short list. Tad came to mind for a moment and vanished just as quickly. If nothing had happened between us after ten years of eyeing each other over the pew, nothing would happen now.

Though things had been intense between Tad and I the

day of Moriah's birth, he hadn't said a peep to me since—
avoiding my e-mails, calls and notes in his Sunday school
mailbox at the church. I really wanted to do more to thank
Tad, but there was enough drama going on. Besides, his connection to Jordan seemed to be growing stronger, and
stronger which meant more drama.

I didn't need drama. I just needed a normal, hardworking
guy who loved the Lord, liked kids and at least wanted to be
my friend—without a bunch of emotional entanglements.
How hard could that be to find?

Am I really even thinking this?

I was. If I was honest, I had been for a long time. As I put
on my purple silk dress for my first outing with the dating
service, a group dinner date I'd signed up for but never really planned to attend, I admitted to myself that it was time
to move on, even if this was a weird way to do it.

According to the dating service, meeting someone new was
as simple as making Christian friends best suited to my "God-
given personality." Sounded like a line from one of those self-
help books Tracey was always reading to me, but I was willing
to give it a try. The questions in the e-mail profile had been
surprisingly insightful: What is your most important area of
common interest—faith, culture, fitness or socioeconomics?

I'd tangled over that one and similar questions for the past
few evenings during Moriah's naps. After giving up on dating for so many years, anything but faith had sort of escaped
my radar when even considering someone of the opposite
sex. Now I took time to give it some thought, trying not to
feel ridiculous. Faith was definitely still first in my concerns,

but I began to think more and more about what my ideal man might be like.

It was a painful exercise, considering that my last fling into the dating arena had been less than successful. The guy had been nice enough, sincere and hardworking with his own limousine business and a dedicated member of a church in town, but as everyone saw so clearly except me, it never was really about romance but about comfort. I needed to tell myself that I could still interest a man, show Jordan that I could. My mind tried to make it more spiritual than that, but that's about the depth of it.

When my "friend" started chilling at my house as if he lived there and sweating on my special sofa, well, you know he had to go. If I asked, he'd start things up again in a minute, but why try to resurrect something dead? I needed to use that kind of Jesus power on the big ticket items. Besides, Jericho disliked the man and would most likely tell him so if I brought him around again. Moriah's birth had mellowed that boy, but he was still a pill.

Now here I was, knotting a scarf around my neck and heading out the door. As I drove to the meeting place, I gripped the wheel, only releasing it when I'd parked in the restaurant's packed lot.

It was time to dive in, to really try and meet somebody. That was my last thought as I entered Ujaama restaurant, where a darker, younger version of Billy Dee Williams held the door open for me.

"Welcome to Ujaama," he said, taking my hand and ushering me into the incensed lobby.

Welcome indeed, I thought, suddenly wishing this waiter would not only seat me, but be seated at my table. I fanned myself. I was getting out of hand. "Thank you. I'm with a group. A Match Made in Seven? They said my name would be on the reservation."

Understanding flashed in his eyes. His fluid movement leading me through the crowd came to an abrupt halt. "Forgive me for being forward, miss, but you don't look like you need a dating service." He started again, this time taking my hand.

Though usually I'd be upset at someone trying to tell me what I needed, I felt inclined to agree. The whole thing was silly, but I was here now. I drank in his confidence in me, standing a little taller than my already looming stature and enjoying the touch of his tapered fingers. I caught a glimpse of his hands as he pulled me forward. Artist's hands. "Thank you for your compliment. I'll keep that in mind."

He gave me a look that made me shiver down to my toes. "You do that."

We stopped at an empty table and stared at each other for a moment, both a little breathless. Most people couldn't keep up with me, but he'd moved so quickly I was truly out of breath. Good hands *and* in good shape. I stopped myself before I made any more notes. "Is this it? Where is everyone?"

He made a snorting sound. "They're mingling. Finding others with their God-given personality and all that. Oh, and I'll bring another chair. Your party is more than seven, tonight," he whispered. "It's a party of ten."

My smile faded. Ten? I racked my brain for the Biblical significance of that number and came up with nothing except for the ten commandments, most of which I'd probably broken since getting here. Not that it made a difference, but such things made me feel better about crazy situations like this.

Steel drums pounded in the background. "Have a seat here, miss…" The last word lingered like a question, but I made no offer of information. I had enough trouble as it was.

I read his name tag. Shan. Interesting name, but I kept myself from commenting on it. "Thank you, Shan. Thank you very much." I looked around at the empty table. The other nine people must have been still mingling or getting food from the International buffet the restaurant was famous for. "You've really helped me tonight. I was very nervous about coming here." I tugged at the scarf at my neck, bypassing the desire to tug at my earrings, much larger than I usually wore.

The server came closer, smelling of ylang-ylang and peppermint, a fantastic but unexpected blend.

I'll have to recommend that one to Dana. Maybe I'll even have her call it Shan. Who would know?

"You needn't have been nervous, miss. As I said, you didn't need to come at all." He paused for a moment, resting his smooth, dark hand upon my shoulder before walking away.

I blew out a breath. If the wait staff was any indication of how the evening would go, things were certainly going to get interesting—

"Funny meeting you here."

The voice, nasal and far too familiar, made me whirl around in my chair. I gasped for the breath to respond. "Tad?"

He chuckled. "It's me. It seems we've found each other… again. I'm glad. I was just about to bolt for the door. Jordan's sister sort of pushed me into this. I'm still not sure what I'm doing here."

That Dahlia. She was something else for sure.

"Me neither." I wasn't sure if I meant it about myself or him. What was Tad doing here? Most of the women in the church would swoon to have so much as a cup of coffee with Tad, let alone dinner. And here he was, looking for a woman? It made about as much sense as me being here looking for a man.

Tad sat back in his chair. "You look stunning, by the way. You can wear purple like no woman I know."

"Thanks—"

A bronze beauty appeared and reached between us, extending her business cards our way. "I know you two were late and first timers, but we're all supposed to mingle, share cards. When the night is over, you go through your cards and contact directly, but not here." Her gold lamé dress crinkled as she slid into the chair between us. "You know, just to give everyone a chance to meet."

Tad pulled his hand away from mine and extended it toward our guest. "Of course. My name is Thaddeus—"

She beamed. "Actually, I work at your station. Imagine how excited I was when I saw you come in…" Miss Mingle's back was toward me now and the conversation had gone off into the world of television, something I knew nothing about.

I scanned the dim room for Shan, the fine waiter, but he was nowhere to be found. Hmm…maybe I should have taken *his* number and called it quits. Or was I trying to get into something that I knew wouldn't work to keep from actually having a relationship? A deep breath filled my lungs. All this self-analysis was tiring. How did Oprah keep up with it?

Lord, what's happening to me?

Thinking it best to go home and figure that out, I stood, trying to remember exactly where I'd parked. This wasn't the side of town to be wandering around alone after dark.

"Is that you, Rochelle?" While Tad's voice had stolen my breath, this tone froze my heart. This party of ten was full of surprises. Already, I smelled the Halston Z-14 floating toward me in the restaurant's simmer of peppercorns and curry.

"It's me, Jordan."

Soft lips grazed my cheek. It'd been weeks since Jordan and I had talked, but looking at him it seemed like a lifetime. His thin frame had fleshed out into the broad shoulders I'd once known. The same honey-colored skin, full beard, chocolate drop eyes...the same dog I'd once fallen in love with. I wasn't sure what had happened, but the old J was back and looking quite at the top of his game. I swallowed hard and deliberately lowered myself back into the chair before I fell down.

He didn't waste any time. "I'm a little surprised—and hurt—to see you here. I'd hoped that if you had any interest in pursuing a relationship, I'd be first in line."

My reserve gone, I dropped my jaw. "Seeing as how you're engaged, I think that'd be a little difficult, don't you? Where is Terri, by the way?"

Jordan took the seat on the opposite side of me. Tad's

voice broke through the ceiling of his huddled conversation
with his coworker. I couldn't make out the words, but he'd
definitely noticed Jordan's arrival at the table. It seemed no
one in the room had missed it. All eyes in the room were on
us, including Shan's. He lingered a few tables away with an
I-told-you-so smile.

If only he knew.

"The last time I saw Terri, she was taking a special deliv-
ery from the UPS guy…in our bedroom."

My hand flew to my mouth. "I'm sorry." And I meant it.
His girlfriend wasn't my favorite person, but I'd finally accepted that the two of them would be together. It had actually made things a bit simpler. Now, I was totally confused.
"How—how are you handling it?"

"Better, now that I'm looking at you again. I'm so sorry
about our last conversation. You deserved better." He looked
beyond me. "Is that Tad?" Waving furiously, Jordan gave his
best smile.

"Tad. So he's here for this thing, too? Wow. Dahlia was
right. Everybody in town must be onto this—"

A handsome white man with a gentle smile tapped Jordan on the shoulder, requesting an autograph. On further in-
spection, I saw he was my podiatrist, but he didn't recognize
me, thankfully. Like most men, it was only J he had eyes for.

"Do you mind?" Jordan kept smiling, but the lines creased
around his eyes.

I shook my head. In truth, I was thankful for the diversion. Most of the "party" had returned to the table by now,
though no one was talking, except for whispers debating if

it was really Jordan followed by questions about my identity. Miss Mingle, as I'd dubbed Tad's coworker, took a break from getting to know Tad better to give me a look that would give small children nightmares.

She added a warning, too, just for clarity. "You just know everybody, huh? Next time, do us regular folks a favor and stay home." She hissed the words through clenched teeth wreathed by the biggest, reddest grin I've ever seen.

The malice was real but so misguided.

As Jordan finished scribbling, I decided leaving probably was the best option if everyone was to meet. Sliding my stack of business cards across the table—the service did check to make sure that everyone had the right amount of cards—and palming the small pile of cards next to my still empty plate, I leaned over to Jordan. "Look, I'm really sorry about what happened with Terri, but take tonight and meet some new people. There are some beautiful, smart women here from the looks of these cards. It's over for us, J. It's been too long." I almost believed it.

"Much too long." He pulled me to him. I tried to resist, but that stupid cologne rendered me senseless.

He touched my finger. My ring finger. The bare one. "Look, I'm too old for this dating thing, so don't sweat it. I just wanted to get out, do something low-key. I'm just glad you're here, because, though we've talked about a lot of things, I've been wanting to make up somehow for ruining your life."

Make up for it? Did he think that was actually possible? "Ruin my life? I've had a good life. In fact, I'm seeing more and more that maybe raising Jericho preserved me, saved me for later, you know?"

"You're definitely well preserved. I'm going to have to take you to the hoop sometimes and see just how well kept you really are." His smile was innocent and he was talking about basketball, but this woman knew fleeing time when she saw—and smelled—it. Though in truth, Jordan's cologne paled in comparison to that cute waiter's scent.

Stop it.

I found the strength to pull away and push back my chair. My podiatrist tossed a card on my pile as did a beautiful tiny woman who smelled of cinnamon. I smiled. Maybe she'd make a good friend if anybody actually followed up on anything besides date prospects. I thanked them and started for the door. I waved to Tad. "Sorry I didn't get to meet everyone, but I have the cards. Have a good time."

Tight smiles and annoyed goodbyes rushed toward me as I ran toward the door. Still, I was no match for Jordan's long legs. He pushed the door open as I reached it. Shan the server followed us with a look that said he'd flatten Jordan in a minute, NBA legend or no. I gave him a reassuring grin. "It's okay. We're old friends, you know?"

He looked at me as though he didn't understand. Maybe he was too young to know how these things went, but I couldn't be sure. He had that kind of timeless handsomeness that denied being pinned to an age. He could be twenty-eight…or forty-eight. I'd go out with him either way…

Cut the waiter bit and ditch Jordan. This was all a mistake. Just get home safe, a little voice warned.

Jordan shook his head and gave me the amazing look. "You know the waiters, too?"

I laughed. I didn't know Shan, but I wanted to, despite knowing it was a bad idea. "Not exactly. He helped me to my seat tonight." From the looks of things, Shan was guiding me to my car, too, with his eyes. He remained in front of the restaurant, arms folded and eyes focused on us like a laser.

Jordan tried to laugh it off. "And people think *I'm* famous. Everybody in the restaurant is after *you* tonight." We squeezed through the maze to my car. The restaurant was nice, but they needed to work on parking. Listening to Jordan, I plotted a way to get out without having to ask anyone to move.

His words cut my exit plan short. "Look, I know you don't want to be with me anymore. I think you've made that clear. But the sacrifices you've made to care for our son mean a lot to me. This thing with Terri really hammered that home to me again."

So that was it. "Sympathy pains, huh? Sweet, but don't bother. You and Terri will be patched up and at the altar in a few months. Don't slow down to tend my wounds. They've long healed." Like a fool, I touched his face. "I think you'd better put some balm to your own hurts."

He nodded. "When I walked in on Terri, I thought about how your face looked the other day at the hospital when you thought I'd left. I'd been trying to wrap my mind around how you must have felt…"

I still felt it, more often than I was willing to admit. "Let's not revisit it." I looked back at the restaurant. Shan was still watching, waiting for me to make it to my car. The shiver

I'd felt inside when our eyes met ran through me again. I brushed it off as the cool night air and fumbled for my keys. I really needed to get home. Church folks who haven't been out in a while needed to take these things in little doses, lest we lose our minds completely.

After an awkward pause, I opened the driver's-side door, praying that I'd be alert to teach Sunday school in the morning. From the looks of things, Tad might not be in any shape to cover for me. He'd told me once he went to bed each night at nine. One more reason I should have stayed home. "Good seeing you, Jordan."

He grabbed my hand as I went to shut the car door. "Don't do it, Chelle."

I jerked back. "Don't do what?"

His eyes bored into mine. "Don't be afraid to love again, even if it means loving me."

Chapter six

Though the publicity was good for business, nothing could have prepared me for the media blitz waiting for me Monday morning. The local TV station had even sent Austin to cover it. Had she told them that she knew me? I hoped not. I turned the key to open my store with a tight smile and an even tighter skirt. Time to go back to the Tae Bo again.

"So, Ms. Gardner, word has it that Shoes of Peace is a business on the rise and you're the new face of Leverhill society. Perhaps even the new love of former NBA pro Jordan Rose?"

Austin sounded like she always did, but one look into her eyes, especially her left one which was blinking and watering like crazy, let me know that she had not opted for this assignment and that she wanted to run inside and lock the door behind both of us.

Not knowing what to do, I pushed open the door. The cameraman practically knocked me down. I rallied and managed a quick breath. "Shoes of Peace has always tried to carry styles from classic to cutting edge. Because of that, we get a wide variety of customers."

Another reporter, one who'd appeared from nowhere, waved a hand. "Customers like Jordan Rose? Isn't it true that you two were high school sweethearts? That you have a son—"

"I'm going to have to ask you all to leave." I summoned my best smile and firmest tone. All the time I'd spent yesterday in the Word must have been in preparation for this mess. I held the door open with my foot, motioning for Austin and her crew to exit as well.

She frowned. "Me, too?"

"You, too." I stepped aside so that the frustrated cameraman could maneuver his way back out the door. Jordan and I was one thing, my family was another. Hadn't the media seen J parading Terri around for months? I never saw *her* on TV. Why me? And who gave them my name?

Somebody at that restaurant, Ujaama. My business cards contained all the ammo they'd needed.

As Austin passed me, she whispered, "Let me get an interview outside. I pulled some strings to cover this. That other guy is out to make you look bad. I'm going to play it way down. A human interest story."

"Fine." How could she do this for a living? What a nightmare. Still, a giggle purred in my throat watching her in that Barbara Walters suit looking all serious. What a contrast to the ponytail and sweatpants woman I was growing to love. She looked like a movie star…or a spy.

Her eyes widened into a look she'd definitely picked up

from Dana, who was conveniently out of town again. The please-not-now look. I shook my head. Austin needn't worry, I wouldn't crack up laughing in her face on TV. At least I didn't think so.

"So tell us what it's like to own one of the only shoe boutiques in town?"

I sat down on the ledge outside my display window, moving until the cameraman gave me a cue to go ahead. "It's amazing. Designing shoes—and selling them—is something that I love. There's nothing like a good pair of shoes—"

"Or a good man to fill them."

We all swung around to find Dahlia in a winter-white knit suit with a fur collar and the coral snakeskin pumps she'd purchased from me the month before. My breathing, already shallow, turned to a panting whisper. "This is Dahlia…one of my customers. Thanks so much for stopping by, but I'd better get in and attend to her."

Dahlia fanned her hand. "Don't let me interrupt. In fact, I think that Rochelle is being rather modest. She always could hook up a nice pair of shoes, even back in the day. Add some beads to those horrid dyeables for the prom, put a cute flower on a pair of flip-flops. She knows how to make a woman look good."

"Thanks, girl." Hand on Dahlia's elbow, I pulled her toward my door. Next, she'd be telling how I'd once taken her mother's bedroom slippers and turned them into wedding shoes when I was starting out. Or those red satin shoes I'd made to go with my nightgown. I still had those. Why do people only remember the embarrassing stories?

Austin appeared relieved when I looked back. "Well, it seems that Rochelle Gardner and Shoes of Peace are well loved by everyone around here. Thanks for your comments, Miss—"

Just as I had her crossing the threshold, my almost sister-in-law wiggled from under my arm. "Rose. Dahlia Rose. I own Urban Interiors, a few blocks down?"

The other reporter looked like he'd just found gold. "Rose? Like the basketball star?"

Dahlia smiled. "The one and the same. I'm his baby sister. Rochelle here almost married him, isn't that right, girl?"

My stomach dropped.

The camera kept rolling.

The bell over the door to my shop chimed, shaking me out of my thoughts. I'd been taping the news for two days but still managed to miss the clip. Jericho thought it was cute. I did not. Right now though, I needed to focus on my customer.

"Welcome to Shoes of Peace," I said slowly, making out the face of my newest customer.

Wearing the paisley bow tie and suspenders that I'd bought him as a Secret Santa gift back in the day, Tad approached the counter with his jacket slung across his arm.

"Do you have anything for men? Shoes, I mean."

Shaken by the thought that he might be here for something other than to talk to me, I stumbled for words. "Y-yes. I have a few men's styles. If you'll have a seat, I'll bring some things out to you."

He buried his hands in his pockets. "Your shoes? Did you make them? The ones you're bringing out?"

I ran a hand across the faux quartz counter. "I don't make many shoes anymore. Most of what I have is from other designers. I do some custom work, but it's pricey."

Tad came closer. "I'm willing to pay, however much."

My blouse suddenly seemed itchy, especially around the neckline. Making shoes for men felt intimate to me. Like kissing. I did it for my girlfriends with no problem, and Mrs. Shapiro insisted on custom work, but outside of my son, I hadn't made a pair of shoes for a man since design school. And I would rather not start with Tad.

"Well, I'm sure you can afford them, but I don't know if it would be practical. You're busy, and the fittings can take quite a while the first time—"

He tossed his jacket on the counter and circled behind it. To me.

"I can make time. Can we start now? With the measurements, I mean?"

As he stepped behind the counter and stood beside me, a sweet, manly scent came from Tad. A plaid sort of smell kissed with spices and plums. For a moment, it confused me so that I forgot what he'd said.

But I didn't forget that he was there. My body reminded me of that.

"We can start now. That's fine."

He smiled and put a hand on the counter, millimeters from mine. Almost close enough to touch me. And it thrilled me more than if he had. Tad was that kind of man, one who made every movement, every word count. After ten years of analyzing his every word and deed, I knew that his presence here meant something, but what? Jealousy? Worry? Maybe he actually needed new shoes.

"I have to admit, I really don't need a pair of shoes," he said as we walked to the seating area.

So much for that theory.

"However, I would like to try a pair of your shoes. Have a chance to see you work. I so respect what you've done here, with everything in your life. Have I ever told you that?"

I shook my head as he pulled his foot from his wingtips. Black silk socks, great thread. Just as I'd expected. Suddenly, I was back in the Sunday school room with roses sifting through my toes. There was so much I wanted to say, but something inside me said to be quiet and take the measurements.

And so I did. I measured his feet. Nice feet, with even, manicured toes. He'd definitely been to the pedicure place I frequented. Who knew? Whatever his foot hang-up was, it wasn't visible now. As I did my thing, Tad did his, something he usually only did with a Bible in his hand or very close by—talking. In fact, I couldn't shut him up, not even with my silence.

"That woman from the restaurant turns out to be someone I work with. I'm so sorry that I let her monopolize my attention. I saw though that Jordan picked up where I was negligent."

Again, I nodded and motioned to his right heel, instead of spewing out any of the words pacing behind my lips like armed soldiers.

He extended the correct foot. "I know that Jordan is in a hard place right now, fresh out of a relationship and everything. He's coming to Bible study and seems to be getting a good bit from it, but it's obvious that being involved with a woman again is foremost in his mind."

I tugged the tape around his other ankle, breathing deep to keep from commenting. These were the most words Tad had ever spoken to me that didn't somehow involve church work or the singles group.

This is getting deep, Lord.

Tad gulped, but I didn't react. He must have taken that as a sign to go on. "I can understand Jordan's desire to get into a relationship as quickly as possible, especially with a beautiful, intelligent, godly woman as a prospect."

On the seat now beside him with a stack of shoe-style photos, it was my turn to gulp. "If you mean me, I—"

"I do mean you. And I understand his feelings, because I've had the same feelings for a very long time."

The photos slid from my lap. "What? Why didn't you say something?" So much for my strong silence.

As my anger hit him full force, I saw Tad almost physically retract into the shell I knew so well. His Bible shell, a safe and wonderful candy coating of his emotions. "The Word says that God gives good and perfect gifts. I'm still trusting Him to make me into something worthy—not perfect, but better."

My hands balled into fists. Worthy? Better? I'd spent last spring dating a chauffeur in tight pants because Tad had some kind of insecurity thing going on? Didn't he know how badly I'd wanted to be with him? Needed him? "Are you out of your mind? Better? Better than what, Tad? I mean come on. It's been ten years. You always preach that God takes us as we are. You're one of the best men that I've ever known."

He stood and started for the door. "That's just it, Rochelle. You really don't know me at all." He paused to pick up his jacket from the counter. "Oh and by the way, you look even more beautiful on TV. I had the pleasure of viewing the clip at the station."

From: *Sassysistah2*
To: *Sassysistah1, Shalomsistah, Sassysistah3*
Subject: I'm Baaaaaaack!

Hey ladies! I know that it's been like forever, but Adrian and I are back from the second honeymoon (hush, Chelle) and the Bath and Body Trade Show. We would have been back last week, but Adrian landed a sizable European account and we stuck around in Chicago to work out the details.

Tracey, thanks for holding on to your baby until we got back and Chelle, I hear I'm a great-auntie! Jericho said he would send pictures but never did and you, well, I hear you've been BUSY. (Right, Austin?)

Anyway, I love you sistahs and I've been missing you. It's been weird living without being online all the time, but I think it's a good thing. I'm even considering getting rid of my high speed connection. (Shut up Tracey, I mean it).

Rochelle, what do you think? Maybe we could even make the devotional list weekly instead of daily? We probably all spend too much time on this thing. Anyway, I'll be in touch by flesh or phone in the next 24. My boo is calling.

In His grip,
Dana

"So spill it."

"Spill what?" I wrapped a hand around my mug of ginger tea and tried to avoid Dana's eyes. Though Austin had played my heartstrings during our little girlfriend get-together, Dana and I went back far enough that she didn't stop to pick up any goodies to soothe me. Or mince any words, for that matter.

From the looks of her manicured nails, neatly braided hair and svelte figure, she hadn't been stopping to soothe much of anything except Adrian, her new husband, another of my longtime friends, though I hadn't talked to him much since he and Dana got married.

Dana took a sip of her tea, still steaming and without sugar. Amazing what a little international travel could do for a person. "Come on, Chelle. I've been gone for over a month and I've seen you post on the list what, once?"

I cleared my throat. "Twice."

Dana shrugged. "Okay, twice. That thing used to be your life. Then Shemika has the baby and you don't tell anybody? If Tad hadn't been there, the church wouldn't even have known—"

I moved over on the sofa. The leather squeaked beneath me. "Well, Tad was there, so I guess the day was saved."

My friend set her tea down on the coffee table, then picked up a coaster and shoved it under. Even in her quiet rage, she gave me that consideration.

We'd gone through a lot, Jordan's little sister and I. When he left that hospital room, he didn't just leave *me*. He'd left *her,* too. Something I'd really only come to understand in the past year. But now she had Adrian, her best friend, her "boo," who she'd almost missed out on altogether.

But God…

God. He was still in my life. My daily disciplines—devotions, prayer, worship—were all still in motion, even with the stiff new Bible I'd purchased. I kept at it every day, hoping that my disciplines would become devotions again, actions of love, deeds of desire.

Tell me, O my love, where are you leading your flock today? Where will you rest your sheep at noon?

The verse from my daily reading became the cry of my heart as Dana looked at me with the same look I'd given her so many times before—an expression of disappointment laced with fear. I smiled, knowing the roads we'd both trod. Smiling was the best I could offer. I was afraid too.

If you don't know, O most beautiful woman, follow the trail of my flock to the shepherds' tents, and. there feed your young goats. What a lovely filly you are, my beloved one!

Goats? Fillies? I had no idea what the Lord was saying, but it sure sounded good.

Dana unfolded her arms. Unlike me, when really upset, she took the time to gather her thoughts before speaking. "I don't know what to think, Chelle. What to say. You're a grown woman. I've looked up to you for most of my life, especially my Christian life. I don't have any children, so I can't imagine what you're going through, but if I didn't know any better, I'd think that you're ashamed of Jericho."

I tried to come up with a response to her simple, soft-spoken accusation, but I couldn't. Not one word of defense came to mind.

Seeing no barrier, Dana probed further. "And not only

ashamed of Jericho, but ashamed of yourself. For what, being a single mother? For having a kid who made some bad choices? For having Jordan come back and get involved with someone else? None of this is your fault. You know that, right?"

Words spun around in my head.

Yes.

Sure.

Of course.

None of those words, those lies were spoken. Instead, a tear slid down my face and into my tea.

Dana took the cup from my hand and pulled me to her. "I'm sorry I wasn't here for you, Chelle. I'm so sorry."

Though I'd let myself break down with Austin, I couldn't relax enough to do it now. I wanted to, *needed* to, but I just couldn't. "It's okay. You have a life now. A husband. Tracey is about to have a baby—"

"Speaking of which, have you talked to her?"

My hands shook. "Not really. With the babysitting keeping me up at night, I'm not really keeping in touch with anyone. I'd forgotten what it's like to have a baby around. When the baby was first born, Jericho and I barely talked to each other and we were in the house together. We sort of met up at the crib and grunted, you know?"

Dana laughed. "I do know. You and I did the same for him, remember?"

I held her hand in mine, remembering, something I didn't do that much. The pain I thought healed was sliced open again by Jordan's presence. "Thank you, Dane. For being there for me then. I realize now that you were just a kid, too. You and your mother hung with me all the way through."

At the mention of her mother, Jordan's mother, Dana stilled. "She was a good woman. She would have been overjoyed about this baby, despite the circumstances. She would have married them off, of course..."

I stiffened at the truth of it. The one thing that had plagued Mrs. Rose more than anything was that Jordan hadn't married me. She was hurt that he'd left, too, but the fact that Jericho didn't have his last name was a disgrace to her. She was known for her deft management of fried chicken shotgun weddings for the expecting couples on our block. And so far as I knew, all of them were still together. Not without hard times, but still married.

"I'm sure your mother would have wanted them married, but that was a different time, when people were willing to work hard and build a family. These kids nowadays want everything they see on TV, and they want it now. To make a marriage last today, you've got to have an education. Shemika needs it as much as my son does."

"So that she can better herself? Or just in case things don't work out?" Dana raised an eyebrow at me, as if in challenge.

Dahlia's talk of not being sure about getting married anymore turned over in my mind. "I didn't say that." Not with my lips anyway.

Dana's cell beeped in her pocket. She gave me an unnecessary nod and picked up. "Made of Honor, Dana speaking—Adrian? Hey, babe. I'm still at Chelle's." She smiled at me and whispered, "He says hi."

I nodded. "Hey, Adrian."

His booming voice came through the line. "Hey Grandma! Where's the baby? I'm still waiting for my pictures."

Dana shook her head. "Don't mind him—honey, the baby isn't here. She's with Shemika at school. Yeah, in the nursery—"

"If you stick around, you'll see her. It's our part of the week now. Jericho will pick her up this afternoon. Shemika's in that training program you used to work with, she's learning to make soap just like you and everything. They get their GED, as well."

Dana looked excited. "That's a great program. I'm even scheduled to get some interns from there. Who knows? Maybe she'll work with us one day."

I nodded, scanned my living room, packed with a baby swing, high chair, play pen and all sorts of other things Moriah couldn't use but we kept around in case we needed them. My life had definitely changed. And though I loved that baby to pieces, there was more than a little truth in Dana's words.

I was ashamed.

I was that hobble-toed, swaybacked eighteen-year-old girl again, knocking on my apartment door, only to find that my mother had moved out and left no return address. "You've thrown away everything I tried to give you," the note said. It was an awful sentence. One that I'd never truly understood until now. Still, I was determined not to run away or duck my head in the sand. Things were what they were—jacked up.

Dana finished her conversation and rested back on the couch that had previously been off-limits. "I'm staying to see my niece. The baby is the highlight of our return home. Although, getting to sit on this couch is pretty awesome. When did this become public domain? I've been eyeing this thing for years."

I shrugged. "Well, with the baby coming, I figured I'd better loosen my grip on some of my stuff. Make it easier on my nerves when it all gets destroyed." With visions of what my son's life was supposed to be flashing across my mind, I hugged my own shoulders and then let go.

"You're giving that baby too much credit. She's not going to destroy everything."

My head hung low. "She already has."

A frantic knock at the door broke the quiet between Dana and I. She leaped to her feet in anticipation. I eyed the diaper stacker and baby wipes container. Both were full. "He's got a key." The least the boy could do was open the door.

Dana wrung her hands and went to the sound. "But he's got the baby in his hand, and oh, I just have to see her!" With that she flung the door back, then covered her mouth.

"Jordan?" We both said it at the same time.

Car seat in hand, he kissed his little sister's forehead and made for the space on the couch next to me. "Hey, Dane. I didn't know you were back."

She went behind him to shut the door. "Well, I am. Bring her here. Let me see her."

He seemed not to hear, talking to me in an anguished tone. "Jericho had a scout come by the school today so I agreed to babysit—"

Already unsnapping the baby, who was eerily quiet, I jerked my head around. "Babysitting? You? Since when?"

"Since a while, okay? Jericho didn't want you to know. Sometimes he has school things to do—"

"He could have asked me." I held the baby to my chest and then out to Dana. She seemed clammy and smelled funny. Where was that humidifier?

"It was during your work hours and my job is more flexible, okay? We'll have to argue about it later. I came over because she doesn't feel right to me."

I stopped short. "Not to me, either. Is she coughing?"

Jordan nodded. "She was. Really bad. Then I gave her some medicine Shemika had in the bag. Pedia something. It worked, but her breathing seems shallow and she's sweaty and she smells—"

"Sick?" Fear knotted in my stomach. Maybe J wasn't totally incompetent after all.

Dana stopped her cooing and stared at us. "What can I do?"

"Hold her while I get dressed!" I screamed, whisking into my room to throw on clothes and shoes. I pulled on a coat and grabbed some extra baby blankets, even though Jordan had some sort of new quilted cover over the car seat. It was October, and the wind was starting to chill. I'd closed the shop early today to prepare for the winter stock arriving tomorrow. I sent up a prayer, thanking God I'd been at home.

When I got back into the living room, Dana wasn't holding Moriah. Jordan was fastening on a fresh diaper.

She apologized. "I told him I had her…"

Before I could say a word, Grandpa snapped Moriah's

clothes back on and put her into the car seat again. Dana and I both stared as he filled a travel container from Shemika's bag with wipes from my container and grabbed four more diapers from the stack. "They keep six, but I like ten to be safe. Sometimes she just goes and goes."

Dana and I both just stared as he tugged a cover over the car seat and shook up a bottle of formula from the powder and distilled water in the bag. Shemika had finally agreed to let us give her some formula a little while back. I wondered now if it hadn't been a mistake. She really looked sick.

"I'll heat it before we go in case she wakes up on the ride. She'll take it room temp, but it's got to be nasty like that, you know?" He pulled the plastic liner down the bottle and noted the looks on our faces. "What?"

"Uh, nothing. Did they give you the doctor's number?"

Jordan sighed. "What do you think I am, stupid? I called the doctor first. I just came here so that you could come along." He shook his head and peeked in the little hole in the car seat cover. "When you grow up, remember that all men aren't dumb, okay? Even though we act like it sometimes."

Even I had to smile then, but not for long. The dread climbing my spine wouldn't allow it. Something told me that this baby who I'd just said would destroy my life might be in danger of losing hers. Jericho had been sick like this once. Pneumonia.

"Don't forget to call Jericho, Dane. And lock up behind us?" I knew she had it under control, but talking made me feel better.

"Got it. Calling him now. Go on."

As we headed for the door, Jordan's eyes locked on mine. There was fear there, too, but something brighter, something better, clouded it. Faith. Something I'd never seen in his eyes before. Something I wasn't so sure was showing in mine.

"We should pray," he said in a calm tone, though his eyes looked unsure. We were almost down the stairs now and into his SUV.

"Would you like me to pray? Or you? I can try and get Tad on the cell if it makes you more comfortable…" The wind swallowed my words as we stepped toward the car.

He hit a button on his keys and the doors unlocked and opened. With one move, he planted the baby seat in its base, shut the door, helped me into the front and was in the driver's seat and pulling into traffic.

"No, I don't need to call Tad. This is my grandbaby—*our* grandbaby. Let's pray for her together." Without pause and eyes still on the road, he started. "Father God, You saw fit to give us this baby, please heal her and make her well. I thought maybe I was overreacting, but now I don't think so. Let the doctor see us quickly and know what to do. Bless Jericho's efforts at his tryouts and Shemika in her training. Help us to look out for this baby—" He paused as we pulled up to a red light. "And for each other. Thank You for Rochelle, Lord. I couldn't do any of this without her."

He stared at me, but I couldn't think of anything to add. Besides, the baby was stirring in the back, where I should have sat. I jumped out and made the switch just as the light turned green. She curled her hand around my finger.

It was all the sign I needed. My part of the prayer came to me like a gift. "Thank You, Lord, for Jordan, who is turning out to be a wonderful grandfather. Help our little Moriah be well, in Jesus' name, Amen."

To: *thesassysistahood*
From: *Sassysistah1*
Subject: urgent prayer/my grandbaby
Can you all please pray for Moriah? She has respiratory synctial virus, RSV, and is having trouble breathing. She's been admitted to the hospital. Pray for Jericho and Shemika, too. They're not taking it too well.
Rochelle
"Far better it is to dare mighty things, to win glorious triumphs, though checkered with failure, than to rank with those poor souls who neither enjoy nor suffer much, because they live in the gray twilight that knows neither victory nor defeat."
Theodore Roosevelt

Chapter seven

"How's she sound?" I asked through the fog in my mind. Moriah had been released from the hospital two days before, just in time for Jericho and Shemika's midterm exams. In an attempt to get the baby well and make sure they both graduated, I'd offered my couch, my special couch, to Jordan. To my surprise, he'd accepted.

"Much better," Jordan said, as his long, brown body leaned into the crib. "That medicine is working, thank God. I can still see her little chest straining, though..."

I nodded, gathering the folds of my robe closer around my pajamas. The doctor explained that although Moriah had only been a few weeks premature, it was enough to give her breathing concerns.

When a bad cold containing RSV had circulated through the nursery at Shemika's school, it hit Moriah hardest. The doctor suggested Moriah be taken care of at home for the next few months, something we weren't quite sure how we could pull off, but we were trying. Tomorrow, our first work-day since the baby was released, would be the first real test.

I clicked off the light in Jericho and Moriah's room. My son was in the bed behind us, knocked out asleep with an Algebra II book opened across his chest and a frown etched into his face.

Jordan took it all in. "Is he doing any better with that math?"

"No," I whispered. Not any worse, but not any better. Still a solid C. I'd usually be ranting, but under the circumstances, I was grateful. "He needs a tutor. Maybe Adrian, he's so good with chemistry and everything. Or Tracey. She's out of town, but there's the phone and the Internet—"

"She's having a baby, Chelle. And these two are trying to sleep. I'll work with him. You've probably forgotten, but math was my best subject."

I hadn't forgotten a thing. Asking Jordan had been my first thought, but I hadn't wanted to fix him into yet another part of our lives. Of my life.

"Come on. These two need their sleep." Jordan took my hand and pulled me toward the living room, where his make-shift quarters were. "I just want to thank you again for let-ting me stay here," he said with wintergreen breath. "I really wanted—needed—to do this. Help with the baby, I mean."

I didn't leave, though I probably should have. "No need to thank me. I do appreciate your help. We're just doing what families do, even families as messed up as ours."

In the dim of the hallway, he slipped an arm around my waist. The stingy light played off the lines around his eyes and the graying shore of hair along the edges of his face. I'd always wondered how he would age. He'd been so handsome as a young man that I couldn't imagine what he would become. Now I didn't need to imagine. It was all right here, warm and breathing, his heart so close to mine…

"You just called us a family. Do you think we could ever be a family again, Rochelle? You and I?"

I stared at the ground. "Again? We never were a family, Jordan. Not until now."

He pressed his palms against mine, threaded his huge fingers through my small ones. "We've always been family, since the day I laid eyes on you. I remember watching you play basketball at the park and thinking how amazing you were."

Here we go with that. "Don't." I pulled away and started down the hall, pausing by the kids' door. Her breathing monitor was hooked up and all, but I had to be sure. Jordan didn't follow me. Tomorrow morning, he'd get up, shower, shave, dress and leave before I got up, leaving his sheets and blankets folded and out of the way. If only he could fold himself up just as neatly, along with my confused feelings toward him. As I cracked the door to look in on the baby, my son's voice called out to me.

"Mom?"

"Yes, honey. It's me."

There was a rustle of papers. A book fell on the floor. "Did I hear Dad out there again? Or was I dreaming?"

I sat on the edge of his bed, took a deep breath. "No dream. Your father is going to stay a while longer. We're going to work together to help with Moriah while you and Shemika study for your midterms."

He jerked up in the bed. "Shemika. Where is she? I was supposed to drive her home after evening service…"

My hand met my son's shoulder, knotted with tension and stress. It was a feeling that often corded my own body, something I'd wrongfully tried to shield him from. "She's in the guest room sleeping. I set up the pack and play crib in there. When Moriah wakes up to eat, I'll take her in."

"You go to sleep, Mom. I can—"

"I'd rather you didn't." My tone was more sarcastic than I meant for it to be, but I was just keeping it real. The last thing this kid needed to do was hand off his baby to his girlfriend while the adults slept. No thanks.

"Mom…I would never disrespect you in your house. Give me a little credit, would you?"

I stood and held a finger to my mouth. He was talking a little too loud. "The only credit I can help you with are the ones you need to graduate."

He sat up in the bed. "Wait. Who's watching the baby tomorrow? I know the doctor said not to take her to the nursery. Maybe I can talk to my teachers…"

I cringed, thinking of my recent conversations with his counselor. The teacher's reports all said the same thing—my son had become more focused, but on his baby instead of his schoolwork. From calling the nursery at Shemika's school during class time to trying to leave school to check on the baby, Jericho seemed to have forgotten that he was still a child himself…*and* a student. He'd need good grades on both midterms and finals to pull through.

"I've talked to the people at school. They all agree that

you need to focus on studying right now. Your grandpa is going to come by once he's gets things settled at the restaurant. Your dad will come back after his last appointment. He has an early day, I think."

I was at the door now and falling asleep on my feet. Dealing with a baby was taking all I had.

"An early day? You two are getting awfully chummy, aren't you?"

My shoulders slumped. Even in all this mess, my boy still called it like he saw it. "We're just looking out for you."

"Yeah...right," he said, as I shut the door.

I couldn't have said it better myself.

The week stumbled forward on sleepy legs. I did the same, rushing home to look after Moriah each evening while Jordan cooked dinner—who had taught him how?—and grilled Jericho for his midterms, now just a few days away.

Though it was our week to keep the baby, Shemika showed up more often than not and, in truth, we were usually all glad to see her. Grandparents are one thing, mommies are another. Moriah definitely knew the difference. Now if only I could make sense of my muddled feelings, we'd be on to something. It probably wouldn't happen today though, not by a long shot. It was Thursday.

Tad day.

Seeing him about this pair of shoes was becoming more and more difficult, especially since Jordan had moved in. Though he'd come the first time in suspenders and a bow tie, with each visit he'd made subtle

changes—loafers instead of wingtips, a shirt and tie with
no suspenders. He'd even grazed my pinky finger while
putting on his coat during his last visit. I'd almost swooned
right there.

Still, nothing could have prepared me for today. As I stared
at his sweater, khakis and all-weather coat, you could have
knocked me over with a feather. I'd never seen Tad dressed
so casually all the days I'd known him. I couldn't even try to
figure out what this meant…or what would be expected of
me in response to it.

"Nice sweater," I said, deciding finally on a safe compliment. And a compliment it was. He'd always filled out his
suits nicely, but this casual twist and perhaps the golds and
greens in his outfit brought out the kindness in his eyes. The
results of his obviously regular workouts were showcased
nicely as well.

I held in my stomach. I was squeezing in Tae Bo three
times a week now, sometimes with Moriah next to me in her
car seat. I hadn't finished the entire DVD in far too long.

"You like it? See the purple here?" He pointed to a rich
thread of color that I'd somehow missed despite its bright-
ness. Once he pointed it out though, it stood out, and beau-
tifully so. "Whenever I see purple, I think of you." He
chuckled. "Whenever I see most things, I think of you."

Something intending to be a smile spread across my face.
I probably looked like a deer in the middle of a highway.
Who was this wonderful, kind man and why had he waited
until now, until I had Jordan on my couch, to surface? And
worse yet, how long did this alien being plan to stick around?

"Well whatever the case, the colors look good on you. Let's get started."

He took his usual seat. "Sure."

I went to the back to grab his things. Tad's shoes were the only pair I was working on currently, something I was both grateful and horrified about. With any other customer, I would have been concerned about moving much faster to completion, but he seemed fine with our current pace, dreadfully slow compared to my usual work. I brought the leather and laces I'd chosen out to him.

Delight glimmered in his eyes. "We didn't even make a final choice on the color last time, but this—this is exactly what I wanted. How did you know?"

Warmth crept up my neck. I'd given myself away. What could I say now, that I'd known what to pick because I'd watched him so closely over the years, listened to him so completely? No, I couldn't say that. His presence here, that sweater, the hungry but humble look in his eyes…all indicated there was much more to Tad than even I knew.

"The Lord helped me choose, I guess." It wasn't a lie. I always prayed when working a new project.

A questioning expression passed over Tad's square jaw into the hazel of his eyes. As he nodded, doubt slid along his spidery lashes.

He knew.

In that second, he comprehended all that I'd felt for him over the past decade. In the same moment, I knew something, too, something I'd never understood fully—that Tad had cared for me, too.

Deeply.

"Thank you," he said with none of his usual inflection. It was a weary but strong voice, a warrior's whisper.

Before I could chatter away his gratitude, he did the most simple, most unnerving thing.

He stared at my feet.

And not just a glance, either. His was an intense look as though he were remembering something. His eyes even grew moist. I almost jumped out of my skin. If he'd kissed me, I could have taken it better. Well, not really, but this was really bad…

Tad set the leather and laces aside and turned his eyes back to my face, set his shoulders squarely across from mine. I looked up at him, then closed my eyes for what seemed like forever. When I opened my eyes, Tad was beside me.

On one knee.

Lord have mercy.

"Rochelle…" Tad leaned in closer, his forearm grazing the ground.

The chimes exploded at the door before he could squeeze out another word. In a fury of pink wool, Terri, Jordan's ex-girlfriend stomped inside, marching right up to us. She pinned the elbow of Tad's sweater to the floor with one of her stiletto boots.

I reached down to try and free Tad, but to no avail. And she didn't even seem to notice. As much as she got on my nerves, I wondered if she hadn't saved me from something I wasn't ready to deal with. Not ready to deal with? Wasn't that what I'd wanted? A proposal from Tad? Evidently not, judging by the relief surging through me. "Terri, what are you doing here?"

She snatched off her coordinating leather gloves and soft, round hat and waved them back and forth. "What am I doing here? What am I doing here! I'm trying to save my marriage, that's what."

Terri shifted her stance and I lunged forward to help Tad free himself. "What marriage?" Was she talking about Jordan or somebody else? When dealing with crazy people, I had to check the facts. Since she was here and yelling, it must have been Jordan, but one could never be sure about these things.

Fists on the hips of her long, pink coat, she snorted. "Well, my engagement then. That's not the question here. What I need to know is why Jordan is living with you?"

A soft purr of thread hissed from Tad's elbow as he snatched himself away. One look into his wide eyes told me that I needn't worry about what he'd planned to say next. Not that I'd wanted to hear it any way (well, maybe) but I couldn't have him thinking bad of me.

"Keep it down, Terri. It's not like that at all. He's sleeping on the couch. We're just trying to get the kids through midterms, helping them out. We all take turns with the baby." I peeked at Tad from the corner of my eye, but he'd focused on the purple thread dangling from his elbow.

She rolled her eyes. "I'll just bet you do. This is so stupid. We were doing just fine the whole time Shemika was pregnant with both of them living with *us.* If you'd just let them get married, none of this would be an issue."

"They want to get married?" Tad inspected the large hole in his cable-knit.

It was my turn to roll my eyes. "That's not the point. They're too young. They need to finish high school. They need—"

"Perhaps they need to obey God." Tad said it softly, but the message was as clear as if he'd shouted it, not to mention the glint of accusation in his eyes.

I turned back to Terri. "Look, I have nothing to do with what goes on between you and Jordan. If you'd handled your business, he'd be at your house anyway." Oops. That was over the line.

She yanked on her gloves. "It's always been about you, Rochelle. Since the day I met him. I guess it will always be about you until Jordan decides otherwise."

Tad stood, still gawking at his sweater. Terri pivoted on one pink heel like a giant Powerpuff girl. I sat stunned for a second anticipating the techno music. She made Buttercup look like an amateur in that outfit.

"Wait, Terri. I don't know what you've been told, but there is nothing between us—"

She turned back, partway to the door. "Nothing? Of course. Nothing but a son, a granddaughter and a lifetime of memories, the only memories he seems to care about. If I hear about your prom night one more time, I'm going to strangle myself."

Prom night? Jordan had told her about that? What else had he told her?

As if reading my mind, she pressed her lips together and crossed her arms, almost knocking down poor Tad, who was trying to put on his coat and escape this whole mess of a conversation. "Everything. He told me everything."

The hairs on my arms bristled. *Everything* was a lot, even with a man telling the tale. Too much, in fact. "Whatever. Look, it's just for a few more days. Then you can have Jordan back to do with him whatever you'd like. Even if there were any feelings still between us, I'd never be stupid enough to let him hurt me again."

Terri jerked on her hat with a satisfied smirk. "I plan to take care of my business. I just wanted to make sure that you won't be interfering again." She tossed her scarf, white with pink stripes, over one shoulder and pointed at Tad, moving past her and out the door. "Keep your altar boy dressed down. He's even cuter than on TV," she said as the chimes announced Tad's exit.

As the chimes rang the second time, I sank to my knees. It made things easier for the falling on my face that was sure to come. I might as well just sleep on the floor these days. Everyone was determined to keep me there.

From: *eventcoordinator@amatchmadeinseven.com*
To: *Sassysistah1*
Subject: Missed Matches
Dear Ms. Gardner:
Your presence has been requested twice in the past month at group gatherings. We missed you both times. Is everything okay? Is there anything we can do to help?

We know that getting to know new people can be stressful at first, but we're committed to helping you make the connection you desired when you contacted us. The next gathering is this Saturday at Ujaama restaurant again.

All attendees will be from your target pool of applicants, so please try and stick around. Who knows? You might make a match made in heaven!

Sincerely,

The Match Made in Seven Event Team

My feet were numb. It seemed like I'd been on a long walk to nowhere for the past week. Tad was back to his old self, barely acknowledging me at church. I doubted he'd come back to the shop about his shoes. That made me a little angry…and a lot relieved. He was one of the few men I could really let myself fall for.

The other two were far more scary: the cute young waiter who kept invading my dreams, and the nightmare from the past, currently standing in front of me.

Jordan Rose.

I had one of those stupid group dates tonight and he'd offered to babysit. I could kick myself for mentioning the outing during our last phone call, but it would probably do me good to get out for a little fresh air. "The baby is in her crib. I really appreciate this," I said, still fiddling with one earring.

Jordan rubbed his hands together, as if taking quick inventory of me. With Moriah feeling better, I'd squeezed in a few more workouts and was looking a bit more like myself. He made a circle motion in the air with his index finger. "Turn around?"

I squinted at him but complied, doing my best diva twirl.

It'd been a while since I'd made such motions, but I managed not to fall down.

"Umph. Maybe I shouldn't have offered to babysit after all. I just wanted you to have a good time, not give some man a heart attack. That dress is a weapon."

Of mass frustration…

My breath came out in a smothered sigh. Why did he say things like that, especially when he was looking and smelling and being so good? I rubbed the stupidity from my eyes.

"Stop it now, J. You've got me in enough trouble already. Terri probably has a hit out on me or something. She's not going to show up here tonight, is she?" My tone was playful, but I was serious. No drama on the home front.

Jordan sobered. "I can't tell you how sorry I am about that. Terri was totally out of line. She won't come here tonight. That much we've straightened out. Besides, I'm going to take her to lunch tomorrow after church. She's probably somewhere painting and lotioning in preparation." He chuckled.

I didn't. Though I was headed for a date with a bunch of strangers, the thought of Jordan lunching with Terri didn't comfort me. How could he take her back so easily? Probably the same way I was stupid enough to let him crawl back into my life.

Into my heart.

Hoping I hadn't shown my disappointment, I checked my makeup in the hall mirror and ducked into the closet for a jacket, finally choosing a black cashmere swing coat I'd got from a catalog back in the eighties. It never went out of style.

Jordan obviously agreed as he ran to help me into it. "What time will Jericho be home from his practice game?"

I put my hands into the sleeves carefully, hoping not to smudge my nail polish. It seemed dry, but I wanted to be sure. Usually I kept my nails short and clear. Tonight, I'd splurged on two coats of pearled mauve. Both arms safely through my sleeves, I turned to answer the question about my son's arrival from his first practice basketball game of the season. "Around nine or ten. And when he gets in, can you two look at his Algebra for a while?"

The look on Jordan's face told the story before he could get it out. "I'll try, but I doubt he'll be up for it. Last time I tried that after a practice, he went to sleep on me. Besides, he passed the midterm. I don't want to push too hard."

Too hard? The boy had earned a C. If *I* had the time and energy to push my son, he'd be getting A's and B's again. "Okay. That's fine. Just listen out for Tracey. And if she calls—"

He held up one hand, knowing the drill about my pregnant and newlywed friend. "I know. I know. If Tracey calls and says she's in labor, call on your cell phone. Not that I know why exactly. What are you going to do, drop everything and drive two hours in the cold and dark? Dana and Adrian are there with her, not to mention her husband. Haven't you seen enough birthing for a while? The little bit with Moriah about took me out."

I smiled, thinking of how strong he'd been that day...only to be reminded of how weak he'd been on another day.

Seventy times seven.

For the first time, I actually did the math on that little forgiveness ditty. Four hundred and ninety. Jordan had used up his forgiveness tickets years ago, hadn't he? I pulled my coat closer, trying to be good, to be gracious. "It's a woman thing. I like going to births. No woman should be alone when she's having a baby."

He followed me to the door. "But she's not alone. I just told you—"

I turned and touched his shoulder. There were some things even I couldn't explain. "J, sometimes you can be in a room full of people and be totally alone." It was a phenomenon I'd experienced all too often, especially in church leadership where I was often the only woman and the only single...besides Tad. I hoped the event I was going to wouldn't be another wallflower experience for me. This time, at least I'd make sure to get some food before running to the parking lot like Cinderella.

As my hand dropped to my side, Jordan took it and kissed the knuckle of my ring finger. "I understand. It was like that for me during my physical therapy in Mexico. Everyone was so kind and patient, but I didn't know the language or what was really going on. So many times, I felt like giving up, but I thought about you and about our baby—"

"Baby?" A small tug brought my hand back to my side where it belonged. This wasn't the first time that Jordan had referred to Jericho as a baby or "little man." If six foot four and growing was *little,* we were all in trouble.

He blushed. "I know that sounds silly to you, but that's who he was to me. My little guy. The last pictures I'd seen of him were when he was four or five, I think. I just wanted to get walking and talking and get home and try to explain…to both of you." He took a step closer. "I had no idea how I'd feel when I saw you again. If it's possible, you're even more beautiful than you were then."

And you're even more full of it.

I turned the doorknob and pulled my coat tight around me. "Well, reuniting hasn't been easy, but I'm glad Jericho got to know you and that you two hit it off. This plus the baby has forced me to make some big adjustments, but God knows."

Jordan held open the door. "I guess He does, doesn't He? As weird as this all is, it seems like I was meant to be here now."

A smile was my best answer before speed walking to my car. I'd learned years before that "why" wasn't the best question to ask. God allowed the inquiry and was very patient, even when I came back many, many times. It was the asking itself that became addicting, diverting me from the blessed assurance of acceptance. Sometimes it was better to ask how, as in, "Lord, how can I get through this?" This year was a long string of those times.

I heard the whispers first.

"That's her, isn't it? The one from the news? Soles of God?"

"Shh. Shoes of Peace. Mind your manners, she's looking."

And that was just in the parking lot. A kente-clad valet met me at my car and escorted me to the door of the restaurant, a big change from my stumble through the car-crammed space weeks before. I looked around, wondering if a red carpet would roll out the door next. The man kept silent as we walked but maintained a curious smile. I stared at the ground, measuring the distance back to the car with each step. Austin and her silly interview…

True enough, the foot traffic in my store had greatly increased since my spot had aired on TV, but I had no idea that my association with Jordan had turned me into some sort of quasicelebrity. With my entrance to Ujaama however, I quickly realized that things were different. Very different.

"Ms. Gardner, thank you for joining us this evening. Your party is waiting in the room down the hall." The gentleman's speech was as crisp as the pleats in his African garb. "There is an Ethiopian buffet already prepared, but let us know if you'd like something else. I'll escort you now if you're ready."

Like a little girl crossing the street, I looked right, left and right again to make sure that this gentleman was talking to me. How had he known my name? Why did the group have a room this time instead of the table in the middle of the dining room? Perhaps the agency was just stepping things up, trying to get everyone more acquainted. Sure, that was it. Besides, I'd missed a few of the group dinners. The staff had probably just grown accustomed to everyone…

"Thank you. I'm sure whatever you've prepared is fine." I looped my hand around his extended arm and trailed through the dining room where the dinner crowd paused to stare at me. It was then I began to wonder if I wasn't being led to a secret taping of Old Maids Unleashed or something.

No matter what happens, don't scream.

In truth, I kept looking for Shan at every turn. Had he quit
or was he off today? Home drawing a portrait with those
artist's hands, perhaps? I almost asked about him, but re-
strained myself. During dinner, I'd think of a casual way to
inquire about him.

We entered the first door on the left. My escort released
my hand. One glance at the food-laden table revealed ba-
nanas, grapes, figs...so much for low-carbing. I hadn't had
one of those in years.

I squinted at the fruit at the top of the pile. Was that a po-
megranate? I hadn't had one of those in forever, either. Not
since my daddy used to buy them. The thought of my father, whom I'd last seen months before my son's birth, tightened my throat. I could still see him on his deathbed, with
disappointment stinging his eyes.

Before I could get too sentimental, the peppery smell of
a hot stew made me breathe deep. I spied a tub of hot flat
bread and grilled vegetables.

I turned to my escort. "Wow."

The man laughed, then took a bow. "Enjoy."

He didn't have to tell me twice. By this time, I was starv-
ing and nervous, not a good combination. A slender woman
with a gold head wrap and matching dress covered with ele-
phants took my coat and handed me a plate. "I love your
shoes," she said with a thick accent, pointing to my pom-pom
sling-backs. "I come by your shop soon."

I forced a smile. "Please do." This was too weird.

Miss Mingle, the woman who'd accosted Tad and looked
daggers at me during the first gathering approached again,

all sugar and spice this time. I flinched and nearly dropped my almost full plate.

Another woman, someone from the service no doubt, approached me next. "Ms Gardner? Sorry to startle you. We're so glad you could make it. Just wondering if you brought your cards?" she chirped. "Not that you need any." A string of nervous giggles followed her last comment.

I scrambled for my cards and handed them to her. "Here you are. I'm sure I need them as much as anyone. I doubt anyone knows me here." My words were intended as much for me as her, but neither of us seemed convinced. One could hope, though. I mean, Leverhill was a small town, but this was ridiculous.

A distinguished man with a salt-and-pepper beard approached and said hello. He had a kind of Ed Bradley appeal going on. Very nice. I shook myself. My years of training myself to ignore men, to look away, focus my thoughts…it seemed as if I'd forgotten all of it.

"May I have one of those, please?" he called after the girl from the dating service. His voice had a trained quality, like a voice-over announcer. Or like Tad. He made me feel comfortable immediately.

Already out of earshot, our kind hostess didn't respond.

"I have another." I put down my fork again, then gave him my card, pulling it back at the last second. "Where's yours?" Was I batting my eyes or was I getting an infection from this new mascara? Either way, this was definitely spiraling out of control. For almost twenty years, the most I'd said to men was "Have a nice day, come again" and now I was like some almost-middle aged madwoman. Well, there was of course that limo driver and those times when I went crazy at weddings....

He laughed deep, sort of like a cartoon pirate. "Here you are. So sorry."

Trying not to crack up laughing in his face, I pulled my head down to my plate. For some reason, that Blackbeard laughter just tickled my funny bone. One fig later, I lifted my head. To my relief, the salt-and-pepper pirate had fled.

To my shock, there was another man sitting across from me, one with black velvet skin and soft-looking coils in his hair.

Shan, my dream waiter.

I tried to hide my surprise, but from the way his smile widened, my bluff didn't go far. Neither did my brain waves. He moved his chair closer, bringing his peppermint fineness too close for comfort. I took him all in—a crewneck and corduroys, both in varying shades of chocolate, made him look like a Whitman's sampler pack. He sat with the posture of a CEO instead of a waiter. The troublemakers always did.

I swallowed hard, trying to contain myself. Jordan's old flames and Tad's slow burn was one thing. This young-old man—I still couldn't place his age—was too hot to handle. "What are you doing here?" He obviously wasn't working.

Shan laid a hand on mine. "What every other man here is doing. Trying to get with you. Who do you think ordered the valet and the private room? I even picked the menu."

From: *Harvardgrad4god*
To: *Sassysistah1*
Subject: Pictures of Tracey's baby/singles group

Attached: LILY.ZIP

Rochelle,

This is Tad. Hope the new e-mail didn't confuse you. Too much mess kept coming to the last address. Hope this finds you well. Ryan asked me to come up and hang out with him. I'm attaching some shots I took of the baby. Seems I'm the birth preacher these days, huh? That's cool. God is always birthing new things in me.

We missed you at bowling night, but everything you set up worked great. No problems with the shoe rentals this time. I explained that you were taking time with your family. Everyone understood. Well, almost everyone. You know how some folks in BASIC can be. Tell Jericho nice game the other day. I didn't catch it all, but I swung by the gym at the end.

Yours in Christ,

Tad

Chapter eight

"I am so sorry, Tracey." And I was. In the midst of being Queen of Sheba and Grandma of the Year, I'd missed the birth of Tracey's baby. And who had managed to be there and even capture pictures? Tad. When he was more thoughtful than me something was seriously wrong. It was like we switched places.

"Don't worry about it, girl. You have the rest of Lily's life to get to know her. And you know I'll hit you up for baby-sitting later. What I need to know is what's the deal with some hot waiter? Austin said you called her at two in the morning!" Tracey sounded bubblier than I'd heard her in months.

A smile spread across my face. Good news traveled fast in the Sassy Sistahood, especially with me offline. No telling what all they were talking about on there now. "Girl…I'm scared to even talk about it. I'm still not sure how old he is. We just clicked, you know? I used to think you were nuts when you and Ryan talked for hours, but that's just what we did. We talked about God, food, politics, art—"

"Sounds like a winner. When do we meet him?"

On my lap, Moriah started to stir. The rocking chair creaked back as I resumed my rhythm. She opened one eye and gave me the sweetest look. Probably gas, but it was a smile to me. "You don't get to meet him, Tracey. He's too young and too—too—"

"Poor?"

I sighed. "No. That's not it. We just don't have enough in common..." Truth was, I was scared of the man, plain and simple. I'd dreamed of chocolate-covered candy canes all night long. He was the kind of guy that made women pack up and move or get pregnant on a whim. At least I didn't have that to worry about.

Ever.

I tried to change the subject, though Shan was still on my mind. He probably would be for a long time. "I still can't believe I missed that baby. I was planning to come up next weekend. At least Dana was there. Come to think of it, Dana skipped out on the wedding preparations, so I guess she got the baby job."

Tracey wouldn't budge. "You're not getting off that easy. I haven't heard you like this since...never. You sound like that waiter swept you off your feet."

More like knocked me flat on my face. "Well, I have to admit, he did it up. Rented a private room, had me escorted from my car...I hate that, though. Probably took a whole week's salary."

"See. Money is an issue."

"That's not it. It's more than that. I'd like to get my groove back—or find it in the first place—as well as the next woman, but I can't. I have a family to consider." My usual craziness was enough. I didn't have time to figure out the foibles of somebody new, not to mention young and broke.

A rough hand smoothed the back of my neck. "I'll put Moriah down," Jordan said.

I started at the sound of his voice, wondering how much he'd heard. The sweater he'd had on last night hung over his arm and cushioned the baby's head. A Bulls T-shirt clung to him like a second skin. I turned away...for both our sakes.

"Who was that? Does Jericho have company? 'Cause I know that isn't who I think it is." Tracey raised her voice on the phone.

Girl, you don't know a thing.

"It's Jordan. He babysat last night while I went out and when I came home he was asleep—"

"O-kay." Accusation mingled with laughter hissed through the phone.

Now on my feet, I shook my head. "It's not like that, Tracey," I whispered. "The kids are right here, too. They're just tired from studying and working."

"Who's working? What about school?"

My thoughts exactly. "Shemika has decided to get her GED. She's enrolled in a program that teaches how to make soap and toiletries. The program has a soap store where she works in the afternoons and some evenings. When she gets done, she'll probably go and work for Dana."

"The Creative Cooperative? Dana told me about possibly getting some interns from there. She has some other single moms from the programs working there already. I think it's too much with her really just recovering from her surgery and all, but you know kids."

I scratched the hair above my ear, watching as Jordan stared down on our grandbaby. Time for a touch-up. When would I fit that in? I was due for a pedicure, too. My feet might be lumpy to the eye, but I still liked them soft to the touch. "She's getting interns from there? I need to catch up. I'm out of the loop."

With one hand, Jordan tugged on his sweater the way only a man can. Memories stabbed at my mind. I grabbed his jacket from the back of the couch and handed it to him. Last night with Shan had burned out most of my brain and Jordan was trying to sizzle what remained of it.

I could tell from the flutter of his tired eyes that Moriah had been up most of the night. One more thing to feel guilty about.

"I'm going to go," Jordan said, zipping his jacket and kissing my cheek. "I'll see you at church. You know how to get me if you need me."

"Hold on, Tracey." I covered the receiver and turned to my handsome babysitter. "Thanks again. See you later." I waved and breathed a sigh of relief. If I wasn't on the phone, I would have walked him to the door, but Tracey had enough ammunition to work with.

My hand slipped away from the phone. "Don't even say it." Now truly cracking up laughing, Tracey could hardly get her words out. "I...don't...have...to." She regained her breath. "You've said it all. Look, you're about to make me hurt myself. The baby is waking up and Ryan will be back with food any minute. Give my love to, ahem, everyone. And tell Tad thanks for being here. That was a lovely surprise."

My mind switched gears. Tad. I had him to face this morning as well. "I'm sure. You'd better get some rest or you'll be feeling it later. I know you feel good, but don't overdo."

"I won't."

She would. "Okay, bye."

From the couch across the room, my son began to stir. "What time is it?"

Time for church, I wanted to say, but we'd had enough of those arguments lately. He'd come to church when he was ready. He talked about God enough, but talk was about the extent of it. "It's about five-thirty, honey. Would you like some breakfast before I leave?"

He sat up and smiled at me, patted the bed beside him.

That was a new twist. Usually whenever I came near Jericho on Sundays, he squirmed away. I pounced on the bed before he changed his mind. "Yes?"

"I'm going to cook you breakfast, Mom. And then, we're going to church."

My son couldn't have picked a better—or worse—day to attend church. The pastor was out of town. (I used to know these things ahead of time). Usually, his son preached instead, which made a lot of people happy. (Except me. Nice, easy sermons were the son's specialty.) Today, I'd hoped for just such a message, an upbeat you-can-do-it kind of talk on the grace of Jesus Christ.

Instead, I'd heard a sermon on the rebellion of Satan.

And the rebellion of Rochelle.

The fact that Tad had delivered the message made it all the more devastating. If there was such a thing as a spiritual Band-Aid, I certainly needed one. My fascination with me, me, me the past few months finally smacked me square between the eyes. Where it hit my son and his girl-friend, I had no idea, but we all lumbered back to the car in tandem.

Shemika broke the silence as Jericho strapped in the baby's car seat. "Mr. Tad came down hard, didn't he? He gave me a lot to think about."

My son ducked his head out of the car. "Yeah. I never thought about how much I've been putting what I want in front of everyone else. Especially you, Mom. I'm sorry."

"I'm sorry, too, Mrs.—Ms. Gardner. About everything. Thank you for all you've done to help us—me," she said.

Hands on the steering wheel and key in the ignition, I could do nothing but stare at both of them. "I don't know what to say. I mean, Tad's words blew me away, but I never anticipated this kind of response from you kids—no, let me stop saying that. You both are growing into wonderful adults. This morning proves that."

The twinkle in my son's eyes made me think of Christmas. Usually I would have had the tree out of the attic by now. I was doing good to know the date these days.

"You don't know how much it means to hear you say that, Mom. I've been trying. We both have."

Shemika nodded as I started the car and eased into the traffic exiting the parking lot.

Trying. Hadn't we all been doing that? For now, it counted for a lot. Sometimes for everything. A year ago, trying wouldn't have been acceptable, not from anyone, including myself. But today, well, it was enough. I reached over and took Shemika's hand. "I know you've been trying. I'm proud of you both. And thank you for sitting up here with me, even for a minute. I know you like to be with the baby—"

"I've got it, Mom," Jericho piped up from the back. "I haven't had much time with Moriah this week and well, y'all need to talk."

Shemika smiled. "Yeah. I guess so."

I adjusted my rearview so I could see my passenger and the road. Now forty pounds slimmer and sporting a short afro, Shemika beamed with the quiet confidence of a woman walking in her destiny. It turned out that attending church this morning had been her idea as well. She'd changed quite a lot and I hadn't had a thing to do with it. God had done it all.

A knock rapped at my window as we inched forward, almost to the mouth of the lot. Tad. He waved as I buzzed the window down.

"Where are you all headed?" he said casually, as if he hadn't just brought the church down with one of the most powerful sermons ever preached there.

"Lunch. Wanna come?" Jericho called out from the back seat before I could respond.

I blinked so hard I almost hurt myself. "I'm sure that Deacon McGovern has better things to do than—"

My son was already out of the car and offering Tad a seat. "Come on, man. Get in."

I momentarily lamented the day I'd traded my Lexus for this Volvo. Before, he couldn't have fit in the car! I waited for the back door to slam and for my blood pressure to rise, but Tad stayed put at my window, his breath fogging the winter air. After a chilly silence, I got it. Tad was waiting for an invitation from me, as well.

"We'd love to have you join us for lunch," I said.

A smile, the one I hadn't seen since that day in the Sunday school room when he'd touched my bare feet, took over his handsome face. "I'd be honored."

Golden Corral was packed with people, but that didn't stop Jericho from drilling Tad with Bible questions right there in the line. Never had I seen him so curious. When Moriah cried in her stroller, he plugged her mouth with a pacifier, the thing he begged me not to do. When Shemika tugged his sleeve, he held up a finger without even looking at her. I should have been happy, hopeful…

I wasn't.

Silly me had the nerve to be…jealous?

"So what were those 'I wills' again, the ones the devil said?" My son was so close to Tad that I hoped he hadn't spit on the man.

With the patience of a tenured professor, Tad answered. "'I will ascend to heaven, I will raise my throne above the stars of God, I will sit on the mount of assembly in the recesses of the north, I will ascend above the heights of the clouds and I will make myself like the Most High.' Isaiah chapter fourteen, verses thirteen and fourteen."

A blond woman behind us picked up a napkin and scribbled down the Scriptures. In fact, everyone around us honed in on Tad's words the way that people had focused on me at Ujaama last night. Was that it? Had I become somehow taken with myself? Is that why all this rubbed me the wrong way?

My son looked at Tad in awe. "And you just know all that? From memory?"

Tad shrugged as the line progressed. "Don't you know lyrics to songs that you play a lot?"

Shemika laughed. "Boy, does he! Way better than the quadratic formula, that's for sure. Ask him to do a song, any song—"

"Sure. I know a few tunes." Jericho gave his girlfriend the "don't say things like that in front of my mother" look I knew so well. He needn't have bothered. I'd long since found his stash of CDs with explicit lyrics. Over a year ago, in fact. Back then, I'd been biding my time for that battle, just happy that he hadn't been having sex. Or so I'd thought...

"Well, Scripture is for me what music is for you. I study all of it, but the passages that focus on my weaknesses stick in my head because I have to read them so often." He took a tray and handed it to me, holding out his hand for me to go ahead in the line.

I took my place ahead of him, but craned my neck to hear more.

"You? Weaknesses? I know you're not perfect or anything, but what do you have to work on? You've smart, you have a good job, can preach your b—"

"Jericho!" I gripped my tray. The boy was almost eighteen and still he said the stupidest things.

Tad chuckled and straightened his tie, a navy silk he wore whenever he preached. "It may seem like I have it going on, Jericho, but sometimes that can be another problem in itself. One of my main problems is pride. That's why I know this passage so well." Though he spoke to my son, Tad glanced my way.

I swallowed. Pride. Considering that it came before falling, I'd say I had a bad case of it myself. I stopped and scanned the room for a suitable table.

Tad pulled up beside me, his arm on mine. How was he holding that tray with one hand?

"You want to know what my other problem is?" he whispered.

My skin tingled. "Not really."

Maybe he hadn't heard me. "Fear. Fear of hurting people. Fear of being hurt—"

My son pointed across the room. "Dad? Dad! Hey, Mom, look!"

I did look, knowing I shouldn't. There they were, Jordan and Terri, smiling and shining the way only they could. As they waved us over, Tad's hand fell away from my arm.

From: *WallofJericho*
To: *Sassysistah1*
Subject: thanks/phone message

Hey Mom,

You're at work and I'm in the computer lab. Don't freak, this is free time. ☺ I just wanted to say thanks for this weekend. It was great to hang out with you and Mr. Tad. Sorry that Terri was tripping so hard. I think you handled it well. In fact, you handle everything well. Coach says a college scout has been asking about me. I'll know more after practice tonight. They may want me to do some visits on the weekends. I'm not sure how I feel about that with the baby and everything, but I'm trusting God. (Did I say that? Yup. Meant it, too.)

Oh yeah and some guy called. Richard, I think? He sounded like James Earl Jones. Are you getting with him, too? Watch out Mom, you're hotter than me. LOL

Jericho

"Richard? H-how are you?" I stared across the counter, trying not to look shocked. Since Tad's sermon, I'd been doing some soul searching and wasn't sure where I stood on this whole dating-service thing, but it seemed that one of my "friends" was determined to make a match.

Sure, the group dates had taught me some things about myself—that I needed to get out more, that I had an affinity for young domestics and that maybe I was even ready to consider a relationship, but I still wasn't sure if pairing up with strangers was the right thing, even Ed Bradley clones like Richard. (Was I the only woman in America who giggled during Ed's sections of *60 Minutes?*)

He smiled like Ed, too. "I'm fine. Just stopped by to check

in since you've been dodging my calls. And then some man answered the phone, so I didn't know what to think."

"Man?" I straightened the thigh-high boot teetering on the display stand next to me. "No, that was my son." Although I had to think hard to be sure. Jordan had come by to baby-sit while I drove up to see Tracey and her new baby. What a precious little thing.

Color rose to the man's cheeks. "Your son? He sounded so—"

"Old?" I had to laugh at this guy, he had a way about him, of wearing his emotions on his sleeve that made me smile. It was refreshing after being around Tad and Jordan. Both of them would drive even a psychiatrist mad trying to read their brains.

Shan sure made his intentions clear, I thought, swatting away the idea before it took hold. More and more he came to mind these days with his dazzling smile and slow, soft talk. I'd taken to chewing peppermints. That boy was dangerous.

"Well, yes, old. You don't look old enough to have a son with that much bass in his voice." He leaned a bit forward.

He meant that as a compliment. At least I hoped so. I took a step back. "Well thank you, but I do have a son that old. He's almost eighteen." The story was too long to get into and even if I had the time to run it down, I didn't have the energy.

Richard looked even more relieved. "That's even better actually. I really don't do well with young children."

"Well, my son does have a—"

A November gale battered my door chimes as Tad stepped

inside, wearing his full-length wool coat and the hat that Dana said made him looked like Dapper Dan slightly askew on his head. He took a look at Richard and me, before wiping his feet and unwinding the chestnut-colored scarf from his throat.

I smoothed my hairline. "Richard, my next fitting has arrived. Let's talk later, okay? E-mail is actually better for me. I don't have much phone time these days." In truth, it was easier to dump someone by e-mail. Wasn't that what I really meant?

Lord, help me.

"No problem, I just wanted to see if we could—"

"Right. Well, like I said, drop me a line." I was around the counter now, extending my hand to take Tad's hat.

He kept it. The softness on his face was already starting to set into the lines on his forehead, Tad's lines of defense. I could see his fortress going up as sure as if he'd laid bricks before my eyes.

Richard headed out the door, shaking Tad's hand as he passed. "Getting some shoes, man?"

Tad agreed, giving the man-nod that only guys understand. "Yes. Some very nice ones."

When the door shut, I apologized. Profusely. "Sorry for the intrusion. I wasn't expecting him. Or you. It's been a while since your last fitting—"

"I understand." Tad smoothed his new beard, one of the reasons I loved winter. I gulped as his glossy black hair threaded between his fingers. How could such a simple motion shake me to my shoes?

"Someone from the dating service?" he asked, taking a seat.

"Yes," I started toward the back room to get his shoes. Though he hadn't mentioned them or come around, I'd been working on them, thinking I'd give them to him for Christmas. "Have you met anyone?" I asked, not really wanting to know the answer.

"Actually, yes," he said as I almost walked into the wall. "Katrina. You've met her. That first night at the restaurant, remember?"

Miss Mingle. No wonder she was so nice to me at the last gathering. But if she and Tad were an item, why had she been there in the first place? And why hadn't she shown up at church yet? Was he bluffing me? I sure hoped so.

"So will she be joining us at church soon?" I called over my shoulder, then grabbed the shoes and started the painful journey back to his chair.

"Probably not. She has her own church and I'm not ready for that kind of commitment."

Commitment? Going to church? "I don't understand." Not that I ever understood much of what he said.

Fear of hurting people and fear of getting hurt.

That I understood.

He bridged his fingers over one knee. Both thumbs pointed upward. "Broken Bread Fellowship is my church home. My family. While this lady is nice, I'm not quite ready for her to meet the folks yet, if you know what I mean." A sadness tinged his eyes.

In that moment, I knew just what he meant. Though he hadn't spent much time with me outside of church in all these years, he'd considered the time we did spend within those walls as something special. And here Jordan had brought himself into the congregation and jumped right into the mix—as my ex-boyfriend and Jericho's father. Had that hurt Tad? I'd never thought about it until now.

"I can understand that. Until lately, I never thought I'd be dating at all."

And if I did date, it was supposed to be with you.

He picked up the left shoe and inspected the chocolate leather. Even I had to admit they'd come out much nicer than I expected. A long, low whistle came from his mouth. "These are excellent. Can you do me another pair? Different color, same style?"

My heart leaped. "Sure." I usually would have discussed price, but that wasn't even a consideration. Maybe this meant that there was some hope for the two of us, despite his new girlfriend or whatever she was. Despite the pain in his face during lunch with Jordan last Sunday. Despite those deepening creases on his forehead.

"These will be finished by Friday. Come by anytime to pick another color." Would they? I guess they would now.

He stood. "Great. Katrina's favorite color is burgundy. I'd like to surprise her." He smiled. "She has a shoe thing, you know?"

I nodded. I did know. I had a shoe thing, too.

And a stupidity thing. "Right."

The knock came just in time. I'd expected Shemika any minute to pick up the baby. And she'd arrived not a minute too soon, either. I could hardly keep my eyes open. Though

Moriah had fared well after her bout with RSV, an endur-
ing case of colic had now overtaken the child. After Jericho's
teacher called about him falling asleep in class and Shemika
missed three days of work, Jordan and I were back at our
posts as the pinch-hitting grandparents. Now Grandpa was
out on a recruiting trip and I was on my own. I hadn't been
to church in a week, let alone touched the computer. Maybe
tomorrow …

"Coming," I said in a faltering voice, gathering my robe
against me. Once again, the belt was tighter than I would
have liked.

I opened the door and turned back for the bed, but
Shemika's footsteps didn't follow.

A look over my shoulder found Dana frowning and Austin with both hands on her hips.

Blondie started in first, sweeping into my place like a little tornado. "You open the door and walk away, just like that?
We could have been anybody—robber, killer, rapist. What
were you thinking? If you knew the stories I'd covered
lately…"

Dana didn't say anything. She just came in, shut the door,
dropped her purse on the couch—the special one, it was everyone's favorite now—and walked over and hugged me. I melted
into her embrace, sagging like a wet noodle. She smoothed the
few strands of hair that had escaped my head scarf.

That made me laugh. "Oh, please. Stop it. You're turning
into your husband. You two are sickening."

Austin joined our little hug. A bag I hadn't noticed before chilled my side as she held it against me. She giggled with

us. "Aren't those two sickening? It's like one brain with two bodies. When I'm in the store with them, it's positively freaky. A customer will be looking at something and trying to decide and they'll look at one another and split into two directions, both finding just what the person needs." She headed to the kitchen and came back with three spoons.

I dropped onto the couch and pulled a velvet throw over me. It had always been for decoration, too. Tonight it couldn't have looked more beautiful anywhere else than on my body.

Dana threw the fringe over my toes, still peeking through. She reached into Austin's bag and handed me a pint of ice cream. Ben & Jerry's Half Baked. It had my name on it, written in purple glitter pen. I smiled and shook my head. "You ladies are a trip."

Austin pushed a coaster over on the coffee table. "Put it there, please," she said in a mock serious tone.

That really made me lose it.

"Sorry I went crazy on you about the door. Just want you to be safe, you know? We're worried enough." Austin's genuine concern showed on her face.

Dana frowned, as if Austin had let something slip.

My eyes blurred with tears as I dug into the ice cream. "What is this, some kind of intervention? Coming over here with Half Baked. And I don't deserve it. I've been such a horrible—"

"Shh." Dana held a finger to her mouth. "Friends love at all times, Chelle. When are you going to understand that? If you could keep it together all the time, you wouldn't need friends. You wouldn't need Jesus."

She had me there. I took another bite, fighting the urge to turn the container around to see if there were as many carbs in this stuff as I remembered.

I'll just eat a little.

Austin sat across from us with that same spill-it smile she'd had after Moriah was born. Dana was talking a mile a minute, about Tracey and her baby, about church, about work, about her marriage…but Austin sat silent. Smiling.

That smile was the last thing I remembered before waking up with my face plastered to the sofa. Dana was gone. Moriah, too. On the couch across from me under one of Jericho's old NBA blankets, Austin perched in front of the TV with a bowl of popcorn.

While I pried my eyelids open, she lifted the buttery mess to me. "Want some?"

I'd better not.

"Sure. What are you watching?" I asked as she howled and slapped her leg. From my angle, the set was out of view. I'd positioned it that way to keep people from sitting there in the old days.

Austin munched so fast I thought she might choke. "*Golden Girls.* It's hilarious. Betty White is so funny. I used to hate this show when I was little, but now it cracks me up."

I sat up a little and reached into the bowl on the coffee table between us. The butter slid off my fingertips. Yummy. "Now we're old enough to get the jokes."

Austin nodded. "Maybe." Her tone grew more serious. "Dana had to go home. Adrian spilled candle wax on himself."

My eyes peeled totally open. He'd done that once before years ago and taken off some hairs on his leg. We'd teased him that electrolysis was cheaper than trying to kill himself. But in truth, that kind of burn could be quite serious. "Is he all right? What happened? He's always so careful."

"He can't function now unless Dana is there. He's okay. It was just a little bit on his ankle, but you know how guys can be when they're hurt."

I snorted. "Big fat babies." Jericho was pitiful, too. As big and strong as that boy was, the sight of his own blood could still make him lose it. How he'd made it through Moriah's birth only God knows. "What about you? Don't you need to get home, too?"

Still laughing at the television, Austin shrugged. "Steve is out of town for work. You're stuck with *moi.*"

"Sounds good to me." A deep sigh escaped me. Though I hadn't thought to ask for help from my friends, I suddenly realized just how much I needed it. "Right. Jordan's out of town, too. He was helping here and there. I guess you'll do for a few hours."

She threw a piece of popcorn across the void between us. "That's what you say now. I've got my overnight bag in the car."

"You're kidding." I sat up on one elbow. This was so something I would do.

Austin stared in the empty bowl, then frowned. How did she stay so skinny eating like that? She licked her fingers. "I am so not kidding. You're like a slow cooker—the goods are tasty but it takes forever to get done. Dana and Tracey spill easy."

That struck me as so funny that I had to sit up to keep from choking on my popcorn. I laughed until my eyes strained at the corners and my belly was sore. "Girl, you know us so well. I'm so glad you're in the sistahood."

She smiled. "Me, too. Now do you want to go back to sleep or should we get a head start on the talking?"

I rested a buttery finger under my chin. "Might as well get on with it. Let's start with Tad…"

From: *RichardMason*
To: *Sassysistah1*
Subject: Dinner
Rochelle,
You said e-mail was better, so I'm writing a quick note. I've been on the road since we last talked, but I'd like to hook up with you when I return. Will Thursday at seven work for you? I certainly hope so. I really want to get to know you better.
Blessings,
Richard

Chapter nine

Austin was a godsend. She cooked, she cleaned and somehow, she even got Moriah to sleep. She drew the line at dishes, which was fine since it's my favorite chore anyway. Now it was time for her to go home to her own place, get changed and meet her husband at the airport.

"You didn't need to do all of this, really. I would have—"

She held up a hand. "I know you would have. You always do, but for a few days you didn't have to. I enjoyed myself, actually. I grew up sort of taking care of things and Steve's mother rarely lets me do that. It's good to be needed."

I shook my head, staring down the hall at Jericho's room. He was out at practice and a friend of Shemika's had the baby, which I wasn't sure how I felt about. "I know just what you mean. I wonder how long it will be before Jericho no longer needs me. Or worse yet, no longer wants me."

Austin sipped the sparkling grape juice in front of her. "I don't know that he'll ever stop needing you or wanting you.

He'll just need you in a different way. A grown-up way. Isn't that what you wanted? That's what you've been telling me."

I broke off a piece of cheese. This was what happened when you let an amateur psychologist with a fabulous memory sleep over. She threw things up in your face. "It seems clear that he'll eventually marry Shemika. Sometimes, I have to admit it seems more practical than the baby going back and forth, but…"

She speared a turkey cube from our little makeshift relish tray. I would have loved plum tomatoes, but this was December and they were five dollars a package. Though I could afford it, I couldn't bring myself to pay it.

Austin paused, searching the tray. Was she looking for a tomato, too?

"I can understand you being worried about Jericho and Shemika, Rochelle. Marriage is a huge move. It'll affect everything—their education, their future—but in truth, having a baby in the first place was a huge move—"

"I know that. It's not just about the education." It wasn't, was it? Shan's velvety brown skin crossed my mind. Okay, so maybe I didn't want to be poor. Or my child, either. I'd gone that route. It wasn't that exciting. That's what movies were for. Ugh. I was starting to sound like—like my *mother!*

Austin dunked a chip through the dip and back to her mouth in a swift movement, probably knowing from the sound in my voice that I'd dive on her and eat the whole pack if she didn't move fast. She circled her lips a few times like an airplane before going for the crunch.

I shook my head. "You are such a kid."

She shook her head in response. "And you are such a mother. Now tell me, if it's not just the education, what else is it?"

The knife trembled in my hand as I spread peanut butter into the groove of my celery. Would I ever get used to Austin's pointed questions? Probably not. Still, they saved a lot of time.

"How can my son have a successful marriage when he's never even seen one? Besides Tad and a few teachers, Jericho never really had a male role model. And his dad—who he adores—makes easy money and has a live-in girlfriend—"

Austin grabbed her throat. "I thought she moved out."

Me, too. "She's back."

"And he's still coming over here to babysit and stuff?"

"Basically."

"Wow. She wants him bad. I should have known when the wedding Web site stayed up that she wouldn't go quietly." She paused to sip her Mello Yello. "Keep going. No male role model and all that."

Wedding Web site still up? I definitely needed to get back on my computer. "Anyway, I keep wondering if I didn't actually hurt Jericho by not dating instead of protecting him."

There, I'd said it. I hadn't even realized that it was in my mind, but now it was out. "I've been an overprotective crazy woman and now the boy not only has a baby, but has no idea how to be in a real family."

Austin reached across the table and took my hand. "Oh Rochelle, believe me, you *have* a real family. I had a father and I still got into trouble. My dad's body was present, but his heart was absent. Jericho knows you love him. You did all you could."

I swallowed back my tears. "I tried, now I need to do something else. This whole dating-service thing started out as some sort of impulse to make myself feel better, but now I'm thinking I should take it a little more seriously. Jericho will be here a few more months. Maybe I can show him something of how a good relationship works."

Like I would know.

Austin's phone beeped. She stood. "That's the Steve-o-meter. I've got to go and get ready for my sweetie. As for you, I'm glad to hear that you want to give meeting someone a chance although I'm not sure I agree with your reasoning—"

I started to respond, but she held up a hand in classic Dana fashion.

We've turned her into a monster.

"No time to argue. We'll have to save that for the next visit. Your black pantsuit is on the bed and your cell phone charged. I freshened up the bathroom."

My head dipped down. I narrowed my eyes. "Pantsuit? Bathroom? For what?"

Keys dangling from one finger and overnight bag over one shoulder, Austin laughed like sunshine. "For your date, of course. It's Thursday. Richard will be here in half an hour."

He was smooth like butter, this Richard, saying all the right things, making all the right moves. Even brought a Bible along. His highest selling point? The man knew the power of a good suit and what colors looked good on him. His mama had definitely schooled him on that. As Dana would say, he was shaped like a high-rise—tall with wide shoulders. I should have been soaking this up, capitalizing on my big chance to make a connection. So why was I still forking through my pasta and eyeing the clock?

"They make the pasta by hand here, a special family recipe," he said between mouthfuls, his job skills as a corporate negotiator once again shining through. Like the best of facilitators, he managed to keep the conversation flowing without monopolizing it.

"It's delicious," I said, taking in the hand-painted mural of Sicily on the wall. I'd always meant to get over to this restaurant, the Italian Grill. Now I wished I'd come alone. The atmosphere was like a wedding reception, with people eating and laughing, moving easily through the tables. The staff seemed to know most of the customers and the customers seemed to know one another. Richard was obviously a frequent visitor from all the winks and waves we'd received.

"Delicious, huh? You've barely eaten a thing." His smile defied resistance.

I smiled back, unwilling to explain that I'd eaten a third of a pint of ice cream before coming. "I don't eat pasta much and I'm just not hungry—"

"Two cannoli to go, please?" He dropped his fork to the plate. "Why didn't you say something? I asked where you'd like to go. Please don't do that. Tell me what you want. What you like." Another kind smile.

This time I didn't return it. I was too busy trying to wrap

my mind around his words. *Tell him what I want?* If only I knew. "It's been so long since anyone bothered to ask that I'll have to get used to that, but thank you. The place here is lovely. We can stay."

He pursed his lips. "Of course not. Why waste the time? I hope to see you many times. This is just the beginning. It could have been better. And it will be better." He walked around and stood at my chair.

I stood, too. He hoped to see me many times? What exactly did that mean? Did he have a wedding chapel reserved or what? Suddenly my legs felt itchy. Was this how men felt around pushy, er, focused women? Who knew? "Thank you."

He took the bag of dessert and left a crisp twenty on the table. I pulled on my coat before he could help me with it. Why could I let Jordan help me into my coat and not this kind stranger? He was one of those people who was very easy to be around. And easy to go too fast with because he did the right things. Like my once-unspoiled couch, if I started up with him, he'd be a hard habit to break.

In the car we listened to jazz and played the I-wonder-what-happened-to game with seventies and eighties singers. I even got up the nerve to admit that I wasn't going to eat the cannoli either, which made him laugh as we parked in front of my building. White and red lights lit my row of town houses as it did every year during the holidays, making my lack of decorations woefully apparent.

"If you need any help with your lights, let me know. I love that kind of stuff. I decorated my house the day after Thanksgiving," he said before rounding the car to open my door.

My spinster sense started tingling. A house of his own, decorating on a schedule, trying to let me pick everything that I wanted…way past mama training. This man had obviously been married. The question was how long ago and to whom? We'd discussed it briefly during our first phone call, but I hadn't really been paying attention.

"My son will help me. He's just a little busy right now. We'll get them up." I stepped carefully over a snowdrift and onto the sidewalk. No ice patch underneath, thank goodness.

Without pause, he started with me for the door. "Young boy like that? Who knows when he'll get time, though I hope he will. If not, you can always call me…or e-mail, of course."

Call him? I hated phones the way some people despised computers. Give me a keyboard and some cocoa and it was on. Though I had dialed the number Shan scrawled on my napkin a few times and hung up before he could answer. How high school was that?

My eyes ran down the row of parked cars until I saw my son's new vehicle, a gift from his father, parked at the end of the row. True enough, the minivan made travel easier, but we'd had words over it to be sure. That and Jericho's new job, helping his father recruit players by watching tapes of college games. True enough, the boy had an eye, but I couldn't help thinking it was another of Jordan's schemes to subvert my authority. How would the boy learn to work for things if he had everything given to him? Anyway, with Jericho home, I didn't worry too much about Richard coming in. In fact, I was interested to see what my son's take on the man would be.

"Rochelle? Are you all right?" Richard looked concerned. I definitely wasn't following his agenda for this date.

"I'm fine, just thinking. Sorry." I raked a hand through my bob, finding every hair spritzed in place. The door opened before I could get my key in the hole.

Jericho waved us inside. "There you are, Mom, we didn't know where you went," he said, shoving a hand toward Richard. "How are you doing, sir?"

"Fine," Richard said, accompanied by that man-nod I could never figure out. Men. If they had their way, they'd probably never speak at all. They'd have to eventually. All the women would be at the mall. It never ceased to amaze me how guys could have a whole conversation in body language. That would never work for us ladies. (Why are you standing like that? Cramps? I've got something in my purse for that.)

"What's going on, son?" I asked as we stepped inside and shut the door behind our guest. A sharp intake of breath followed our entrance. Austin had picked up the house before leaving, but the only thing fresh now might be the bathrooms, though I doubted it. Baby blankets, the swing, diapers, wipes—stuff was everywhere. Baby food in every flavor cluttered the table at one end. Jericho's homework was scattered at the other end. I turned to Richard to explain, but it was his turn to stare off into space. Shemika jumped off the couch and started picking up.

I gave Jericho a questioning look. The two of them weren't supposed to be here alone, though many times it was unavoidable. We'd sort it out later.

Richard's skyscraper shoulders wilted. He wobbled a little.

Don't fall on me now. "Do you need to sit down? What's wrong?"

He clutched the chair beside him. "You have a—a baby?"

I hung my coat on the back of the chair opposite him. "She's my granddaughter. Moriah. And this is her mother, Shemika."

She waved from the floor, folding up the bouncy seat. "Hi."

He managed a feeble hello, then turned to me with that same stricken expression. "I told you, I don't do young children. I'm allergic to them. It's a medically documented condition."

Jericho exploded with laughter and slapped his baby-food splattered knee. "Allergic to kids? You've gotta be kidding."

Shemika curled up her nose like she'd sniffed one of Moriah's diapers too hard. She looked at me with wide eyes. "He *is* kidding, right?"

One look at Richard let me know he definitely wasn't kidding. With eyes as big as eggs, he dug into his pocket for his wallet and pulled out some ragged piece of paper, a photocopy with a doctor's signature.

A psychiatrist's signature.

Mr. Mason has an unreasonable fear of children twelve and under, much like a physical allergy. I recommend that he limit contact with them, especially babies.

If that didn't beat all.

I folded it back up, handed it to him. "Sorry for the confusion, Richard. This just isn't going to work. Thanks for din—"

"Mom? I think someone is at the door." Jericho craned his neck. "Someone who really wants to come in."

"Might be the kids from two doors down wanting me to unlock their door. That key is supposed to be for emergencies. They're just getting comfortable now. Hold on, Richard." With my best mother-face, I opened the door, only to find the biggest, prettiest woman I've ever seen. And she wasn't alone. The man next to her, balding and smirking, held a TV camera on his shoulder. Had the reality shows of my nightmares finally found me?

Jericho ducked. "That's the guy from *Your Cheating Heart!* Shut the door, Mom!"

And so I did. On reflex and too tired to think, I slammed the door in those poor people's faces. Before I could open it, a rain of knocks pounded on the front door.

"Richard! I know you're in there. You said you loved me, that you were going to marry me. Now you're out here riding around in the cold with some woman. And she's such a scrawny thing, too—"

Babies? Marry her? There were so many things to fixate on here. Me, I grabbed the insult. "I am not scrawny!" I stared at my son for some clarification.

Already checking for another exit, the man offered not one word of explanation. "Is there another way out of here?" he half whispered.

Jericho stood between us and shook his head. "Look, man, I don't know what kind of game you're running, but whoever that is doesn't need to be yelling at my mother, who is not scrawny, by the way. Go out there and handle your business like a man. Or are you allergic to that, too?"

Okay, maybe I did something right with this kid.

I peeked around my son's shoulder. "Who is that anyway?"

He paused at the door, with his hand an inch from the knob. "My ex-fiancée," Richard whined like a kid caught stealing candy.

"I'm *still* your fiancée, fool. Now open this door!"

When my guest didn't respond, Jericho opened the door and pushed Richard outside, but not before I heard the reality TV cameraman say something about this being the home of the Jordan Rose's ex-wife. I sank into the nearest chair and dropped my head on the table.

Shemika peeked out the curtain. "Ooh-wee. The sidewalk is full of folk. And all the neighbors have their lights on—and uh-oh."

I lifted my head about an inch. What else could happen? "What?"

She pressed her lips together. "Jericho's daddy, we called him for help because we didn't know where you were—"

"You called him? But he was out of town!"

Shemika shrugged. "*Was* is the operative word. He's pulling up now."

"What kind of craziness is this?" Jordan slammed the door behind him after forcing his way through the crowd in front of my apartment. The sprinkle of gray at his temples seemed suddenly whiter than I remembered.

I swallowed, thinking I'd better check my own scalp. Nights

like this could leave me white-headed. "Some guy from the dating thing. Seems he was engaged to someone—"

Jordan snatched off his gloves and tossed them on the table. "Engaged? Didn't you ask about that before you went out with him? And what did you bring him back here for? It's late. The baby isn't feeling well. And you have some man up in here?"

Straightening from where I'd been slumped at the table, my top lip slid to one side. Was he raising his voice at me? "Look, the man took me to dinner. That's it. I had just told him that we shouldn't see each other again when our little company arrived."

"He's allergic to kids," Jericho piped up from the couch, where he held the baby on his shoulder.

I looked for something to throw at that boy. Finding nothing, I shook my head at him instead for even repeating such foolishness. This was embarrassing enough.

Jordan shrugged out of his leather coat. "Allergic to kids? Okay, see this is totally out of hand. Do you realize that's a national show, Rochelle? And that they're depicting you as my ex-wife? I know that I went to that little dating dinner too, but let's cut that for now, okay? You're messing with my livelihood, which, in case you've forgotten, is helping take care of your son." He pointed toward the couch.

The couch was empty. Even Shemika ran down the hall on that one. Jordan should have been so smart.

He gave me a puzzled look at their reaction. "What?"

I stood.

Slowly.

Both hands firmly planted on a place mat, I found my voice. "*Your* livelihood? Taking care of *my* son? He's *our* son. Don't do me any favors. I've been feeding, clothing and caring for that boy for seventeen years—"

"My money didn't hurt, either." He folded his arms.

My voice went an octave lower, the key in which I sang the most sorrowful of our church songs. In a minute, a chariot was going to have to swing low and escort Jordan's body out of my kitchen. "That 'money' of yours was gone years ago. I invested and scrimped and saved and worked like a dog to preserve your life in that Mexican hospital, to put your sister through school and to keep your son cared for."

He touched my arm. "I know. It's just that what you do affects all of us. Maybe you need to consider that maybe God doesn't want you with anybody."

I froze. Hadn't I considered that very thing for most of my life? Hadn't I even believed it for the past decade? Didn't I even wonder about it now? But it wasn't Jordan's place to say it.

"Have you ever considered the same?" I stared into his eyes, so much like those I'd once known except for the lines feathering the corners. Honest eyes, I'd thought to myself on a prom night long ago.

What a fool I'd been.

I wouldn't be one again now, too. "You know what, Jordan? It's always about you. My life is changing and I need to change with it. I'm not sure what God is doing, but I'm trying to follow the best I can."

He pulled his hand away, sank into the chair I'd been sitting in. "By going to dinner with strangers, Rochelle? By handing out your business cards to men we know nothing about? That's how you're following God?"

We? Most of what he said got past me, but I didn't miss his implication. Not at all. "Oh, I get it. It's okay for you, but not for me?"

Jordan pounded his fist on the table. "No! Well, yes! You are good, Rochelle. You always were. You don't need to get a guy that way when—"

"When I can have you?" Might as well get down to the meat of this bone we were picking at. I walked around the table, creating more distance between us. That cologne was starting to distract me. "You're getting married, Jordan."

He wilted. "It's complicated, Rochelle. I came back here with nobody. You wouldn't even talk to me. I didn't plan it, okay? Terri was just there and then she was there again and after a while she was always there. And I do…care for her."

Care for her? What about love? That's what I'd been expecting to hear. He was right. This *was* complicated.

"Can you two keep it down?" our son whispered, emerging from the shadowed hall. "I just got her to sleep."

We both stared at each other and then at him. Jericho shook his head. "Fine. I'll tell her that Grandma and Grandpa are having a fight in the sandbox."

I sighed as the door shut down the hall. "I'm sorry," I said, pressing my hand to my throat.

On his feet and rounding the table, Jordan agreed. "Me, too. Do you forgive me? I shouldn't have raised my voice, or even said anything. I have no right. I'm not your husband.

And who am I to give advice on relationships? The best one I ever had was with you."

Thanksgiving, a blur of bland restaurant food still sour in my memory, had passed quietly. Christmas, formerly my favorite holiday, approached without invitation. For the first time in months, I had to face the singles group for the Christmas Eve get-together that I'd naively planned a year ago, dutifully securing our place on the church calendar. If only I'd known then how much would have changed.

The past few weeks were a blur of working every spare moment at the store, whose foot traffic had suddenly diminished after the *Your Cheating Heart* episode aired. It seemed that where Austin's interview had been intriguing, that show had been a turnoff. I hadn't worked this hard since starting out eight years ago. And then there was Moriah's colic, which sometimes responded to the doctor's medication and sometimes not. The sometimes not seemed to always land on my watch.

I entered the church basement, drinking in the smell of apple cider and the beauty of the gold and violet ornaments I'd bought on sale after Christmas last year. I'd forgotten all about them, but someone hadn't. I turned into the room to find a three-tiered gold candle stand with more of my purchases in perfect array. Tad, looking more handsome than when I'd seen him two Sundays ago, lit them one by one. The scent, Cranberry Relish, was a bestseller in Kick!, a line of candle stores Dana's husband Adrian owned. The aroma of one of my holiday favorites took my breath away. I walked up behind Tad as he lit the last one.

"The decorations are beautiful, Tad." My voice, worn-out from midnight lullabies and long talks with teachers, came out more breath than words.

He turned with surprise, not having seen me behind him. With both hands he grabbed my shoulders. "Rochelle! I didn't think you'd make it."

I paused for a moment to record the memory of his strong, peaceful hands holding me up. "I didn't think I'd make it, either. Funny, huh? I planned the thing."

His smile widened. "It's not funny at all. It's my turn. You've done the planning for this group for so long, while I—well, I'm not sure what I was doing."

Avoiding me, that's what. With me out of the way, Tad could do things without having to worry about our strained phone conversations or awkward meetings.

"Well, I thank you for taking up the slack. The baby's had colic and the store, well, since that TV show, things haven't been going so well. I've even had problems with some of my suppliers and other designers whose shoes I sell. It hurt business, even for Christmas."

He sobered, putting down the long-handled butane lighter, but not before he switched on the child safety. I frowned. Why did he always do that? The youngest person here was thirty.

Tad shrugged as if reading my thoughts. "Just to be safe."

Safe? Though I knew that under God's arms safety existed, danger and pain were again real, too. A year ago, I'd stood in this room reciting my verses in total confidence, having shut out the world all together. I'd become "churchy," as Shemika called it. I still wasn't sure if anything was wrong with that exactly, except maybe forgetting what "church" was really about—Jesus.

As others milled into the room raving over both the scene and the scent, he leaned into me, lowering his voice to almost a whisper.

"I'm very sorry about what happened with that show. I did put in a call to their producer and the owner of A Match Made in Seven. That man should have been screened properly and the journalistic tactics used by that host were totally unprofessional."

My mouth opened, but I didn't know what to say. I'd spent so much time defending myself to everyone that it hadn't occurred to me that I needed someone to believe in me. Or that Tad would be the one to do it. What had happened to him this year? He'd changed, too. I bit my lip to keep from crying. "Thank you. You didn't have to do that. Really…" My voice cracked.

"This place looks great, Brother Tad—Rochelle, is that you? Merry Christmas, baby. Come on here and give me a hug," Deacon Rivers said. Still the oldest and most vibrant member of the singles group, he never missed an outing, much to the dismay of the women in the Seniors Bible Study, especially Mother Holloway, whom I needed to call about Shemika's Christmas gift.

I accepted the older man's embrace while Tad looked on. Were his eyes misting up, too? It had certainly been a long time since I'd come around here. Too long, in fact, though Deacon Rivers still doused himself in half a bottle of Old

Spice before coming. Some things never changed. "Merry Christmas to you, Deacon."

By now the room was almost full and everyone stopped to hug me and pat Tad on the back. Even the women who'd given me sideways looks whenever Tad and I taught together or worked on a project for the group, smiled at us both and made little remarks.

"Brother Thaddeus, I see your prayers have paid off," one of the group members said before turning to me. "Merry Christmas, Rochelle. We've missed you. Call me. I have something for your grandbaby."

The reception was so kind and gracious that with each second I came closer to a total meltdown. Though these people had often seemed thankless when I spent my days praying for them and planning activities, the love they poured out to me now was genuine and came just when I needed it most.

"Are we ready to begin?" someone called.

Tad raised his hand after another brief handshake. "Just one minute."

He leaned over to me. "I called that show because they made the grave mistake of casting a shadow on your integrity. I know that you're hard on yourself, but you are a good and godly woman. I couldn't have anyone thinking otherwise."

Not even you?

"Thanks. Now go on. Everyone is waiting."

He nodded and wound through the folding chairs to the microphone.

"'O come let us adore Him…'"

I closed my eyes, allowing myself to go back to that stable, to see past the fear in Mary's eyes, the stink of the animals. Right there, in the most unlikely of places, in the most difficult of circumstances, was Jesus. And He was right here, too. As peace flooded me, I felt a hand on my shoulder. And I smelled…peppermint.

I opened my eyes to find a dark, clean-shaven face. The happy face so often in my thoughts.

Shan.

I hugged him quickly, though I hadn't meant to. "What are you doing here?"

He released me quickly and took my hands in his. "Well, you won't take my calls or e-mails, so I had to turn detective. I thought, where can a man find a fine woman with a good heart? The answer was easy. Church."

Chapter ten

To: *thesassysistahood*
From: *Sassysistah1*
Subject: Cheating Heart Show/new devotional
Renee,
No, I did not watch the *Your Cheating Heart* episode. I didn't watch the show before, so I see no point in starting now. Thanks for the heads-up. Pray for me, that's all I can say. Everyone else, the devo I promised is below. Kiss that baby for me, Tracey.

Unshaken

"And this expression, Yet once more, denotes the removing of those things which can be shaken as of created things, in order that those things which cannot be shaken may remain." (Hebrews 12:28, NASB)

Life can be a series of quakings and upheavals, clanging our faith against the walls, our convictions against the ceiling.

It's sort of like one of those amusement-park rides where the floor drops out, only you can't get off. And you know what?

It's a good thing.

When dictating our own plans, we can forget THE plan, the one God has for us. But when all our preconceptions are shaken, many of the "created things" turn to a smoothie of nothingness before our eyes.

So if you're in a lifequake, let go of the walls. Open your eyes. Meet God today on your shaky ground. I'll do the same. After all, to get to the seed of thing, you've got to shake off the hull.

Rochelle

"Surviving is important. Thriving is elegant." Maya Angelou, Poet Laureate and sistah extraordinaire

"This is Dr. Walter calling. Do you have a minute?"

I bristled at the voice on the phone. My podiatrist? I'd been avoiding him, hoping he didn't want a date, too. That'd be too weird. No need to be rude, though. Phone to my ear, I poked through my organizer boxes for the birthday card I'd picked out for Jericho months ago. As I found it, I scrambled to reply.

"Dr. Walter. Sorry I missed my last appointment. My life has been, well, a little hectic lately."

He cleared his throat. "So I've heard." He followed it with a chuckle, but the damage was done. Definitely a *Your Cheating Heart* viewer.

I pulled the birthday card onto my lap, seeing now how juvenile it was. How inappropriate. It was not a card for the man my son had grown into. Oh well, I'd have to do what I both hated and loved—impulse buying. Being healed of that habit had helped me go into business and buy my town house. I tried not to do it often. "Yes, well. I'm not sure I'll reschedule, either. I don't know anymore if I want my toes broken or not."

Wasn't a broken heart enough?

His chuckle grew more robust. "What, does the ex like the old feet? They definitely have character. Still, I'm more concerned with the health of your feet than their appearance. There are other options. Come in and let's have another look, huh?"

Relief rushed out of me. The past few months had hobbled me enough. "Okay."

"Great, and don't worry, when I'm ready for my date, I won't call as Dr. Walter. I'll be Larry then."

It was my turn to laugh. "After my date tonight, I'll be clearing my plate for a while. Though if I were willing to hang out with anyone, it might as well be you, uh, Larry. Still, I think it'd be awkward since I'm your patient."

"Why do think I'm calling about your feet? You won't be my patient forever."

Great. Just what I needed. My own personal foot doctor. Okay, so I did need that, but still—the thought was creepy but funny, too. My shoulders relaxed. I pressed the top back onto my tote box full of cards. "You're funny. It's one of the reasons I chose you in the first place. I'll call soon for an appointment."

"I'll do you one better and send you an appointment card. If the timing doesn't work, just let me know."

I nodded. "That'll be great. See you sometime soon."

The thought of going to dinner with Shan tonight almost made me want to redial the doctor's office and beg them to break my toes right now. Why I'd agreed to the date I'm not sure except to get out of yet another odd situation with Tad where another strange man showed up. I tell you, I haven't had this much male attention since my body blossomed in sixth grade. And sometimes the parallels run a little too close. I could almost feel a pimple straining to break the surface of my skin.

"I'm too old for this," I said to no one in particular as I stared out the window of my apartment.

So many years of singleness hadn't prepared me for the intensity of dating, let alone pursuing a relationship. People wanted so much time, so much talking. It was enough to make a girl want to give up. I wasn't looking for a girlfriend, just a nice guy to spend some time with now and then. I'd long since given up on that get-married-for-Jericho thing. Finding a man was one thing, but finding one that I liked and liked me back, well, that was much more difficult than I'd anticipated.

Jericho would be eighteen in a few weeks. Soon after, I'd turn thirty-seven. Was I really interested in spending the kind of time it would take to find a husband, let alone get to know that guy?

Probably not. These days, sorting my socks was challenging. Being a grandma had rocked my world enough. Moriah also raised another concern. Did I really want to bring another man into my world with a young child—a girl, no less—so often in my care? One part of me said that it was my overprotective mom thing in action again, but in the guts of me, the broken parts, I knew these were things to consider.

And what about Jordan? Though he and I had fought about it, the truth was, some of my actions did affect his reputation. The media had seen to that. Although I couldn't say Terri and I would ever be tea-toting friends or anything, she'd cleaned up nicely from that painted-on dress she'd worn the first time I'd seen her. By the time Moriah was old enough to notice such things, Terri might even be wearing clothes she could fit into.

Well, that was probably pushing it, but anything could happen. Look at me, Spinster of the Midwest one minute and reality-show home-wrecker the next. It'd been a long time since I'd been on this side of the fence, my hand out for a drop of grace, my mouth dry for a sip of understanding. It made me realize just how graceless I'd been to my son, to my friends, to people at church, to Jordan…but mostly to myself. In my quest to be more like Jesus, I'd somehow switched to trying to be Him. Perfect.

Sure there's that fury and the justice thing. I still said that the fear of the Lord is the beginning of wisdom, whichever way you choose to interpret it—reverence or knee-knocking-scary fear. I'd experienced both. Like Dana and even Tad had been trying to tell me for years, there is a special love that Jesus wanted to pour into me. I'm trying now to reach for it, even if it's just an ounce at a time.

After tonight, I'd give myself room to be still, to move slow, to crawl if necessary. All that really mattered was staying on the path, keeping my eyes on Jesus. Looking down at the road made the trip seem faster, but it could also make a girl naive and overconfident, made her trip and fall. And fall hard. I'm realizing that it's not just about the destination—getting married, making money, reaching goals—it's also about the road on the way there. The process. God cares about that, too.

I'm also learning that sometimes the road leads you back to where you started but the second time around, you're just glad to be there.

Across the living room, Moriah let out a piercing scream in her portacrib. At the same time, the doorbell, the new and louder one I'd recently installed, blared. With a smile, I went to Jericho's room, leaned over and gathered Moriah into my arms. Six months ago, I might have gone for the door first, not wanting to keep anybody waiting. Now I'd realized that the urgent thing wasn't always what's important.

Love was important.

"Be there in a minute," I said, fingering the folds on Moriah's blanket as I went. She seemed so big now, so long. Her face changed every week it seemed, switching from one of Jordan's family members to another. Shemika and I just shook our heads and gave up looking for any resemblance to us.

"Don't be surprised if the baby don't look like you," my mother had said when I told her I was pregnant. "Them Roses got strong genes." Mama didn't lie on that one. Not a bit.

I stared through the peephole, squinting one eye to make out the giant face on the other side. It only took a second.

Shan. Two hours early and he didn't call. Normally, I would have walked back to my bed and lain down and let him play a tune on the doorbell. Today, I shrugged, prayed and opened the dead bolt, then the regular lock.

"A little early, aren't you?"

He smiled, but not at me. At Moriah. "Oh, my. Is she yours? She's gorgeous."

I stared at him in disbelief. "She's my granddaughter," I said, prepared for the comments about not being old enough and a whole sob story, the one I'd avoided with Richard but wouldn't mind telling Shan. He was that kind of person. The kind you could be real with. What else could be done with him, I wasn't sure, nor did I want to find out.

Before I could invite him in, Shan reached for the baby. "Do you mind?"

"No, just be careful. She's heavy."

He lifted her easily. "Heavy? She's a peanut. Aren't you, sweetie?" He smoothed the back of her half silky, half curly head, about the only thing she *did* inherit from me.

I pushed the door shut behind him and watched in awe. Moriah never went to strangers without pitching a total fit and sometimes she wouldn't come to those of us who cared for her all the time. She took to Shan like breathing, cooing and giggling like crazy. He still hadn't commented on the grandmother thing. I liked that about him. Unlike me, he was able to take something as it was and let it be. "Not everything requires a response," as he'd so wisely told me after I'd asked him why he was so quiet after Tad's inquisition of him during the Christmas program.

Tonight I was grateful for his policy. With a sigh, I plopped down beside him on the couch, watching as he held Moriah, playing with her toes as he talked to me. "I just came over to ask how you liked your barbecue—spicy or sweet?"

Midway through a monster yawn—did I really do that?—I almost choked on my own breath. "You came all the way over here for that?"

He stood, walked to the diaper bag on the other couch, took out a diaper and wipes and handed Moriah to me. "Well, so far I've learned that face-to-face communications are best with you. Your answering machine was on, which meant that you were probably home, but your IMs are blocked on the computer, so you were definitely laying low and in deep need of barbecue. The question is will it be spicy or sweet?"

"You are something else." Amazed at his correct call that Moriah needed a diaper change, I went to the other room, wiped her up and deposited her on my hip so that I could wash my hands. Shan peeled the baby off me and shooed me away.

I rubbed my damp palms together, wondering what his baby aptitude might mean. He was good with her. A little too good.

There's always something.

But hey, I had my "somethings," too. So what if he had a child? I was only willing to consider the possibility of playing stepmom to one at this point, but it was probably more. He was too nice. And hadn't I always wanted more kids? Whoa…this train of thought had streaked out of the stupid station and was about to arrive smack in the middle of crazy. After tonight, I was going it alone, wasn't I?

I reached out for the baby, but she turned her head, curling into Shan's shoulder. My mouth dropped open. "I can't believe it. Did you see that?"

Shan turned back from the window. "Don't take it personally. Babies just like me."

My mind started queuing up the questions. *Okay, Mister Nice Guy, just how many kids do you have? And where do they live?*

His child support is probably enough to run a small country.

Shan was right. Everything didn't require a response. Or an explanation. Why not just let it come out? He didn't seem to be the hiding type. And why did I care anyway? I had no idea why, but I did care. Suddenly, I cared very much. Sure he was too young for me, too broke and too cute, but hey, at least he was saved, right? I tucked my bob behind my ear. I was doing it again. Dreaming.

His hand touched mine. "So which is it?"

"Huh?" That smile had blinded me. What was he talking about?

"Spicy or sweet? The barbecue?" He whispered now because Moriah was nodding off to sleep against him.

For a second, I envied her position.

This is definitely my last date. I'm not strong enough for this. I never will be. I've got to keep it real.

"Sweet." Why did I say that? Sure I'd relished my mother's sweet ribs back in the day, but now I spent hours in the summer making my own low-carb sugar-free variety. "No, make that spicy. I don't know what I'm thinking."

"You weren't thinking. You were feeling. It's okay to do that sometimes. Even Jesus says so. Sweet it is." He squeezed my hand before placing Moriah in her portable crib with such tenderness, my knees almost buckled.

"Bye, sweet girl," he said, turning away. He paused to give me a smile. "And bye to you too, sweet lady."

I swallowed hard, staring at his silky skin. How did he get to shine like that? His hair, in small coils around his head, had the same sheen. He was pretty sweet himself. How could he be so young and have me feeling like this? It was all so 1985.

I still didn't know how old he was.

I brushed away the thought and watched Shan head for the door as if he hadn't blown my mind…again.

He paused on the step that led down into my living room. "Forgive me for coming without calling. I'll be back to pick you up at six. Oh yeah, and bring the baby."

Sweet didn't begin to describe it. From start to finish, my dinner with Shan was the most fun I'd had in years. I'd waffled about taking the baby to a place I'd never been, but after praying about it, I felt it'd be okay, as long as I drove myself. That would also give me the option of leaving early if I wanted to.

I wouldn't want to.

In fact, I wouldn't want it to end at all.

"So what restaurant should I meet you at?" There were a few barbecue places on the west side of town where Shan lived, a part of town that had become what my neighborhood had once been, an international neighborhood peppered with churches, mosques and Jewish temples, all with curry and hot sauce swirling from their chimneys. With his restaurant experience and great location, I was sure he'd pick a nice barbecue spot.

Shan sucked his teeth at me through the phone. It made the same clicking sound as one of my Jamaican customers when she was checking the prices on my shoes. It sounded much better on him. "Woman, you just don't get it, do you? I'm not taking you to any restaurant. I'm bringing you to my house. I wouldn't serve you someone else's food on the first date."

I held the phone up and looked at it, then at the blanket of white on the ground outside, deeper than when I'd checked earlier. "Shan, it's winter. How are you going to barbecue?"

He held the phone a bit away from his mouth as if he was turning around. "She says how can I 'cue in the winter, y'all. What do you say? Can I do it?" There was a round of laughter and then he brought the phone back to his face. "Miss lady, my balcony is one of the finest grills in this city. Let me come and pick you up and you'll see."

Checking Moriah's bag once more and leaving a note for Jericho, I stammered. "I, uh, I'm going to drive if you don't mind. Give me the directions again?"

He groaned. "No way. What kind of man would send a woman and a baby out into the cold alone? In fact, since the temperature has dropped so much, I can just bring the dinner to you."

My heart sped up. Shan and I alone? "I don't think—"

"If you can accommodate my whole crew, that is," he added.

"Crew? I thought we were having dinner alone."

"Alone? I'd make a fool of myself. Besides, all that dating

stuff is so fake. You can't get to know somebody like that. Not the right way, anyway."

I know that's right.

My mouth went dry. "Well, I don't mind if you don't mind. Who are you bringing?"

"Hold on. Turn that meat over, will you? No, the chicken on the bottom—I'm back. Sorry about that. Bringing? Let's see. Me, my mom, my brother and his wife and my pastor if we can squeeze him in the car—"

There was a swishing sound and a strangled male voice in the background.

While I tried and failed to pull myself together, Shan came back to the line, laughing between his words. "Sorry. I almost got myself in trouble there. Anyway, the food is done and ready to roll. What do you say?"

What could I say? The man was bringing his mother and his pastor. "I say come on."

And come they did, baked beans, potato salad, sweet meat and all! His mother brought macaroni and cheese. The real kind, the kind that stays square when you cut it. And they didn't let me do a thing. Just came into my kitchen like they'd lived there, throwing compliments around about things that nobody else ever noticed.

"Oh, girl, this kitchen was on the cover of *Country Living.* The surburban chic issue. I'll never forget it. Did you do it yourself or hire somebody?"

Trying not to talk with my mouth full of macaroni and cheese, a substance foreign to my body but happy to my mouth, I only managed a short reply. "I did it."

Shan stopped pouring punch. "Really? It's a great design."

I shrugged, not knowing what to say. I hadn't expected his mother to have a subscription to *Country Living* or for Shan to recognize the merits of kitchen design. In truth, I hadn't expected much of anything.

…for he who comes to God must believe that He is, and that He is a rewarder of those who seek Him…

"I redid the kitchen a few years ago when I started low carbing. Lately, though, I haven't been cooking much."

Shan's sister-in-law swooped on me. "The no-bread thing? Did that work for you? I tried it but—"

The pastor, who'd been standing silently in front of my bookshelves, waved her off with one hand. "She's tried it about as much as I have," he said, patting his paunch. "Exercising is what does it for me. I must get back to it."

Marching to the table with a satisfied smile, Shan's mother graced the table with a platter of fruit carved as deftly as any gourmet chef.

As everyone reached in, I rubbed my chin. "Did you bring that platter with you?"

She shook her head. "No, honey, this was in a back cabinet. And crystal no less. You spent a lot of money for that. Don't be afraid to use it."

My jaw hung slack. I'd bought that platter and a punch bowl set for the youth ball the church had sponsored a few years back. Several people had been on the committee, but I'd ended up putting on the whole thing alone. I'd pushed the platter—and the memory—into a dark corner. Amazed at how she'd created such beauty from my estranged back cabinets, I reached in among the spirals of red pepper and lemon zest to take a bit of apples, oranges and kiwifruit, all of which had been near death in my fruit bowl.

Shan's mother smiled apologetically. "Sorry about all the carbs. He didn't tell me. I can do you a veggie plate if you want. You've got some good stuff going bad in that bin. Don't sweat the mac and cheese. It won't hurt this once. I make that for the boys. They like it with their barbecue."

Shan nodded, ladling barbecue sauce over his macaroni. "We do like it. Right, brother?"

Shan's brother, chin deep in his plate and a thicker, lighter-skinned version of Shan, made just a slight nod.

Their mother, Betty, who liked to be called Bett, shook her head. "Don't choke yourself, son. Nobody is going to take the plate away."

Shan giggled and winked at me, turning to smile at Moriah in the bouncy seat beside him sucking her fingers. I tried to breathe, remembering what my son had said to me a few months earlier. *Family. I just want a family.* Being part of this one, even for a few minutes, made me want a family, too. Or maybe more of one. What if Bett or someone like her had been my mother…

I tried not to think about it, choosing instead to watch Shan's brother guard his ribs from the preacher.

"See! That's how he does it. That's why I have to eat fast, 'cause Pastor Shields will sneak up on you."

My eyes pinched shut as I tried to hold back my laughter.

Shan put a hand on my back and leaned in to me. "Go ahead and laugh. It's okay. It's good for the digestion."

So I did. And once I started laughing, I couldn't stop.

Shan's brother kissed his wife and shook his fork at their pastor. "Now see what you've done? Get the girl some water, Shan, so she don't choke." The brother got up and made another plate and pulled up a chair on the way back to his seat. He handed it to Pastor Shields. "Here, Brother Pastor. Have some dinner...so you don't have to have mine!"

With that we all cracked up. Even Moriah, though she had no clue why.

"Why thank you, brother, I believe I will take this plate. And this seat." With a grace unusual to a man his size, the man sat down beside me.

Everybody stopped laughing then. Except me. Within a few seconds though, I collected myself, but not without effort. As I did, I realized that no one had commented on my wild, loud laughter. Usually people stared in horror the first time they heard it. I turned to Shan. "Is something wrong?"

He handed Moriah a small piece of bread he'd rolled up with his fingers. "Pastor never takes a plate of my barbecue. He wanders around and eats my brother's when he's not looking. It's their game. You must really have some good books over there to get him to sit down and get to know you."

The pastor looked at me with gentle eyes. "She's got some books over here, all right. Some that I have yet to read. I can see why you pulled out the special sauce. She's worth it."

Special sauce? I wiped the laughing tears from my eyes, thankful that I'd taken Shan's advice and changed from my cute pantsuit to jeans and a T-shirt. I had to really search to find a pair of jeans, but they were so comfortable. More than I could say for the rest of me. "What's he talking about, Shan?"

Miss Bett beat him to it. "Humph. The sweet sauce takes almost a month to make—you have to infuse the vinegar with sage and pepper—"

"Just hush, Mama." For once, Shan looked put out.

I, on the other hand, was taken in. I swallowed hard. "A month? Why that must have been—"

"Christmas Eve," Miss Bett said. "When he skipped our service and went to yours. Came home and started brewing sweet sauce, so we knew you had to be something."

Shan stood and started clearing the table. "Will y'all quit it? Let the lady eat."

They all made a cooing sound, like little kids do on the playground before they start singing, "Shan and Chelle sitting in a tree…" If I wasn't so shocked by this information I would have been crying-laughing again.

The pastor even got up and pinched Shan's cheek.

Shan rolled his eyes. "See how you people are? Try and introduce you to someone and look how you act." He marched off in a mock fury that just made them laugh harder.

The sister-in-law, Lee Ann, I think her name was, took the seat next to the baby and nodded for me to follow him.

She needn't have bothered. I was already half out of my chair.

In the kitchen, I put a hand on Shan's wrist and made him put down the plates he was carrying.

He wouldn't look at me. "If I rinse these now, the sauce won't stain."

I pried the plates from his hand. "What if I'd chosen spicy?" I said, trying not to lose it.

Shan leaned down, pressed his forehead against mine. "Sweet is all I made."

To: *Shalomsistah*
From: *Sassysistah1*
Subject: Emergency Girltalk
Hey,
I think you said that Steve is out of town every Thursday this month? If that's true, can you come over tonight? I really need to talk.
Thanks,
Chelle
P.S. Bring ice cream.

Chapter eleven

Austin held her spoon in the air. "So let me get this straight. He spent the last month making that sauce for you? And he's good with babies? Loves Jesus? Sorry, Chelle, but I'm *not* seeing the problem here." She shrugged and swooped her spoon back into her Chunky Monkey.

I squeezed my pint of Half Baked, for once giving no thought to how it would look on my thighs. "There *isn't* a problem, *that's* the problem!"

Well, there was that waiter thing, but we could work around that. Surely Dana's husband Adrian could find him a good job somewhere. Shan was smart as a whip. And fine as—

"So you're upset because there's *not* a problem? Worried that this is someone you actually could fall in love with? Is that what you're telling me?"

My ice-cream carton clunked onto the coffee table. I rose and paced around the couches. Austin's directness was usually refreshing, but tonight it was giving me a headache. "No, that's not it. Well…" I made a face. "Maybe."

Austin nodded. "So lets do the itemization—sorry for the money words, but my husband is rubbing off on me." She took the back of a junk mail flyer and folded it in half. I tossed her a pen from my purse.

"He's a Christian—"

"As far as I know," I interjected, now pacing again.

She smirked. "He brought his pastor on the first date, Rochelle. Give the guy a break."

"I know. I know. But sometimes that's just a front. Crazy people always act nice at first. How do you think they get women in the backs of those vans?"

"By scaring them and lying to them, not feeding them barbecue—is there any of that left, by the way?"

Nodding, I started for the kitchen.

She held up a hand. "Not yet. Let's get through this…and the ice cream. He's also cute, funny, loves kids and is a gentleman. Would that sum it up?"

I wrung my hands. "Pretty much."

Austin nodded. "Now on the other hand? He's a little younger than you…"

Calm enough to sit, I perched across from her. "A little? His mother told me he's thirty-one. That's a lot. Five, soon to be six years."

"Isn't Jordan older than you?" She waved the spoon again. That was getting really annoying.

"Okay. I see your point, but it's still an issue—"

"Mom?"

Rapt in what we were doing, neither of us had heard the door open. Jericho and Shemika stood in the doorway, both with sheepish smiles. Moriah slumped over her mother's shoulder.

"Hey guys." Austin waved. "Oh, and happy birthday, Jericho. Sorry I missed it."

He managed a half smile. "No prob. Thanks for the check."

She laughed. "I'm sure that's all you wanted anyway. I remember eighteen."

So did I. That's what worried me. Neither of them had moved from the doorway. I stood.

Slowly.

"Why don't you guys come on in?" I tried to sound calm.

Shemika stared at the floor. Jericho stepped back. "You have company. We'll come back."

Gathering the rest of her things, Austin started for the kitchen and assembled a plate of barbecue in record time. She squeezed past them at the door. "Don't mind me. I was just leaving."

"Sorry," I said softly. "But thanks for coming."

She wagged a finger and lifted the pro/con sheet. "I'll be back. We're going to finish this. We have to."

I nodded, but suddenly weighing Shan's merits didn't seem so important. As Austin shut the door behind her, my son and his girlfriend trudged toward me. Their legs moved as though the floor was made of peanut butter. I gripped the arms of my sofa, tugging one of the now-fraying stitches. They didn't need to tell me. I already knew. "You did it, didn't you?"

My son knelt in front of me, put his head in my lap. I held his face in my hands, trying to stop it from moving up and down, from nodding.

"Yes, Mom," he said. "Shemika and I got married."

This time, I ignored the doorbell. It was Shan. I could feel it. My in-box was full of his e-mails, but I had no strength to reply. In a few minutes, the ringing at the door stopped and I managed to walk past Jericho's room, where he slept with his "family." For months, I'd kept them apart with the "you can't sleep together under my roof, you're not married" speech. Now what could I say? I knew they were on the way to Jordan's when they'd stopped by. And honestly, maybe they'd be better off there. He could certainly do more for them financially. Still, it was their walk with God and their educations that concerned me.

Heart pounding, I went to the door and opened it, planning to stare into the street, to take in the fact that someone had just been here—for me. I didn't get the chance for contemplation. When I opened the door, Shan was still there.

He wasn't smiling. "Just tell me that you're okay. That's all I want to know."

"I'm okay." I bit my lip.

His head jerked slightly. "Fine." He started to turn away.

He tried to turn away, but I grabbed his collar with both hands. "It's not okay. I'm sorry…" I melted into him, shaking and sobbing.

With almost no effort, Shan pulled me into his arms and carried me into the house. As he smoothed my hair, his scent stole my breath. A brisk fruity something worthy of Dana's shelves. I inhaled again. Peppermint and...mangoes? Weird, but good.

We sat on the couch in the Saturday morning stillness. He held me but didn't say a word. More than anything, I wanted him to kiss me, to touch me. Or at least I thought I did. Just when I thought he would, he pulled away and went into the kitchen.

He didn't return until my teapot had whistled long and loud. He brought me white pear tea—my favorite—in my best china. The flavor, a dash of lemon juice and two Equals, made me sigh. And laugh. I'd ordered the same thing that first night at the restaurant. I laughed, in spite of my tears. "You don't forget anything, do you?"

He clasped his hands in front of him. "Not the things that matter. At least, I try not to."

The things that mattered? Did I matter to him? I pulled the cup to my mouth, drowning my emotions the best I could. Sure that dinner had been amazing, but that had just been a fluke hadn't it? No one could feel like this—like that—so fast, could they? Sure it happened on TV, but it had never happened to me. My hand trembled.

Shan helped me get the cup back to the saucer. "Be careful. That's pretty hot."

So are you.

I nodded, not knowing what to say. He took off his well-maintained and always shined loafers and took up residence at the opposite side of the couch. I closed my eyes, thankful for once that my son's height had forced me to buy this giant sofa. It could turn into a sectional, the man at the store said, but I never arranged it that way. There was just something about that forever leather running against the wall. Something that had made everyone keep off it. Until lately. Tonight, with Shan's big toe resting against mine, I was glad to have declared open season on the couch. Shan tossed the velvet throw over us both, again pressing his feet against mine.

It occurred to me then that I'd padded to the door in my bare feet, which meant that he'd seen my lumpy toes in their full glory. He didn't seem to have noticed, but I knew better. He was observant if nothing else. He pressed against my big toe with his. I stared at him in astonishment. "Are you playing footsies with me?"

He nodded. "Yep. And I'm winning."

I pressed the sole of my foot against his larger one with all my might. "Oh, no you're not…"

He pressed back even harder, sending us both toppling to the floor and tangled in the blanket. Our laughter tangled, too. It must have been louder than it sounded in my ears because Jericho and Shemika came pounding down the hall.

My son looked surprised. And angry. "Mom? Are you all right?" There was a *who is this fool* unsaid between his words.

Still giggling, I pointed to Jericho. "Honey, this is my friend, Shan."

On his feet now, my guest reached out to shake my son's hand.

"He's the one who made the barbecue," I whispered, but Jericho didn't seem impressed.

He was greeted by a lukewarm reception, but that didn't

seem to be his concern. It was Shemika in her nightgown that seemed to concern him. And rightly so.

"And this is his new wife, Shemika," I said softly.

Shan's face lit up. "You have a beautiful baby. And you two are married? That's nice. Real nice. Congratulations. No wonder your mom wouldn't talk to me. She was too excited."

A thin smile eased over my son's mouth. "You could say that."

"Humph." Shemika couldn't help but grunt, I suppose.

Puzzled, Shan took another look at me, a longer look at what must have been my swollen eyes and drawn face. With his investigative skills, he might have even noticed my scratchy voice, still hoarse from last night's screaming. His eyes widened as it all came together for him.

He covered it well. "I guess I should probably go. I just wanted to make sure that your mom was okay."

Jericho shrugged. "I haven't heard my mom laugh that hard in a long time. Stay as long as you like if she doesn't mind." He was already starting back to his room.

"Please do stay," Shemika added before following. "And thank you for the food. That sauce was—"

"Mika!" Jericho called behind her.

"Well, anyway, nice to meet you."

Shan nodded. "Same to you."

I was on the couch now, sitting flush with the high-backed sofa. "It's a long story," I said without looking at him.

He sat down and tucked a wayward coil behind my ear. "I'm sure."

As was his way, Shan let the silence settle instead of nervously stuffing it with words. It was comfortable, this quiet. Re-assuring. "Is it okay if we don't talk about it? It's just that—"

"Shh." He pressed a finger to my lips. I would have liked it better if he'd shushed me with a kiss, but God knew best. "We don't have to talk about anything. I just want to be here with you. In fact, I'm going to go to my car and get my Bible CDs. We can just sit here and listen to that, what do you say?"

I sagged against him. "I say yes. I'd like that very much."

He smiled. "Good. I hope you like the narrator. Some of those voices can be a distraction."

"Tell me about it. I had to give a set away one time. Don't worry though. I trust your taste."

On his feet now, he narrowed his eyes. "Don't speak too quickly on that. I haven't listened to them yet. I wore out my last set and I picked this one up last night." He winked at me. "Something told me I might need it today."

I'm turning into an old woman. I'm even starting to wear sensible shoes. My podiatrist demands it. During my last visit, he showed me pictures of feet damaged from pinched-toe shoes and too-high heels, something I've always won-dered about. I've even pointed my customers away from some of my more cramped and cute purchases—not Terri, of course—she could wear all the ankle breakers she wanted.

Okay, I don't mean that, but she and Jordan aren't very high on my list of people to like right now. Seems that she and Jordan both subsidized and supported the little teenage se-cret wedding, but neither of them want to have anything to do with planning a grown-up public church ceremony. I suppose they're too busy quibbling over the details of their own on-again off-again union. Usually, I'd be in a rare state because of all this, but not today.

Today is Valentine's Day and for the first time in a decade, I have a date with someone other than a serving platter. I usually spent my V-day serving dinner to the couples at our church.

These past few weeks with Shan have not only taken the edge off my disappointment about Jericho's wedding, but it's brought out a new side of me as well. Sometimes, I'm even happy for my son and his wife the way Shan seems to be. Then the two of them do something like lock the baby in the car and charge the locksmith bill to my VISA or oversleep for work or school and I see this marriage as the disaster it is—two kids with a kid and no clue how to live. And again, all on my watch.

Do all things without grumbling or complaining.

Ugh. There it is again, that grumbling verse. I really needed to work on that. Was I always this cranky before? Why is it that I never noticed until now? Having a man around is weird that way. Not that Shan says anything when I launch off into the deep waters of my womanhood, but he does have this crooked smile and a half laugh that's his response to my hormonal rages. That and when he arrives the next night with chocolate-covered popcorn and chick flicks. His mother trained him well, that's all I can say.

More like some woman trained him well.

There was that of course, the mystery chick factor, but I tried not to think about it. Shan knew secrets he shouldn't, like hair-salon prices. I'd worn a hat for a week last month when Moriah had that cold and Jordan went on four college visits. Shan didn't say anything to me. Instead, he gave me a business card with a stylist's name and an appointment time. And at my favorite shop, no less. When I got there, the bill was already paid.

Knowing he couldn't afford to do that, I'd tried to give the money back, but he insisted. The crazy thing? The stylist he suggested, one I'd been walking past for years to get to my own hair girl, turned me into a new woman...and in half the time.

Shan's mother does her own hair so he didn't get the hair scoop from her. Miss Bett proudly detailed her home beauty rituals when I complimented her on her past-shoulder-length mane. I listened, but only for her sake. If I tried to relax my hair from a box, I'd be bald and blind. The one time I'd tried it, it'd taken over a year for my hairline to grow back. Like Shan and his knowledge of babies and beauty salons, some things were just too good to be true.

Still, roses were roses and the ones filling my shop—peach, pink, white, yellow and yes, red—had turned my head all the way around. The last bouquet brought in by the florist, the red ones, came with a dinner reservation clipped to the card and a handwritten sentence scrawled at the bottom:

Wear red.

I read it again and squealed with delight and shimmied across the floor. Metal chimes clanged over the door. I sobered quickly, but not quickly enough. Tad, now inches from me, had caught a glimpse of my I-got-a-man dance.

He nodded. "I see that you're having a good day. I came to pick up my shoes."

"I'm doing well. And your shoes are right here." My heart was doing the cabbage patch dance in my chest as I reached under the counter and produced his latest pair of oxfords. "I hope Katrina likes them."

Tad ignored my mention of his new girlfriend, or friend, or whatever she was. He still hadn't deemed her worthy to bring to church though Shan had joined me several times already. His congregation only met on second and fourth Sundays, giving us twice a month to worship together. I hoped to visit his church when the youth choir took over in March and my voice wouldn't be missed. I couldn't move too fast. People were giving me questioning looks as it was. One Sunday, I'd thought Pastor was going to lock Shan in his study for a full inquisition.

Tad sneezed as I passed the shoes over the counter. "Excellent," he said, without even looking down at them. His eyes stayed fastened on the ocean of color raging behind me. "Someone cleared out the entire florist's shop, I see. Jordan has excellent taste." He handed over his Visa as I punched up the cost on my register.

Surprised at his veiled inquiry about who had purchased the roses, my words tumbled out before I'd quite arranged them. "Not from Jordan, but they're pretty, aren't they?" His card zipped through my machine. After punching buttons furiously, I handed it back to him.

"So I take it then that these are from the handsome waiter. He is certainly smitten with you, I must say, but don't you think it's mean to lead him on like this? Why, he'll have spent his whole salary by the time you dump him." An unsettling grin fastened on Tad's mouth as he slipped his credit card back into his wallet.

Tad was back to his old self.

I blinked. "It's not like that…"

It wasn't, was it?

Nah.

Tad tipped his hat. "Of course not."

Out of desperation, I grabbed a rose, a peach hybrid, and jammed my face into it. This was a gift from kind, funny, handsome Shan, who wasn't afraid to hide behind some church pew veneer—who wasn't afraid to show me that he cared. My head filled with the scent of his gift. "Not that it's any of your business, but Shan has two jobs. He works at Destiny Architectural Design as well as the restaurant." It was news I'd only learned recently—overhead from a cell call, actually—but I was thankful to have it in my arsenal. When in this type of mood, Tad could be difficult to subdue.

With a swagger I hadn't seen in months, Tad started for the door. "Destiny Design, huh? I'm sure he does well sorting the mail. I saw your little chauffeur ex-boyfriend the other day, too. He said to tell you hello. Perhaps you should send him a rose, too. For old times' sake."

With that, Tad slammed the door. The door frame rattled.

I fumed.

What happened to the sweet, protective man who'd called that horrible show and chastised them for maligning my virtue? Why was it okay for him to buy new shoes to wear with some woman, but it was a crime for a man to buy me flowers? I steeled my shoulders and brought the rose to my face again. Tonight was to be my first date alone with Shan without the baby or family to keep us company. A night when my many questions might be answered. I wasn't about to let Tad or anyone else spoil it, especially when he'd never made a move to ask me out.

Mentally scanning my closet for an appropriate outfit, I settled on a red velvet skirt and silk blouse along with the ruby earrings Jordan's mother had left me. I'd never worn them until now.

There was that issue of shoes though…everything that fit the doctor's orders was downright ugly. I'd have to make up something myself. One look at the clock told me there wouldn't be time. I tapped my foot, hoping for a brilliant idea and praying for guidance. Yes, I pray about shoes. Often. Just as an idea came to me, the phone rang. I fumbled with the receiver, finally bringing it to my face.

"Hello, Mom?"

Jericho. Didn't he know I was on the edge of a fashion breakthrough? "Hey, honey. Can I call you back?" I checked the clock. Lunchtime. He was using daytime minutes at that.

"Sure, Mom. I just wanted to let you know that we'll be dropping off Moriah at six. She'll be bathed and fed—"

"For who? I'm going out tonight."

"You're what?" He sounded downright shocked. Sure Shan usually came over to our place, but was I that much of a homebody?

"You heard me."

"But it's Shemika's and my first Valentine's Day as a married couple. We're going to the couple's dinner at the church. Mother Holloway bought us the tickets."

Usually that would have broke me down, the Jesus factor. Since the baby's birth, I'd used any bait I could to get Jericho to church. Usually, mention of his attending service for any reason made me like jelly on bread—sweet and spread thin. Not tonight. "How nice of Mother Holloway to buy you those tickets. The dinner there is always lovely. But I'm afraid I can't help you. Why don't you ask your father?" He and Terri were living together, after all. They could have their romance anytime.

Static crackled through the line. "I—I can't ask Dad. He and Terri are coming to the church, too. I just figured that since you and Shan usually hang out at the house…"

I swallowed. Hard. The boy had figured wrong. Nobody had ever filled my shop—or my life—with flowers and fun the way Shan had. Being a grandma was a job I cherished, but this time, the kiddos would have to fend for themselves. This morning, a woman had come in with a T-shirt that said, "Mothers are people, too." I should have asked where she bought it.

Turning my back to the door, I wound the phone cord around my fingers. "Look, Shan has been more than considerate about all our craziness, I can't ask him to change his plans. This is too much."

Strong, cold hands touched my shoulder, turned me around. Peppermint essence brushed against my face as Shan, wearing a suit bad enough to make me swoon and the purple and teal tie I'd painted for him, reached across the counter and pecked my cheek with a faint, sweet kiss.

Our first.

"Hold on, Jericho." How had he managed to come in without me hearing the chimes? I shook my head and covered the phone. That man had a soft touch to be sure. Rose still tucked in my fingers, I searched his face. Had he heard? "Jericho, I'll talk to you later—"

Laughter danced in his eyes as he took the rose from my hand. He kissed my finger. My ring finger. "Something tells me there's been a change of plans."

Chapter twelve

What started as a simple choice of going out or staying home turned into a nightmare. To facilitate Jericho and Shemika's night of romance, Mother Holloway babysat Moriah in the church nursery during the dinner. I was to bring her home while Jericho and his wife went to a movie, which also meant my Valentine's Day dinner would be shared among friends.

In my church's basement.

To say that I wasn't looking forward to it would have been an understatement, but when I saw Tad at the door with that stupid so-you-brought-the-waiter look on his face, well, I wanted to run.

Tad however, looked amused. "Welcome to our celebration. Would you like your blood pressure taken before dinner? A healthy heart is part of healthy love." His words whistled through his teeth.

My voice stilled in my throat. The blood pressure checks.

The Senior Bible Study did them before and after services once a month, but with several members having strokes—including my friend Dana last year—the pastor asked that we incorporate health checks into other events. Being the Girl Scout I was this time last year, I'd signed our group right up.

Little did I know…

With a smile, Shan held out his wrist and motioned for me to do the same. "Go ahead. You can never be too careful. We'll have to try this at our church, too. Digital bracelets, huh? I'll have to pick up a few."

Tad snapped the band around Shan's wrist and rolled his eyes at me. (Yes, he really did.) No doubt, the gesture was in response to my date's last comment.

"Your pressure is fine," he said, removing the bracelet from Shan. "Your turn, Miss Gardner."

I brushed imaginary lint off my skirt. "After dinner, perhaps. Thanks." It was embarrassing enough that I'd committed the singles' group to have blood pressure checks and then forgotten to tell anybody. Tad didn't have to rub it in. And that *Miss Gardner* bit? Please.

As we walked off, Shan squeezed my hand. "Don't let him rattle you. He's just mad he let you slip away. I feel his pain."

His breath tickled my ear. I giggled. "Maybe—"

"There you are!"

The words stung my back like the spray from a BB gun. It was Terri's voice, from across the room. I waited for Shan to squeeze my hand again, tell me something comforting, but he didn't. Instead he let me go. True, he'd never met Terri, but I hadn't expected this type of reaction. Sure she had a nice body and everything but not *that* nice.

As Terri approached us, the astonishment spreading from one of Shan's ears to the other turned into something different.

Terror.

He yanked his keys out of his pocket. "Maybe we should just get the baby and go home. It'll be late after this and cold—"

I frowned. "She'll be fine. Mother Holloway doesn't watch Moriah much, but the baby is used to her. Besides, she's asleep."

His jaw tightened. "Still…"

Terri was almost upon us when she stopped short and covered her mouth. "Shannon, is that you?"

My heart dropped through the church basement. Shannon? I'd only learned yesterday (also during an overheard cell conversation. I really need to start leaving the room, but he says not to go) that it was his full name. How on earth did Terri know? And why was she looking all crazy like that? And *why* wasn't Shan saying anything? He looked like he'd been hit with a stun gun.

This couldn't be good.

I pinched his wrist. And mine. "So you've met Shan, Terri?"

She nodded, pouty lips in full affect. "Met him? He and my girlfriend practically lived together for—"

"Good to see you, Terri, but I'll have to catch up later." He loosened his tie and grabbed my hand. I'd like to see what that blood pressure machine would register now. The man looked ready to pass out.

I know I was.

Terri's eyes flashed as she took everything in, piecing things together as quickly as her dense mind could. "*Oh,* yeah. I get it. Well, you look good anyway, Shannon, considering. How's the baby—"

"Fine, as far as I know."

An alarm went off in my head. Little women in sailor outfits started jumping ship in my mind.

Mayday! Mayday! Houston, we have a problem.

"Baby? What baby?" I talked through my teeth like Tad. Not quite at spy level, but good enough.

"We'll talk about it later," Shan said, louder than usual as he tugged at my sleeve, moving us around Terri and down the length of the table. The tablecloth, white instead of red, hung at an odd angle. I passed in a daze, not even stopping to straighten it.

Shan's hand, so warm it felt feverish, clung to mine in desperation. Or at least that's what it felt like. Each squeeze as he scanned the name cards for our seat was like him screaming, pleading for me to wait for his explanation, one that I knew wouldn't come until we were clear of this building. He was just like that.

We walked for what seemed like forever through the endless sea of heart-stickered name cards until we found our own. (Handwritten at the last minute of course. At least it wasn't my job this year.) The ones on either side of us were blank. For that at least I was grateful. This could get ugly.

Once we sat down, Shan buried his head in his hands. "I can explain. Really."

Before I could answer, a man's voice did the job for me. "I sure hope so, bruh, because the lady doesn't look happy."

I closed my eyes at the sound, recognizing the voice immediately, unable to look as the familiar cologne settled beside me. Jordan.

With one basketball-palming hand, he turned over the placard I'd thought blank. Printed neatly above the hearts and crosses was *Jordan Rose and Guest*.

It only got worse.

Once Terri realized where we'd be sitting, her face took on a maniacal glow. She'd been waiting all these months to sink her teeth into me and tonight, well, she had the chance to swallow me whole.

And she took it.

As tasteless courses of our dinner arrived and Terri reached across Jordan to spout yet another "remember when" at Shan, I listened.

And learned.

So far, I knew that my fine little waiter was not only an architect at Destiny design, but the former boyfriend of local-girl-turned-supermodel Aida, whose bare body mocked me from billboards on every corner. I stabbed at my lettuce so hard I bent the fork. Shan didn't look my way, only bothering to nod or provide Terri with a dutiful yes or no. She gleefully supplied every detail, all while slathering her baked potato with Heinz 57. Fat-free to be sure, but *eww.* I tried not to make a face.

Jordan, on the other hand, seemed to find the whole thing quite amusing. As would Tad when he found out, if he didn't know already. Terri's voice carried better than a microphone. The entire length of the table was leaning our way. I kept trying to swallow my food, but my stomach felt as though someone had injected me with some kind of bio weapon. Giving up, I put down my fork.

Terri leaned back a little, whittling away at the fourth of a steak she'd generously allowed herself. She elbowed Jordan. "Oh and baby, you should see the house he built for her. Remember that picture of me you liked so much, the one in the pink halter?" She smiled at me and dabbed the corners of her mouth.

"Well, that's the house behind me. All wood floors, open space. Oh, and the nursery…" She held a hand over her chest before lunging across us again. "Will you promise to do our house, too? The nursery, at least. We're getting married in May and I hope to be pregnant by—"

Jordan cleared his throat. "Honey, let's just eat, okay? We'll talk to Shannon about the house some other time. Let them enjoy their evening." His voice sounded strained.

And rightly so. As it was, I was fingering my steak knife. The question was, which one to go for first. Shan was the closest to me and Terri the most deserving, but I had known Jordan the longest…

Um, you can't do that, Christian woman!

Across the room, my son waved a forkful of steak my way.

He looked to be having a grand time. Good. I'd hate for everyone here to be miserable. I managed to lift my right pinky and feign what started out to be a smile but never quite worked out.

Soon, they'd start the program. If I could just survive until the worship…

Architects.

Babies.

Supermodels.

Babies.

Nah. I'd never make it and if I did, I wouldn't hear a word of it. This was more than I could take. More than I wanted to take. I needed to get away from here before it hit me…

A baby. I couldn't match that no matter how hard I tried. Not ever.

Terri would soon have a daughter for Jordan. Or better yet, another son, one he would play catch with and kiss goodnight. A boy to replace my own. And that skinny wench who Shan built a house for had his baby and a nursery with hardwood floors. And what did I have? Nothing. Not even Jericho. He had his own family now.

What did Dana say in times like this?

For this, I have Jesus.

At that thought, a tear escaped me. I pushed back my chair. I *did* have Jesus and I needed to be alone with Him. "I have to go."

Shan grabbed my wrist.

Jordan did, too. "I'm so sorry about all of this. Wait. Please."

I shook both their hands away and pushed my chair under

the table, taking a deep breath, one big enough to drown my tears until I could get outside.

Shan stood. "Let me come with you—"

"No, you've done enough don't you see?" Jordan snarled like a beast. He turned to Terri. "And you, too. Why can't you ever shut up?"

With that, he held out his hand to me. "Come on, Chelle. I'll take you home. Jericho will have to catch that movie another night."

Shan questioned me with his eyes. *Make a choice,* his eyes said. *Right here. Right now. Make a choice.*

I turned away and took Jordan's familiar, weathered hand. The one freely offered to me. The people around us stopped talking, stopping to watch. They all knew the story. Their eyes gave away their surprise. I shrugged as I passed them on the long walk to the door, my hand in Jordan's. Sure it was the grip of a snake, but at least I'd already tasted the poison.

Why had I let my guard down, allowed myself to be put in this position?

There is no fear in love.

"Is everything okay, Rochelle?" I heard Tad ask as we walked past him, holding a tray of red velvet cake. Last year, I'd carried it. Baked it, too. I should have done that again. Played it safe. This whole thing was a big, sad joke. Shan had a baby. And by a model. I would have run out, but I didn't have the energy. All I could think of was that he'd seen my feet.

"She'll be okay," Jordan said to everyone assembled as we continued toward the door.

Cold bit through my blouse in the parking lot, but I didn't shiver. I couldn't.

Jericho followed, shouted behind us. "Mom? What's wrong? Are you sick?"

Jordan waved him back inside. "I'm taking her home, son. You're going to have to get the baby. We'll talk later." He draped his suit jacket around me and led me to his SUV.

The heat fogged the windows once we were inside. For a long time, neither of us said anything.

Finally, he took my hand again. "I can put on a movie if you'd like." He filed through his DVD collection and flipped down the overhead TV.

I shook my head.

He put the key into the ignition, but instead of turning the car on, he turned back to me. "I figure we've been through the 'I'm sorry' thing so many times that you don't want to hear it again, but if it helps, I really am. Sorry, I mean. About Shan, too. He seems like a really nice guy. I hope you two can work things out."

The leather squeaked beneath me as I shifted in the seat, trying to get warm. "I doubt it," I said in a raspy voice.

And I did doubt it. I wasn't sure why. Shan had told me he'd had a serious relationship for five years, from twenty-three to twenty-eight, I think.

Jordan turned on the car, clicked on the heat, but rested back in the seat. I did the same, closing my eyes, trying to re-member everything Shan had told me.

Shan had wanted to get married. The girl didn't. He kept waiting but he finally gave up and moved out—rededicating his life to the Lord. Not long before he'd met me, his pastor preached on how having a wife was a "good thing," something God was willing to provide. The Lord began to nudge him about a wife, but he wasn't interested.

Then, he'd said with a smile, I'd come marching into that restaurant looking fine. He said he'd gone home that night and prayed like a crazy man. Inside the church, he was probably doing much of the same now.

Or not. The look on his face when I'd left had been final and he hadn't chased after me. Maybe he was more like Tad than I'd thought.

Either way, I didn't hold out much hope for us. The hopeful, happy girl he'd brought here tonight was dead. A hopeless, hapless woman I'd once been had replaced her. Why had I done something so foolish as to date in the first place? Didn't God tell us to humble ourselves, sparing Him the job? Now I'd been shamed before the whole church, in front of my family. Tad was right. I should have been more careful.

But love isn't careful.

And love Shan I did.

"Rochelle?"

I opened my eyes but didn't speak.

"Before we go, I want to say something else. About that baby thing. Terri never should have said anything about me having kids with her. Especially not in front of you."

I shrugged. "Have all the babies you want. Somebody should." My voice broke up. Why had I left with Jordan? He didn't need to see me like this. A hoarse cry exploded from somewhere inside of me.

Jordan pulled me to him from across the gears between us. "Oh, Chelle. Dear, sweet Chelle. I was such a fool."

"You still are," I whispered in the midst of soaking his shirt with my tears.

"Maybe," he whispered, bringing his lips to mine. "Maybe not."

Years melted away as we tangled up in that front seat like stupid kids again. Parsley and Italian dressing breath blew across my cheek as Jordan held me close. This couldn't be a good idea, I knew, but I was tired and needed somebody to hold me.

Anybody.

I will never leave you or forsake you.

The thought came as our lips almost touched. I froze and made a gasping sound. Had I just almost kissed...Jordan? Sure it was a bad night, but not that bad. Nothing was that bad. Or was it?

The look on my face must have been pretty bad because Jordan pushed away, shaking his head. "I'm sorry. I shouldn't have done that. I shouldn't even have walked you out here. Jericho would have brought you home. It's crazy. As messed up as Terri is, I love her. And in some other impossible way, I still care for you, too, as the mother of my son."

As I fell back to my seat speechless, a face showed through the streaks in the fogged window.

Shan's face.

To: *thesassysistahood*
From: *Sassysistah1*
Subject: Don't

Don't come over.

Don't call.

Don't bring ice cream.

Just don't.

This is something only Jesus can fix.

I love you all.

Rochelle

"Love hurts." Rochelle Gardner

The phone started ringing Monday morning.

But it wasn't Shan.

When I locked the door of my store to go home, another call beckoned me through the glass. I stood long enough to hear the female voice, a new customer's voice, on the answering machine before trudging to my car. Though today's brisk business had been a blessing, Shan's silence mocked me by the hour as memories of a man I'd become so used to, so comfortable with, gnawed away at me. Was he feeling like this, too? Or was he already shaking the vinegar for the next one, making sweet sauce for someone new?

It's for the best.

This was true, I knew, but the love in my heart dragged her feet against facing it. She kept whispering to me, putting nonsense into my head like, *There's still a chance, you know.* If I hadn't been swamped in work all day, I might have done something crazy like call him. But I was swamped, all because of those silly Valentine shoes.

Who knew when I'd slapped a flower on my old bedroom

slippers before going to dinner that it would be the hit of the season?

I locked up and took myself home, not at all surprised to find Austin waiting for me. I opened the door, took one look at all those roses I'd brought home from Valentine's Day, now in staggered stages of wilt, and collapsed while she made hasty lattes. Though not scared off by my "Don't e-mail," it seemed she'd at least honored the no-ice-cream clause.

Done with the brew, Austin sprinkled my coffee table with rose petals, then sat on my good couch, sipping a mug of steaming white chocolate. Amusement creased the corners of her young eyes. Without looking, I knew stress lurked in the corners of mine.

She took another sip. "So let me get this straight. Shan sends all these flowers, invites you to dinner, then you take a pair of satin bedroom shoes and dress them up to match your outfit…"

I nodded. The story sounded good so far. If only it could end there.

"Then you go to the church dinner and get totally humiliated by Terri, break down and run out with Jordan, kiss him in the car, see Shan standing outside and—"

"Sort of. Not a kiss exactly, but um, yeah…" A moan escaped me as pain stabbed through my abdomen. I folded over, hugging my waist.

Austin grabbed me. "Are you okay? What is it?"

"Ulcer," I said, barely able to speak. "Every now and then it acts up some. Scar tissue." It stopped. Any longer and I'd have had to call my internist for a barium swallow or some-thing. Ick. That *dye* should be called *die* instead.

Austin sat back on her heels in front of me. "I'm sorry. I didn't mean to upset you. I'm just amazed at how the Lord brought something good out of a not-so-good evening."

"He did, didn't He?" I took a deep breath. How many orders had I received today? Counting the phone messages, e-mails, calls and walk-ins from my church ladies, I didn't have an accurate count, but it was more shoes than I'd sold the whole month of January.

Austin's quick smile, before she jumped and raided my bathroom for Pepto-Bismol, lifted my spirits. I accepted the medicine gratefully and took another deep breath, thinking about the unexpected success of my "Valentine shoes," as every caller had described them. Why they'd made such an impact, I couldn't figure. I'd put more time, money and thought into all of my other designs. What made these throw-togethers any different?

"I don't get it, Austin. I've created top-of-the-line foot-wear for years. Now, I put together some cheap, cute slides and I'm the talk of the town. What gives?"

She shrugged. "The Lord gives. Sure, He also takes away sometimes, but He gives, too. And there's one other thing."

I lifted my head. Just a little. "What?"

Another smile. "Love. You didn't make those shoes to sell. You made them to look good for your man. They were com-fortable, confident and—dare I say it—appealing! You know church ladies like to look good, too."

That made me laugh, despite not wanting to. Maybe she

was right. Since Austin hardly ever said stuff like that, she probably was. Maybe I had been so intent on making a product that I had forgotten about the process. Sometimes it's not always about the end result, but the journey and even more important, what put you on the road in the first place. Whether Shan and I got back together or not, I had him to thank for putting some love back into my work again.

And into my life.

Austin pushed my latte toward me. I brought it to my lips reluctantly, knowing she wouldn't give up until I did. "Ah. That's good. Thank you."

"No problem. Did it bother your stomach?"

I shook my head. "I think I'm okay. Probably more heartache than stomachache now." I could tell by looking at Austin that she wanted to say something else, but she was holding her tongue. Since that was not her strong suit, I took a minute to think about what it could be. A chuckle parted my lips.

The shoes. She wanted to see them, too.

"They're in my room, on the floor somewhere." I rolled over, turning into the couch so she couldn't see me cry.

I heard her boots hit the floor and then halt. "Wait a minute? On the floor somewhere? You? This is really bad, isn't it?"

"Worse." My face was almost smothered by the couch cushion, but I didn't care.

When I heard her scream in my bedroom, I knew I was onto something. One thing about Austin, the girl had good taste. One hour in Dana's store and she'd summed up her target market and sales potential. I'd been skeptical, but she'd been right on. Though minutes away from a nervous break-down, my work brain kicked in. Usually when I made a pair of shoes, I wrote the process down in my notebook. This time though, I'd been too busy getting ready to be bothered. Besides, nobody was going to wear them but me, right? Wrong. I stuck my hand in my purse for my ever-present notebook and pen and scribbled down what I could remember.

About three years ago, I'd made myself a pair of red satin slippers to match my favorite robe and gown. Since then, I'd lost twenty pounds and rarely wore the combo or the shoes. But on V-Day, with the scent of Shan's flowers buzzing in my nostrils, the idea had come to me to dress up those low-heeled mules by attaching satin pom-poms to the front. Shan went right for them when he picked me up. "It's a good thing we're going to the church. No good could have come from me, you and those shoes alone together."

What I wouldn't give for him to say that to me now.

There it was again, my heart, the stupid, naive part of me that left me bleeding in a hospital bed with nobody but a girl who wasn't my sister and an old woman who wasn't my mother to care for me. And now, Jordan's mother was dead and Dana had her own husband, so if I had any sense—lately one couldn't be sure—I'd leave well enough in the same place Shan had left me.

Alone.

At least I had the shoes. God certainly did have a way with surprises. With all the mess at that dinner, I'd never given those shoes a thought. If this morning's calls were any indication though, every woman in the room had certainly given those shoes some serious consideration. Brides, girls going to the prom, upcoming graduates, even the pastor's wife—they all wanted a pair.

Austin, now tipping past me with her heels hanging off the back of my shoes and a dreamy look on her face. "Now see, I hate that you had a bad evening, but these here? These are mine. One size bigger, but just like these. My first anniversary is coming up at Christmas and between these shoes, Adrian's candles and some of Dana's Oatmeal Raisin body lotion, I might just get me a baby."

That jolted me up. "I thought—I thought there was no chance." Though our infertility was never discussed between us, it was silently understood and commiserated. For a second, joy surged through me.

Please, Lord. Give her a baby. I know just how she feels.

At least God had blessed me with one.

"There is a chance, but I've been scared to even think about it, let alone talk about it. Remember when I went for surgery early in the summer? They say things are good enough for a chance. Not a great chance, but a chance."

I nodded, sensing she wanted to leave it there. "You're turning into me, you know. Saving everybody from their troubles but hiding your own. Watch yourself." I put my hand on hers as she took a seat beside me.

She looked away. "I'll keep that in mind."

There was more to say, but I left it, knowing that she talked to Dana about such things, though probably not enough. In our relationship, it seemed she was more comfortable as a listener and that was fine with me. I needed one. The talking would come.

She leaned over to her purse and pulled out a 3 Musketeers for her and a sugar-free chocolate bar for me. I batted that nasty thing down like the plague.

Austin smiled and reached in again, this time producing a Snickers. "So did any of the callers mention your, er, departure from the dinner?"

I ran a finger through my bone-straight hair, still fresh from my new stylist, no doubt one of Aida's former *do crew*. "Evidently it was my walk of shame that did the trick. As one woman said on the phone, 'Even when some mess breaks loose, if your feet are looking right, a woman can hold her head up.' Said she didn't think having the most handsome men in the room fighting over me was a problem."

Austin covered her mouth with her chocolate-smudged fingers. "Now that is funny."

It was funny, both when the woman said it and now. Despite my feelings at the time, I couldn't help but laugh and take the lady's order. What was her name? Monica. She was a new member of the church and recent addition to the singles group. Maybe when I talked to her again, I'd invite her to join the Sistahood list. Right now, my mind was splintered in every direction.

Especially one.

Austin cleared her throat. "So, has he called?"

I shook my head.

"Are you relieved about that?"

A nod, followed by a shake of the head. Another nod. I sighed. "I don't know."

"What about Jordan?"

"You're asking all the big-money questions aren't you? Reporters. You're all alike." I added a smile to that to let her know I was kidding. Mostly. "I've heard from Jordan. Or from his florist anyway." I motioned around the corner to the ridiculously large centerpiece on my dining room table. Purple coneflowers stuck out of it like swords, extending off the edge of the table.

Austin got up to take a look. I heard her gasp before returning. "Okay, he is really, really sorry. And I'm sorry, too—for the florist who had to make that thing."

That got a little laugh out of me.

And her. "If anybody tries to break in, you can always throw it. If the plant didn't get them, the vase would crush them. *If* you could lift the thing, that is."

I hugged my belly as I laughed. "Hush, silly."

She didn't. "Seriously, though, how do you feel about Jordan? You did almost kiss him and everything."

Yeah. And everything. "Now why do you have to try and get all deep on me? It was just a moment of emotion. Of need. That's all. Jordan is, well, Jordan. We're just friends."

Austin felt the outside of her mug to check the temperature before bringing it to her mouth. She plunked it right back on the table and made a face. Guess it was too hot. "I don't kiss any of my friends." She stared up at the ceiling as if really considering the statement for accuracy. "Not on the mouth anyway."

I threw a pillow at her. And missed. "It's complicated."

She gave me an accusing look. "Hmm…now you're talking like him."

My chest fell. She had me there. With Jordan, things were always…complicated. Not so with Shan. No matter how crazy something seemed, he never flinched. He trusted me to tell him when I was ready. How many times in the beginning had I given him my "it's more drama than I can explain right now, but if you stick around, I'll tell you the whole thing" speech? Wasn't he trying to say the same thing the other night? To wait and let him explain?

Maybe. But the explanation wasn't really what troubled me. It was how the whole thing went down. He wasn't who I thought he was. After seeing me tangled up in that lip lock with Jordan, Shan was probably thinking the same thing about me. "Let's not talk about him, okay?"

Her eyes pinched shut, then opened again. "Can I ask you one thing about Shan before we close up shop?"

"I know I'm going to regret this, but okay." I wound the throw from the back of the couch around my shoulders. What Austin was going to ask next, I had no idea, but I had a bad feeling about this one.

She set her cup on the table. Gently. Not a good sign. "I'm just wandering why it was so easy to fall for Shan when he was just a waiter who made barbecue, but so unthinkable to love him now that he's an architect, a supermodel's ex-boy-friend and, quite possibly, a father? I know there's the trust issue, but there's something else, too."

I stared at the wall. And the ceiling. As my head lowered

to the floor, I shook myself, trying to find something to say. Was I afraid of Shan because he was someone I could actually have a future with? She was wrong, totally, terribly wrong.

Wasn't she?

"You're right."

"Wow. I actually called it. Maybe I am turning into you after all."

I grabbed her hand. "Stop biting your lip. You're creeping me out."

"You still didn't answer my question though," she said, pulling away from me to attack the last piece of skin. "And stop talking like Shemika. You're creeping me out."

That did me in. I started laughing and couldn't stop. After several months of working at the vocational center, Shemika's speech had moved from Ebonics to Valley Girl. It wasn't an improvement.

Austin tapped my shoulder. "Back to the question, please."

"Right. I don't know. I never thought about it before. It's not like he's too good for me now. Maybe it's just…risky? Before it was safe because I knew it might be temporary?" I shrugged. "Self-analysis takes too much energy. The Lord will have to reveal it. I have thirty-two pairs of shoes to make this week. I've got to go to bed."

Austin patted my leg, then stood and took the dishes to the kitchen. "I'm happy about that, at least. The shoes. I know that show really hurt business for a while."

I nodded. It had hurt business more than I'd let on, but my down-time savings had pulled me through. By Easter, it would have been gone. This flurry of orders, though lower than my usual prices, was the boost I needed. "I'm happy about the orders, too." Stretched out on the couch again, I turned over and closed my eyes. Tonight, sleep would find me here, still in my work clothes. There was a first time for everything. "Lock the door on the way out, would you?"

Austin touched my head on her way to the door. "Absolutely."

I heard the door open, but it never shut.

Too tired to turn over and look, I called out instead, "Austin?"

A man's voice answered back. "It's me, Chelle."

My stomach tightened.

Jordan.

Chapter thirteen

"First of all, I want to address the other night." Jordan sat on the edge of the couch, which was much, much too close. Thank God I'd kept my clothes on. Becoming a bum had its advantages.

"It's over. Done with. You don't have to apologize." I sat up now, tucking my bare feet under me.

He grabbed my toes and pulled my feet onto his lap, and despite my loud protesting, began to massage them. "I said I want to address it, not apologize for it."

No apologies? Well, I had some. I was sorry that I'd ever sent the money to keep his sorry behind alive in that Mexican hospital. Jordan's hands were playing my knobby toes like a church organ. And in a few minutes, I'd be singing like one if I wasn't careful. With a firm jerk, I managed to get one foot away.

He held on to the other with an iron grip and flashed a dangerous smile. "Don't you agree? That we should talk about this?"

With him kneading my toes like dough, I wasn't sure what I knew. "It's complicated."

You could say that again.

His eyes narrowed and he leaned forward. "Are you trying to use my own words against me now? This is serious, Chelle."

My eyes took in his face, the one so long etched in to my mind. What had happened to the gray in his temples a few nights ago? Gone to the same place my here-and-there gray had fled to, I guess. I touched a hand to my own mane, freshly rinsed in Auburn Spice. "I don't know what there is to say."

His hands moved in small circles on my ankle. In a spot where I'd had an off-again-on-again pain for months, something popped. As I sighed in relief, Jordan lowered my feet to the floor. "There might be a lot to say. It depends. How do you feel about me?"

What a question. I'd spent most of my life loving Jordan, though he'd been physically present during very little of that time. Everything I knew about love, about releationships (dare I even go there?), I learned from him. He'd also taught me about rejection, abandonment and single motherhood. I loved him…but I hated him, too. "Jordan, I don't know how to answer that. It's—it's—"

"Complicated?"

We both laughed, but I stopped first. "It *is* complicated. My feelings for you are all mixed up in the past. I don't know what's real and what's just a memory. Can you understand that?"

He lifted my hand and kissed it. "Totally. That's how I feel, too. But what if it is real? What do we do then?"

Wherever this was headed, somebody was sure to get hurt. Most likely me. "I don't see what we can do, Jordan. You're about to get married. I'm in a relationship—"

"So you two are back together?" He dropped my hand.

I paused. Shan and I were anything but together, but I needed to steer Jordan off the course he was heading down. He'd thank me later, when his new son was bouncing on his knee. "Not officially, but there's still a chance we can work things out."

Whew. No lies there. With God, anything was possible.

"So you're cool with him having a kid, the ex-girlfriend, everything?" His fingers brushed my toes, peeking from under the cover.

My stomach hurt again. "I don't even know if it's his child—"

"The man didn't deny it."

Jordan had me there. "He didn't claim the baby, either. Look, I really don't want to get into this with you. Thanks for the flowers, thanks for being there for me the other night, but I think you'd probably better go."

"I should go, but I'm not sure I want to." Jordan smoothed a hand over his head. Shame about that gray hair. It had added character to his face, made him look like his father.

His arm looped around my shoulders. I eased forward on my seat. "How's your dad? Tell him thanks for watching Moriah those few times for me. I'll have to get over to his restaurant and have some gumbo—"

Jordan's embrace silenced my words.

Now, after all these years, one would think that the firecrackers might be stale and the blinking lights broken, but let me tell you—they weren't. Not a one. Though I'd tried to deny it the other night, this time Jordan had me.

In more ways than one.

It'd been a long time since I'd been kissed. Eighteen years, to be exact. The morning of Jericho's birth. That's a lot of woman to unleash, if you know what I mean. And that this was the patient, intense kiss of a grown man instead of the anxious slobberings of a teenage boy didn't help matters, either.

The lioness in me growled as he kissed my ear. I tugged away, knowing I couldn't risk letting all that repressed emotion roar. Not only would I be guilty of some serious sin, but I might kill the man.

"Stop," I whispered. "Please."

He pulled back immediately, with a silly smile. "Which one is it? Stop? Or please?"

I swatted his shoulder playfully, but knew I was on shaky ground. I could see that chunky robot with his arms flailing screaming, "Danger, Chelle Gardner! Danger!" He didn't have to tell me. I knew.

Inside, my heart was breaking. How could a kiss bring everything back so vividly? Jordan's teasing. That silly smile. We were so much older. So much was different...

He rubbed my thumb. Knuckle. Knuckle. Tip.

So much was the same.

I was on him like a cat.

Matching me kiss for kiss, Jordan somehow managed to get out of his coat and kick off his shoes. We were halfway down the hall before I came to my senses. Though the lioness has released her fury, she was no match for the other lion in the room.

The Lion of Judah.

For this is the will of God...that you abstain from sexual immorality. My anthem, 1 Thessalonians 4:3 rifled through my mind like a bullet.

"Noooo!" As Jordan turned the corner to my room, I clung to the doorway. With both hands.

This time, Jordan didn't let go.

"It's been a long time, Chelle. Too long. Let me love you, just this once. I owe you that."

Now why did he want to go and talk that kind of trash at a time like this? My left hand slipped, only hanging on by a pinky. My right hand held sure, but slid down the door frame, just as Jordan's hand slipped upward...

Tae Bo time.

"Ow!" He grabbed his head.

On the floor, where Jordan dropped me, I echoed his sentiment. I checked for bleeding on both of us. My floor was pretty hard and my bunions? Well, he could be wrecked for life. I'd nailed him good, much worse than Tad. Satisfied that neither of us were injured, I pushed myself up.

And out.

There was no time for explanations. I had to run, get away from that man and away from that bed.

Behind me, Jordan had the nerve to be laughing. "You didn't have to kick me, you know. I would have put you down. That really hurt."

Almost down the hall now, I mumbled an apology while straightening my skirt. I had to get to the front door and get that man on the other side of it. Then, I had a date with a very long, very cold shower.

Or so I thought.

When I rounded the corner, the scent of herbed vinegar and sugar hit me like brick.

Sweet sauce.

Shan stood on my landing with a toothpick hanging from his mouth. Next to him on the floor was a paper bag. Red oozed from the sack onto the floor like a puddle of blood. My breath caught in my throat as I stepped forward. He straightened slightly, adding a mango scent to the barbecue cloud filling the room. The peppermint was absent.

I tripped on one of the pumps I'd kicked off on the way down the hall. Jordan, barefoot and flushed from neck to brow, ran up behind me and, at the sight of Shan, he tripped over my ankle, going down, too—all six feet five inches of him. Most of that landed on me.

We looked like a very bad game of Twister, and I was definitely losing. I held up one hand. "I can explain. Just give me a chance." The words sounded eerily familiar.

Shan moved the toothpick from one side of his mouth to the other. "Some things don't require an explanation." His leather trench swept in an arc as he turned. "Oh, and next time, lock the door."

From: *monilovesjesus*
To: *thesassysistahood*
Subject: Intro

Hey, I'm Monica Sutton. Thanks Dana for inviting me (that candle is burning right beside me). And hi, Rochelle. I ordered some shoes from you last week. I don't know if you remember.

Anyway, sorry to jump right in, but I need some prayer, y'all. I hate it when women say they've found their husbands (I mean really, really hate it) but I guess it's my turn to join the club. He's a little stuck-up sometimes, but cute. One of our deacons. He does the weather too on channel seven? Anyway, he's the one. Y'all pray with me that God will let him know it.

Again, sorry for crashing the party. ☺

Moni Love

Though Jericho and Shemika almost bit their fingers off eating the barbecue they'd rescued upon returning home, I couldn't bear a single bite. Pepto-Bismol chewables and Moriah's infant Tylenol comprised my current menu. And a little toe-pioca, of course. I had so much foot in my mouth I couldn't get it all out if I tried.

And I did try.

Calls, e-mails, notes, flowers—I know he's a man, but everyone likes flowers—everything short of a sky writer, I tried it, including putting in a call to Shan's mother. As the phone rang the second time and she picked up with a sad hello, I held out hope.

"I don't know what you did, honey, but for now, just leave Shannon alone. Praying is all you can do. I've only seen him like this once."

Being the fool I am, I had to ask. "When he left Aida?"

Her answer floored me. "No. When she left him."

That threw a day's worth of antacids tumbling around in my belly. "I don't think I'm following."

She sniffed. "I'll say. For someone so smart, baby, you're awfully slow. But that's your mama's fault. Anyway, Shan was crazy for that girl, only she was just plain crazy. Slept with anything that moved. We tried to get him away from her, but he wouldn't come home. Not even when she got pregnant."

I dropped the shoe I was working on, Monica's pink ones, size eleven. The heel banged my own toe. "W-what? The baby isn't his?"

Running water sounded through the line. What was she cooking now? I wondered.

"Potato salad," she said, as if reading my mind. "The mustard kind. Now about that girl's baby—Lord no, that child isn't Shannon's. He acted like it was, went to every doctor's appointment, caught that child with his own bare hands…"

The room started to spin. He'd done more for a baby that wasn't his than Jordan had done for his own. We'd just left complicated and arrived at just plain crazy. And I wasn't enjoying the view. "And she wouldn't marry him."

"Nope. I've got the bad knees to prove it. I went to bed praying and woke up that way, too. It got so bad that Shannon's father said I'd be mumbling in my sleep, 'not her, Lord. A good thing. Please. Bring my boy a good thing.' I thought that was you. Time will tell."

My hands shook as I pierced Monica's shoe to attach a pom-pom. I should have stopped working, until this call was over, but if I stopped moving, I might faint. My cologne, Good Thing, the only thing I purchased from Dana on a regular basis, wafted up to mock me as I moved my arms. Miss Bett said time would tell, but something told me I didn't have time. "What should I do?"

She popped what sounded like the lid of a jar. Probably mayonnaise. "You have to ask Jesus about that, honey, but pray hard for sure." She lowered her voice. "Shannon hasn't slept here in three days. Pastor and some of the other men are here now, praying for him."

My fingers went numb. The past three nights I'd hardly slept. Every time I closed my eyes, there was my nightmare, Shan, spooning up sweet sauce…for Aida.

God, please.

"Sweetie, you there?"

I wasn't, really. "I'm here."

"Don't let this throw you, hear? The enemy is busy, but he loses in the end. Just keep your eye on that. Shannon's daddy tried to wander from me once or twice, but I prayed the man back every time. Sometimes, that's just what you have to do."

"Okay," I said mindlessly, trying to process her words. Shan carried a picture of his father in his wallet and every time he opened it to pay for something he paid his father a compliment. But the sentiment he always ended on, his mother had just affirmed. "Daddy was a good man…because he married a good woman."

I swallowed hard and said goodbye. Making the call at all had been a stretch. I barely had time to eat lunch. What had been a flurry of orders had become a steady stream. So much, in fact, that the other business owners around me were complaining about my customers taking up all the parking spaces. Though I tried to smooth things over, the notice about the rent almost doubling was the last straw. I didn't have a rich husband like Dana to buy my building. It was business as usual, me and Jesus. I wasn't sure how I'd swing it, but suddenly, moving my store was a real possibility.

I'd thought about it so many times that I had two fat files—downscale or expand. Even a month ago, the decision would have been simple. Err with caution and go smaller. But that was before I fell in love.

Now, something new drummed inside me.

Something big.

On the mall parking lot, an auto tune-up place had gone out of business. Today was their last day and both the owner and the mall were anxious to fill the spot. My mind couldn't think past the oil smell, but it hadn't stopped me from making an appointment with a Realtor and taking a look. Whether inside the mall or outside on the lot, the location was closer to my house, Jericho's school and Moriah's new day care, which in my efforts to avoid Jordan, I'd had yet to visit. His drop-offs ended on my porch as well.

Our last encounter had taught me just how vulnerable I was. It also reminded me that although Jordan was going to church, he still had little to no idea what this Christian thing was all about. And how could I fault him? It'd been ten years for me and I was still sorting things out.

Though my neglected nerve endings had done a happy dance in response to his touch, Jordan's interests in common with mine ended there, except for our son, of course.

Lovemaking was not what I needed right now. A mental game-show buzzer sounded in my head, signaling for me to try again. Okay, let me rephrase. That wasn't all I needed. Let's be real. It'd been eighteen plus years and I'd preheated my hormonal oven a little too much the past few months. Sistah girl was on full broil. But it was because of that long time of celibacy that I didn't want to blow this.

God had spent these years working on me and in me, preparing me for something wonderful, teaching me to love Him with no expectation of love from anyone else. He didn't bring me this far to have me answering booty calls again. If it was time for me to have a husband (and I could only hope so or I'd be in some serious trouble) then I wanted all of it— spirit, soul and body. The whole man.

The entire good thing, specifically the one currently absent from his own bed. Even Austin couldn't make me feel better about that one. There isn't that much mocha on earth.

And if for some reason I couldn't have Shan, then I'd sell an awful lot of shoes to distract me. From the look on the Realtor's face as he bounded in the door, it seemed as if I might get to do just that.

I craned my neck sideways. "Mr. Gold? I thought you were going to call."

He wiped his shoes, sedan-blue and well polished, on the

front mat. My chest hurt. Shan used to do that, too. Every-one else, including me lately, walked right over it.

The slight man pushed his glasses up on his nose. "I thought I'd be calling, too, but I had to come on over with the good news."

Good news? "I could certainly use some of that."

He nodded. "Well, this should definitely brighten your day. Remember your concerns about oil smell and the construc-tion costs?"

I nodded cautiously. "Yes."

The man's hands clapped together. "Well…the seller has agreed to rebuild it to retail specifications."

Blink. "For free?"

"Well, you'll have to buy the property, of course, but, no, you won't be responsible for any of the costs."

Double blink. Figures started floating in front of me. Sales-per-square foot. Franchise possibilities. Was this the break I'd been waiting so long for? Without the cost of the rebuild, the building was dirt cheap, in a great location and at 2500 square feet, the perfect size. If the expansion flopped, I could partition and rent the space to someone else. Maybe Dana. "Is there some kind of catch? Are there termites or some-thing?" I cleared my throat. I sounded like Shemika again.

He laughed. "Of course not. You've been all over the in-spection sheet yourself. In all my days as a Realtor, I've never seen a more thorough walk-through. If you ever get out of the shoe business, you should consider real estate."

I managed a smile. "I'll stick with shoes for now."

He looked around. "As well you should." His Adam's apple

bobbed in his throat. "Those pink ones there. Do you have those...in a six and a half?"

I tried not to laugh. These pom-pom slippers did that to people, men included. I walked him to the side table where they were stacked and picked out two, one orange and the other baby-blue. "Sorry about the colors, I can—"

He snatched the orange pair from my hands. "My wife will love these. How much?"

I shook my head. "Consider it a gift."

No sense in everybody being sad tonight.

If it weren't for the headlines, it wouldn't have been so bad.

Aida Home for Good?

I hoped not.

Supermodel Enrolls Son in Local Preschool

Why didn't that make me smile?

Local Architect Designing for Aida's Heart?

That one hit me the hardest, especially the picture—a side shot of Shan in dark shades, carrying Aida's son in one hand and his briefcase in the other. I needed a long session with Billy Blanks after that one. And a long talk with whatever lunatic kept taping those horrible articles to my door—my friends, of course, just trying to keep me informed. When you see a stack of unread papers in someone's recycling bin, do you think maybe they're not looking to be informed at the moment? I would. Maybe. Okay, so probably not...

Still, with friends like them, Aida was just a placeholder. No doubt, they thought they were doing me a favor, just as they thought taking me out tonight to celebrate the new store was going to make me feel better. Perhaps it would. Stranger things had happened.

They were all so excited about my new success. Why wasn't I? I had been at first, but since the ink had dried on the documents, I'd lost some of my enthusiasm. The dream I'd worked for—all through nights of design school, and the hours before hawking department-store shoes—had finally come true. Still, none of it excited me as much as the e-mail I'd found in my inbox yesterday. A poem.

> *Loveprints*
> *Your love beats against*
> *The shores of me, refusing*
> *To be washed away*
> *Your feet, covered before*
> *Run now, pacing across my*
> *Flesh, pressing into me with*
> *Brown strength, fresh holiness.*
> *In sleep, your heart pursues,*
> *Relentless, piercing howling lies*
> *And confusion. Then I awake*
> *And find you gone, sifting through*
> *My fingers like so much lost time.*
> *In your dreams, listen carefully.*
> *When the ocean stills, you'll hear me*
> *Chasing what's left of you and me,*
> *Swimming in living water, drowning*
> *In what could have been.*
> *Listen.*
> Shan

Already I'd memorized it, though I didn't like the ending. What could have been? That sounded too much like a discount greeting card. Did he not feel anything for me anymore? Love had been thrown about, but…it hurt my head to think about it.

So I didn't. I buttoned my best blouse instead, hoping March would choose today to go out like a lamb. Outside a man paused to brace himself against the wind. Nope, still a lion lurking out there. I went into my art closet and picked a scarf, fuchsia and gold to match my outfit. The paint I'd applied to the fabric three days before was dry to the touch. I swirled it around my neck, knowing the weather wouldn't stop the Sassy Sistahood. Once those girls put their minds to a thing, nothing could stop them.

And today, they'd put their minds to me.

I braved the weather and the drive to the restaurant, Abraham's, a new kosher place Austin chose. I parked next to Dana and slipped inside, turning against the wind as I walked. A deep breath prepared me for the next few hours of giddy girl talk. Most of my pep had left me weeks ago, but I'd get through this, probably end up having a good time.

Thank God for good friends.

Inside, the aroma of falafel and hummus, a scent often embedded in Austin's skin (along with Liz Claiborne perfume and peanut M&M's) met me in full force. The restaurant, a bustling café that contradicted its quiet exterior, teemed with people of every hue.

A woman in a violet-and-orange sari squeezed past me on her way to the bathroom. I tried not to stare and promised myself again that I'd get up the nerve to wear the one hidden in my closet. Some of the other secrets in there could use a good wearing, too. But that was for later. Today was about my sistahs.

With every waiter occupied—they all nodded in greeting, despite their arms full of food—I followed the wall into the next section, a quieter, but no less full room. Harp music laced with Hebrew praises echoed from a speaker above my head.

Someone behind me grabbed my hand. "There you are!"

My mouth opened wide. "Tracey! You drove all the way down for this?" I hugged her close. With her new baby and my mess, we didn't talk often and I missed my sweet, quiet friend. Her presence indicated she missed me as well.

Shifting baby Lily so she wouldn't be squished between us, Tracey hugged me back. "Of course I drove down. Wouldn't miss it for the world. I've been meaning to get here since Valentine's Day. We had those few short talks on the phone, but we need to really catch up." She winked and stepped aside.

A tear trailed my cheek. The first ten years after Jordan had left, I'd focused my life on raising my son and bringing women together, both on the Internet and in little get-togethers. The list had dwindled with the marriage explosion—followed quickly by the baby explosion—but now it seemed to be growing again.

Only Jesus had given me the faith to start the Sassy Sistahood, to belong to people and let them belong to me. And it was still hard for me, especially letting someone else do the leading, the loving. This year, I didn't have a choice.

"I'm so proud of you, girl." Dana hugged me and tucked a bag into my hand. Sure that it was candles or some of her Vanilla Smella lotion, I scooted into the booth and dumped the bag over into my lap.

A red satin nightie, two sizes smaller and shorter than the one abandoned in my closet, fell onto my skirt. I tapped one foot against the floor as my friends' laughter walled up around me, hedging me in. My mouth opened and closed once before I kicked Dana in her shin, though careful not to run her stockings. She'd get me for that.

She leaned her head onto my shoulder and twined her arms around my neck. "We figured you're making all these love shoes and everything, so you needed something to wear with them."

I fanned myself and turned to face the rest of the ladies—Austin, Monica, Renee, Dana's old assistant and part-time employee at her shop, who never posted, Tracey, Dana and even, Naomi, Dana's old boss, another lurker. I turned the bag over again and shook it. "You forgot the husband, didn't you?"

Dana tapped my shoulder, but I ignored her, holding the nightgown up to the light. The back cut down to the waist in a perfect V. The ladies, except for Austin, who was blushing like crazy, banged their plates with their silverware in homage to my gag gift. I shook my head, taking in the daring style. Who did they think I was, Aida?

Dana flicked me this time. "Chelle—"

Though not long ago, I would have been so embarrassed I might have burst into tears, I waved Dana off and shook the nightie extended from my fingertips. "I'd need two or three husbands to wear this mess. Hel-lo?" I raised my hand for a high five, but my once-cheering-but-now-horrified friends didn't lift a finger. Ever have that feeling that the bad guy is standing right behind you?

Hand still in the air, I turned slowly. But not slow enough. One by one, they slapped my palm. The hits, nothing more than a graze of flesh, stung my heart. Man hands, all three.

Tad.

Jordan.

And Shan.

The nightgown slipped from my fingers. Tad looked away. Jordan looked at Shan, who reached down, picked it up and dropped it into the bag Dana so graciously extended his way.

He pulled a toothpick from his pocket. "Hello, yourself, Rochelle. Good to see you."

Chapter fourteen

From: *shantheman*

To: *Sassysistah1*

Subject: Running into you

Hey,

I just want to apologize about the other afternoon. If we'd known that you were going to be there we would have gone somewhere else. And please don't be mad at Jericho. I saw your face when he walked in. With what I've been going through, I needed some men to talk to and since most of it concerned you, I chose the men I respect most, it just so happens that they just so happened to be your ex-boyfriends and your son. Funny, isn't it? Pastor Shields and my brother turn up sometimes, too.

Congrats about the store. Aida thinks it's going to be a smash. I hope so. You deserve it.

Peace,

Shan

www.keepersofthedoor.com
Men guarding their hearts through prayer

From: *pureTNT*
To: *thesassysistahood*
Subject: Room for one more?
Hi ladies,
Most of you know me. I'm Terri, Jordan Rose's girlfriend?
(Hi, Rochelle.) Well, we've decided not to live together until
after the wedding and I'm trying to get some understanding
on this Jesus thing. I can understand if the rest of you don't
want me here, but Austin said she thought it would be okay.
I hope so. I have a lot of photo shoots coming up, so I won't
be saying much, but if you let me stay, I'll be here reading.
    Terri

"So, let me get this straight. You, your dad and Deacon
McGovern have been meeting to pray every week?"

My son folded baby blankets from the laundry basket with
lightning speed, but not fast enough to escape me. "That
about sums it up."

It did not sum it up for me. I needed far more information. God only knows what those guys were saying about me.
Especially the big lug in front of me. "For how long?"

He cleared his throat, looking down the hall as if willing Moriah to wake up and save him. I blocked his view.
He walked around me. "For a while, Mom. After all that
stuff went down on Valentine's Day, I went and had lunch
with Shan—"

My knees buckled, but I managed to stand. "You did what?"

Attacking the towels now, my son shook his head. "It wasn't about you, Mom. Really. This whole marriage thing is harder than I thought and I needed to talk to somebody. I usually talk to Deacon McGovern but—"

So much for standing. "What?" The question escaped me as I landed on the couch atop a pile of baby T-shirts. He'd been talking to Tad, too? Lord have mercy. What next?

Jericho tugged the clothes from underneath me and checked his watch. "Look, Mom. I don't want to get into this. Just know that despite your thoughts to the contrary, this is not about you. These guys, the Keepers, are all men that I respect. They're also men who've made mistakes. Many of those mistakes just happened to be with you. I'm sorry about that, but if I'm going to make it, I need these guys. Now, I have to be at work soon and tutoring after that, so we'll have to cut this short."

Work? Tutoring? "Are you helping your dad recruit? And who is tutoring you?" With the new store and my fresh heartache, I'd only given Jericho's grades a cursory glance. I'd grown tired of trying to fight him and keep him straight. He was a man now, somebody's husband. I hated to do it, but I'd figured letting him crash on his own might be the best lesson. Only he wasn't crashing, he was flying.

With help from all the men I'd ever loved.

I picked up a washcloth and started folding.

Jericho did the same. "Dad wanted me to help him recruit, but I can't miss school to go on the road. Videos don't show everything. When a player catches my eye, I still give him the heads-up. My new job is at Destiny Design, in the copy room. Mr. Tad is helping me with my Algebra and SAT prep."

My hands stilled. How many times had I begged him to study for the SAT instead of trying to depend on his basketball skills to get him into college? My pleading had fallen on deaf ears. Coming from the Keepers of the Door, however, the same instructions seemed to have become divine wisdom.

With one eye on me, my son layered the clean clothes in the basket then smoothed a hand over his hair, freshly shorn and, by the look of his edge, low on his forehead and tapering to sideburns on each side, that too was some of Shan's handiwork. Wasn't it bad enough that he'd taken over my life? Did he have to take my kid, too? Well, what was left of him. Jericho had let go of me months ago.

Jericho's long arm reached out and pulled me to him. "Don't be like that, Mom. I know things are difficult right now. But if it makes you feel any better, it's hard on the fellas, too." He pulled back and gave me a crooked smile. "I never knew you were such a heartbreaker…" He let me go and ducked down the hall.

I threw an abandoned sock behind him. "Boy…" I said it in my play voice, but in truth, I wanted to chase my son down the hall and jump on his back, beat the truth out of him.

A heartbreaker? Me? What was that supposed to mean? Jordan had Terri, even if she had moved out. Tad had the girl from the TV station, plus Monica and well, himself. And Shan, from his last e-mail, he and Aida seemed thick as thieves. Since that day he'd walked in on Jordan and me, Shan acted as if anything between us was just a memory. But then he'd gone and started a prayer group with Jordan? How did that work? Why am I the one who gets punished and cast aside? Men. First to cast the stone and last to leave the table.

Jericho poked his head out of the linen closet. "Don't look like that, Mom. It's…complicated."

This time he didn't duck.

And I didn't miss.

A wadded-up dish towel, one of my best, cocked him right in the mouth.

And he laughed. "Nice aim. Work on that throw though. Kinda weak. I hear you're better at kicking." He took off into his room.

"You!" I slid down the hall in my socks, banging on his door and holding my stomach from laughing. I would wake up the baby, but I didn't care. "See, boy, you aren't right. Not at all—"

He laughed on the other side of the door. "Wait, Mom. Did you hear that? I think there's somebody at the door."

It was such a poor diversion tactic that I stopped to listen. Sure enough, the doorbell. I took the hall again in one slide and stormed the door, still full with the wildness Jericho had stirred in me. I hoped this wasn't a vacuum salesman. For his sake.

My eye pressed against the peephole. No salesman. A sistah. Just what I needed. My hands worked quickly, releasing the dead bolt and pulling back the door. Monica had never been to my place before, but she obviously knew where I lived.

She didn't waste a second coming inside. "Girl, girl, girl! I'm sorry for coming without calling, but I just had to tell somebody. I mean I had to. 'Cause I need to know that it's real and—"

"What? Slow down." I grabbed her shoulders. And I thought I was losing it. Monica was always sort of like this with that big, beautiful way she had about her, but this time she had me totally stumped.

She extended her left hand to clear things up. "I mean I knew God told me, you know. It's not like I doubted or anything, but I mean, I just, well I didn't think it'd be so fast."

Neither did I. The room that is. It was spinning for sure. The brilliance of the carat solitaire on Monica's fat, brown finger blurred into the background of my mind like a disco-ball. She reached out to steady me.

I held on. With both hands. "Th-that's from Tad? That ring? Right there?"

She dabbed her eyes. "Girl, yeah. That little tramp at his job was all over him see, but I wasn't studying that a bit. I just kept claiming that man every time I saw him, working hard right beside him and being myself. I had to call him for the singles group to schedule things and, finally, I just came out and asked him was he going to marry anybody or what."

The air in the room felt thin, like we'd suddenly changed climates. How many times had I wanted to ask Tad the same thing? Wasn't that off-limits? "But you're not supposed to ask a man things like that. You're supposed to—to wait and let them pursue you and all that." My Christan Woman's Etiquette was rusty, but that much I knew for sure.

Letting her left hand drape her side while I clung to her right, Monica pursed her lips. "That's why you still single, honey. Probably always will be. You let everyone else determine who you are. Getting saved didn't take away my personality, it just evened it out some. Still, I'm going to always be me and I have to know what I'm dealing with."

I stared at that ring again. Whatever she was dealing with, I wanted to be dealing with it, too. This was enough to make me straight sick. Wait until Dana, Austin and Tracey heard about it. This might require a conference call.

"So what did he say?"

Monica licked her lips, smearing her pink gloss. "Girl, he said he wanted to be married, but he was a little shy and the kind of woman he wanted to marry didn't always go for the quiet type."

My eyes urged her on.

"So I asked what kind of woman was that—the kind he wanted to marry…"

I pinched my eyes shut and let go of Monica's arm. This was too much, I tell you. Too much. I tried to get away, but her voice carried.

"He said he wanted a big-footed woman. Can you believe that? Mr. Harvard Grad talking like that? But that's just how he said it. Said he wanted somebody who knew how to be beautiful when needed, but knew how to get her hands— and her feet—dirty. Said if she did, he knew how to clean them up. Well, you know he didn't have to tell *me* twice."

One of my dining-room chairs screeched as I dragged it across the floor. The couch was closer, but that would have been too comfortable. I needed to be sitting straight up to hear this madness. "What then?"

"Humph. What then? Don't you know? That next Sunday after service when he was done counting the money and I was done washing dishes, well it was just he and I in the hallway—not that I cared who saw, mind you. I took off my shoes just as big as you please and showed him my feet, bunions and all—"

She started to kick out of them for me now so I could get the full effect, but I shook my head. The stretched leather humps protruding from her shoes told the story well enough.

"I asked him if these feet would work for him and he smiled, said they would do just fine. I took that as some hope for the future and just kept on doing what I've been doing since I came to the church, helping out wherever I could. We talked on the phone a lot. I even sent him some of those devotionals y'all send out. Told him he should start something like the sistahood for men. They need prayer, too, you know."

I stared down the hall, waiting for Jericho to scream amen, but no sound came from that direction except for the shower and later, the slamming of drawers and closets. Monica was right. Men needed prayer, too. Especially men who'd come in contact with me.

"It's probably my fault that they ended up at our restaurant, too. I told him about it, but I didn't think they'd come on the same day. I'm sorry about that, but who knows? Maybe you can still get your man back." She held up her ring to her face. "Nothing is impossible with God."

Especially if you've got the right claim ticket. Too bad I

didn't. It'd certainly be convenient. Still, she was right. God could do anything.

My son, smelling of the ocean and looking like a million bucks, entered the room. At the sight of Monica, he broke into a wide smile. He pointed to her finger. "Oh, snap. He gave it to you? Already?"

Monica nodded, her eyes filling with tears.

My son grabbed his keys and shook his head. "See, Mom, it's like you always told me. Prayer changes things."

From: *eventcoordinator@matchmadeinseven.com*
To: *Sassysistah1*
Subject: Your last meeting
Ms. Gardner,
Thank you for taking time to talk to us on the phone Tuesday. We do understand the pace of your new business, especially during the Easter/Advent season. We have, however, scheduled a group that we think is a great fit for you and request your presence at dinner at Abraham's the first Saturday evening in May at seven o'clock. Please give us one more chance to make your match!
Sincerely,
The Match Made in Seven Event Team

April rushed in, ripping the last shred of denial from my eyes—my new store was ready and my relationship over. May brought new truths to face—everybody was getting married and leaving me behind.

Even Tad.

When I'd nominated him and Monica to take over my spot with the singles group, Tad quickly shot that down. "Sorry, but I don't think we'll have time. The Married Fellowship has already extended us an invitation to join," he'd said, before whistling past me (yes, *whistling*) to his seat.

The newspapers and TV served me a steady diet of Shan and Aida's photo journal of their new life. Though Jericho assured me that Shan wasn't living there, the only confidence he'd broken from the Keepers of the Door. Still, something lived on between Shan and me. Something strong.

Even Jordan, who'd met with me for coffee to discuss Jericho's church wedding, seemed to think so. He started right in with the Shan business. "All I'm saying is why not come to the house and have some dinner. He's been over a few times now, just not with you."

Of course. He was with Aida. No doubt Terri was there, too, for old times' sake.

I sipped my white-chocolate latte, thinking of Austin's look of delight the last time she'd had one of these. We were at the Daily Grind, a café across from Dana and Adrian's shop, Made of Honor. Out the window and across the street, I could see Dana and Adrian moving around in their store, preparing to open. Though I'd done many of the same things last night before closing, my heart pined to get on the road toward my own store. I also knew that my two friends would be kissing any second—they always did—so I turned my head, staring at the coffee bean logo behind Jordan's head.

Daily Grind was right.

I couldn't have described today better. Even for a Saturday. "Jordan, thanks for the invitation, but I don't think so. I still care for Shan but—"

Jordan snorted into his soy latte. "*Care* for him? You two are crazy about each other. And I hate to think that I somehow came between the two of you. I'm really sorry about that whole thing, Rochelle. That day at your place. After this time studying with the guys, I realize how out-of-bounds that was."

I nodded. We'd never addressed that day directly in all our discussions about Jericho, but a layer of ice had definitely formed between Jordan and me. Maybe something like that was what it took to put our relationship back where it should be. Finally disconnected. "Jordan, I apologize, too. For the way I've acted since you came home. We're all making adjustments. As for Shan and I, I don't know. And besides, I have Jericho's wedding to get together still. That's what we're supposed to be talking about. It'd be a major squeeze, but there might be a spot on the church calendar this week…"

Jordan rubbed his hand across the ribs of his turtleneck. "About that. The wedding thing, I mean. You knew Terri moved out and everything. Well, I've really been praying with the guys about what to do."

I cleared my throat. Did I really want to hear this. "About what?"

He shrugged. "About Terri. About Jericho." He paused. "About you."

A gulp of chocolately stuff. Check of the watch. Eight-twenty. And I didn't open up shop until ten. Nowhere to run. "Me? I don't see what I have to do with anything."

He cleared his throat. "You have a lot to do—with everything. See, Terri was right. I really couldn't move on with her until I figured out my feelings for you—"

"You don't have to do this." In fact, I'd rather he didn't.

"But I do have to. And so do you. Even though that night at your place was out of order, it really showed me something about the nature of our relationship. Even in a moment of madness, all I could say was that I wanted to make love to you because I owed it to you. Ever since I got back here, I've been trying to atone for things I can't change, to exchange sacrifice for the obedience I neglected."

All I could do was nod.

"Only Jesus can make things right. And He already did. On the cross. I respect you, Rochelle, but I don't love you. Maybe I never did. Until lately, I didn't even know what love really was. Though Terri and I didn't start off right, I do love her. And if things are going to work between us, I need your support as the mother of my son."

My stomach clenched. The mother of his son. But Terri would be the mother of his sons. And Aida the mother of Shan's. Jordan was right. Jesus was the answer to all of this and I was going to have to lean on Him with all my strength. "You have my support, Jordan. I truly wish you both the best. And thank you for being honest with me. To tell the truth—" I leaned over a little and looked both ways. "I'm not sure if I ever loved you either. I loved a basketball star, a mythical superhero who was going to whisk me away to a castle where we'd live happily ever after. If nothing else, the time Shan and I were together taught that true love is pos-

sible…and what it feels like." Though I doubted I'd be trying to recreate that feeling any time soon.

Jordan nodded, then sighed with relief. "Right. Well, back
to Jericho's wedding. If it's all right with you, Terri and I
would like for Jericho and Shemika to be married with us—
a double ceremony."

My spoon clattered to the floor. "Are you serious?" I'd been
holding on to this wedding and its planning as the last special
time between Jericho and me, but in truth, I didn't have the
time or the energy to plan it. I waited for that jealous anger
to come, as it usually did when Jordan did things like this. Peace
lingered instead. Still, my mind stretched to grasp his meaning. "But Jordan, that's too soon to do both. There's no way…"

He smiled. "I'm totally serious and everything is taken care
of…if it's okay with you. All you have to do is show up. The
kids just didn't want to upset you. And neither did Terri. She
worked really hard on it, though."

I wiped away an unexpected tear and stared down at my
inky fingertips. So much for the waterproof mascara. "I'm
not upset at all. I'm grateful. Thank Terri for me, okay?"

Jordan stood and motioned behind him. "Thank her
yourself."

My neck jerked as I turned to see Terri in a pink pleated
skirt, sitting at the other end of the bar. She must have come
in after us. Though she tried to blend in, Terri was hard to
miss in any setting.

And so are you, Daughter.

One look at her face and I knew that Jordan hadn't only
shared our little "moment" in my apartment with his prayer

group. And all this time on the list, she'd never said a thing. Maybe that meant she saw it for what it was—nothing. Still, I felt bad. "Hey, I just wanted to say, I'm sorry. For everything."

Instead of the smirk I expected, Terri looked at me with downcast eyes. "Don't be sorry. For anything. Being on your list has made me understand a lot, about you, about Jordan, about Jesus. I'd been so concerned about *my* feelings that I didn't really think about what all this has been like for *you*. Forgive me for any disrespect on my part." Her manicured hand extended in front of me.

I grabbed her into an embrace instead. Many things to say crossed my mind, but only one word seemed appropriate. A word we all needed to hear. "Forgiven."

Chapter fifteen

Though I hadn't planned to attend, several evenings later I found myself taking the road to Abraham's again instead of heading for home. The e-mail had stated that this was to be my last group gathering for A Match Made in Seven. I didn't hold out hope for a match, but I wasn't ready to go home just yet, either.

My day's work had filled the cash register but left me feeling empty. Jordan and Jericho's announcement had arrived yesterday and the flurry of phone calls from questioning church members and friends left me too drained to go home. If I did, I'd have to face a harsh reality.

After the wedding, I'd be alone.

"We've loved staying with you, Mom, but after the wedding and my graduation, we're going to move in with Dad for the summer. It'll make it easier for us to work and give you a break."

He didn't say a break from what: babysitting, motherhood

or having a house full of people. Not that I minded any of it. The chaos had kept me sane in the hard times of the past few months, distracted me from my own loneliness. I tried to protest, but Jericho wouldn't hear of it. After tomorrow, I'd be alone, something that would have made me happy a year ago.

Now it only brought regrets.

Regrets I took with me to my last meal with the dating service. I had a good life—a job I loved, great kids, good friends and though a man might not be in my immediate future, I knew that I could still pull one. Though I wasn't sure I'd want to. All the men my age seemed to be allergic to children, afraid of commitment or otherwise insane and men Shan's age would want babies, something I couldn't give them. So, tonight would be my date with the One who'd always love me.

Jesus, my perfect match.

Inside the restaurant, I spied Katrina, Tad's friend from the TV station, piling tabouli onto her plate.

She waved, if you could call it that—her hand moved like it was broken. Her eyes looked a little glazed over. "Hey, good to see you again. I guess you've heard by now about Thaddeus?"

Thaddeus? It sounded strange to hear her call him that outside of church. "Tad? Yes, I've heard. Sorry about that." Considering the contents of my purse before strapping it over the back of one of the last seats at the table, I took a plate and joined her in line. Like the Ethiopian buffet, this Middle Eastern spread drew me in, mounds of grapes, hunks of bread, bright olives and tomatoes and the rich, smooth flavor filling the air. What it was exactly I wasn't sure, but it smelled good.

Katrina shrugged. "It's okay. When I started trying to analyze his every word it occurred to me that he wasn't that into me. I could have pushed things, but it would have been a project. And I'm too old for those."

I had to laugh at that. She looked twenty-eight at the most. A smile slid across my face. "Honey, you're never too old for love. Don't sweat it. Love God and love yourself. Love will find you."

As we returned to the table, she stared at me in amazement as though I'd said something quite profound. From the way her eyes darted right and left, I must have.

"Funny you would say that. God, I mean. My friend has been sending me e-mails from this list, the sassy sister-something. Heard of it?"

I tried not to choke.

My food slid down my throat without my tasting it. "Yes. I've heard of it. I'm even a member. You should join."

Oh, my. Now I was sounding like Dana and Austin. It always seemed weird to me to promote the list, because the women who needed to be there always seemed to find it—or find one of us.

"That's what my friend was saying. She's getting married tomorrow—"

"Terri?" With a mall and plenty of new construction, Leverhill had fooled me into thinking it was growing. It wasn't. The place was still just too small.

She paused to say hello to a man and woman seated across from us. First-timers, I could tell. All the veterans weren't even trying to date, they were just chatting with folks they'd met before. Maybe this was why I'd gone through all this, to meet Katrina.

"Not Terri. Shemika. She's a young mom who works at the shop where I get my body products. Tad told me about the place."

I smiled and took a deep breath. I'd told Shemika about the list months ago, but she never acted interested. With so many new members these days, I'd stopped noticing who was joining unless they introduced themselves. Wow. I'd have to take Shemika to lunch soon. "Shemika is my daughter-in-law. And Dana, who owns Made of Honor, is my best friend—well, one of them." The correction surprised me, but Austin had grown almost as close to me as Dana. In some ways, closer.

Katrina almost bounced in her seat. "Are you kidding? She's a beautiful girl. And so talented. When I go in the shop, I always look for the products with her initials. Dana's stuff is incredible, but Shemika puts a little twist on everything. She's amazing."

Was she? I'd never bothered to ask, except to make sure she'd attended her training sessions and made it to work on time. I hadn't asked anybody much of anything lately. Not about themselves anyway. It'd been all about me. "See, now you're telling me things that I don't know. I appreciate that. Come to the wedding tomorrow."

She looked confused. "I thought they were already married."

"They are, but tomorrow they're having a church ceremony—with my son's father and his fiancée. I'll e-mail you the details when I get home."

The chair next to me scraped back. "Can I come, too?"

I clawed the table as the scent of mangoes washed over me. "Shan?" My voice cracked.

His didn't. "The one and only."

You got that right.

Katrina shot up from her chair. "Yeah well, I'll see you tomorrow."

Still not able to look Shan in the eye, I glared at Katrina. "You don't have to—"

"It's fine." With that and a thumbs-up under her plate, she was gone.

And Shan was here. In all his fine glory and wearing the pair of Levi's I'd given him for our one-month anniversary. I looked down at my skirt, the one with the flirty, swaying hem. Hadn't he bought me this, too?

I tried to remember the instructions from the infant CPR card on Moriah's diaper bag.

Clear the airway.

Swallow.

Listen for breathing.

I hear it, but only his. Am I alive?

"It's really good to see you."

My mouth suddenly needed patting with the napkin on my lap. If only I could cover my whole head with it. "It's nice to see you, too. You look good. I see you kept the jeans."

He put his hand on mine. "Of course. They're a perfect fit."

Okay, it was bad enough he had me at first sight, but the smile that followed these words was enough to make my body want to have babies again. All I could do was smile back.

And agree. If those jeans did anything, they fit. I was about to pass out and the man was just sitting down. If he got up to fill his plate, I'd have to run for the door. His shirt, black silk and snug across his chest, didn't help things a bit.

Notice I didn't mention his touch. Let's just say that I wanted to shed the cardigan to my twinset with the quickness. Either I was having a hot flash or he was going to give me a heart attack. It was dangerous either way.

"Look. I came tonight because I wanted to have a good dinner and clear my head. When I saw your car in the lot, I was glad, really glad. The guys keep me up-to-date on things with you, but I really miss talking to you."

I pushed my plate away. "I miss it, too."

His coils, almost fully locked now and an inch or so longer than when he'd started them, made me want to grab his collar and kiss him. Instead, my eyes traveled over his face, inspecting his eyes for Aida and any light she might have placed there. "Do you love her?"

My heart almost exploded. I hadn't meant to say it, but I needed to know.

Shan threw his head back and laughed. The sound made me dizzy. I closed my eyes, committing it to memory.

He pulled his chair closer and took a drink of the water in front of him. "I see you haven't changed. Still right to the point. Do I love Aida? No. Does she love me? Yes."

I fumbled for my water. Why did Aida's loving him bother

me more than if he'd said he loved her? Maybe because then I could have accepted things as they were.

He lifted my other hand to his lips, kissed it and let it go. "No comments on that?"

"Everything doesn't require a response..." I managed.

"Or an explanation." We said the words together, but neither of us laughed.

He picked a grape from my plate...and my heart right out of my chest. "Maybe I need to rethink that saying. There is a time for explanations. Valentine's Day was one of those times. And I would have explained—when we were alone. I thought you knew me well enough, trusted me..."

Oh, this was getting bad. Like stomach-hurting-run-to-the-car bad. But I couldn't run. I'd done enough of that. "I did know you well enough. I didn't know me well enough. When Terri said those things about you, I was seventeen all over again, abandoned in a hospital bed. That's where trusting men had gotten me, Shan. I couldn't think any further than that."

He pulled me to him with a gentle crush, the kind that even makes people watching cry. If I'd been able to see through my own tears, maybe I might have checked for onlookers. But I couldn't. I didn't. I could barely breathe. My heart was breaking in a room full of people. And for once, I didn't care.

"Oh, Rochelle. I'm so sorry. Please forgive me. There just seemed to be something between you and Jordan and you never would tell me everything that happened between you—"

"You…didn't…ask." Breathing like a little kid after a good whipping, I could hardly get out the words.

He pulled my shoulders back and stared into my eyes with a look that shattered what remained of me. A look I'd longed to see in my mother's eyes and prayed to see in my husband's—a look of unconditional love.

"I didn't want to ask. It shouldn't have mattered. It would have come out in time, just like the stuff with Aida. I never should have followed you to the car or come to your place that night, either. I should have trusted you, trusted your love."

That pulled me up short. In all our time together, I'd never told Shan that I loved him. Until tonight, he hadn't told me. Still, I wasn't surprised when he said it. It had been understood.

He agreed. "You didn't have to say it, Chelle. I know when somebody loves me. It's more than flowers and dinners. It's risking, sacrificing, laying it down. We did that for each other."

Didn't we, though?

My mouth grew salty with tears. "You'd better go up and get something to eat before they take down the bar."

He shook his head. "What I'm hungry for they don't have up there."

I fanned myself with my napkin.

Shan laughed. "I'm not talking about that either, though you're looking mighty luscious in that skirt. I'm hungry for some resolution between us. And for some explanations. From both of us."

So was I.

And so we filled the air and our bellies with stories—our stories. For once, I told all of mine: my mother and her drinking, my father and his running. His dying. The comfort I'd sought with Jordan and his family and the sorrow it'd brought me after. I even pulled off my shoes when I got to the part about my pregnancy.

He reached out and grabbed my toes. "So that's it. I never could figure out what was up with the foot thing. When you kept talking about breaking your toes, I thought you were kidding. I'm glad you decided against that."

"For now. I'm wearing better shoes and doing exercises. We'll see." I slid my foot back into my shoe. And none too soon.

Still nodding for no reason in particular, Shan narrowed his eyes at me. "That was one of the first things I noticed about you."

Oh goodness. "My shoes?"

"Your feet. The cologne was first, of course. And that smile. But I liked that your feet looked sturdy—like my mama's. Like you could walk a long way, carry something. I admire how you do that. Carry Jesus to people. It's a gift."

We were quiet for a long time after that. Eventually, I started again, telling my tale. Shan leaned in so close, his hair brushed my cheek. When I got to the part about the emergency surgery after Jericho, Shan dropped to his knees in front of me.

A waiter stepped right over him and kept going, not dropping so much as an olive. This restaurant was so cool.

I reached down and touched his tear-soaked face. "It's okay, really. I—"

He shook his head, pinched his eyes shut. "It is not okay. Aida and her son, that was it, wasn't it? The baby thing. Oh, man." His voice, a hoarse whisper, told the truth better than I could tell it myself.

"Yes. Even though her baby isn't yours, you were born to be a father, Shan. And I'm sure that child is attached to you. You're the only father he knows."

As if he suddenly realized he was on his knees on the floor of a restaurant and crying no less, Shan pulled himself back into the chair and turned away from me. "That's the messed-up part. Aaron knows I'm not his dad, but I think he wishes I was. When I'm not around, she ignores the kid. It's hard."

My breathing slowed. How different could Jericho's life have been if he'd had a man like Shan in his life? And how miserable would a man like Shan be without a child? The answers to both questions stung me with a truth I'd known all along. Things could never work between us.

From the look on his Shan's face, he thought otherwise. "Maybe I could—we could—adopt him somehow." The fact that there was no "we" currently didn't seem to factor into this theory. But there was really. There had been something between us since that first day at the restaurant. Something we could build a life on. We both paused to acknowledge it.

No matter how indifferent Aida was toward her son, she loved Shan and the child was her only tie to him. She would never let him—or me—get off that easy. "Shan …"

He nodded. "I know. Not likely and I can accept that. God brought me to help Aaron at the beginning of his life. He can bring someone else, too. Jericho is like my son now. All of you are part of my family."

He laced his fingers between mine. "Especially you. I love you, Rochelle, and I want to you to be my wife. My sweet sauce. My good thing."

Lord, I love him so much, but…

My scalp suddenly felt itchy. "I—"

In the booth behind us, a baby cried out.

I slid my purse off the back of the chair. "I'm not ready, Shan. I don't know if I'll ever be."

He turned away. "You're ready. You just don't think I am. I can live without a baby, Rochelle. I can't live without you."

From: *Shalomsistah*
To: *Sassysistah1*
Subject: wedding/Shan
Hey!

I saw your post about Jericho's wedding. What a great idea. I can't make the ceremony, but I'll be at the reception.

I need to tell you something else. I probably shouldn't, but I feel I must. Here's a clip from this morning's society page:

Word has it that supermodel Aida has asked local architect Shannon Inman to marry her. Sources close to the couple say that they could wed as soon as next week, when Aida will be on location in Italy for her first film.

Though Inman declined all questions pertaining to Aida, when asked if his custom design of the mall's new shoe store reflected his feelings for the store's owner and his former girlfriend Rochelle Gardner, he had this to say: "If the shoe fits…"

If the shoe fits.

It did fit and it fit well. I'd spent all night tossing and turning, thinking through what Shan had said to me, what he'd meant to me. I'd even called him and talked further. Being faithful to who he was, Shan put the ball in my court. "I proposed last night. I'm going to keep this ring I bought in my pocket. When you're ready, you let me know. As for the children issue, I always wanted to adopt anyway. My concern was that I'd fall in love with someone who wouldn't want to. Trust me, Rochelle. I've thought this through."

We talked more about his architectural firm and how he'd founded it. How he worked at Ujaama for a college friend whenever they needed help. Usually, I interrogated everyone around me, but for some reason, Shan and I had been content to know the basics. We talked into the wee hours learning more.

That he'd been the one who'd designed my new shop blew me away. It'd been so perfect. Too perfect. How could I have missed Shan's hand in the special touches in my store? From the vaulted ceiling and hanging chandeliers that I'd pointed out to him in a magazine to the children's play area and accessory corner he'd often heard me wish for, everything was there.

Everything but him.

He'd recently acquired the building and was looking to sell it when the Realtor explained about my wanting to buy it. Though we'd been estranged, he still wanted to bless me. And he had. Now it was my turn.

"Mom, have you seen my cummerbund?" Pain knifed

through me as my son ran from room to room trying to get his things together. Morning had long since come and gone and today was the big day, not that you could tell it to look at me, still in my pajamas. Normally, I would have been running, too, probably even yelling a little. But not today. My body stuck to the couch like glue, even when he ran past me out of breath, holding his kente cummerbund over his head in victory.

"Found it," he said. "When I was in Aunt Tracey's wedding and didn't care, I had everything in place. Now, it's like I'm losing my head."

I feel you.

"Sorry, honey. Let me get up and help you—"

"No. Don't, Mom. I'm going to clear out. The guys are going to help me get ready."

Why didn't that make me feel better?

"Okay. What about Shemika?"

"She's at her grandmother's with Moriah. The women from the church are on the case. We've got it covered. Seriously. I told them that you're weren't to do anything but show up and look pretty." He made a little face. "You might need a little nap for the look-pretty part. What happened, you fall out of the bed last night? On your head?"

Jericho ducked, but I didn't throw any pillows this time. He was right. I looked pretty bad. But I felt wonderful. Last night, talking to Katrina, I'd realized what a great life I had and that being alone wasn't a bad thing. In those moments, I'd looked forward to getting to know my "amazing" daughter-in-law and watch my granddaughter grow. As quickly as I'd embraced that thought with contentment, love had come back to me, called to me. Even now, I could hear it calling to me, sparking down my arms and legs into my house slippers.

I'd carried a lot of burdens in my time. Tired feet. Guilty feet. Even beautiful feet, according to Tad. But cold feet wasn't a mantle I was willing to carry any longer. God had brought me something special and there was no way to get ready for it. I smiled at my son. "I had a late night."

He picked up his shoes and put them in the chair next to me. "So I heard."

I closed my eyes. Would I ever get used to all these guys being friends? "He called you?"

My son waved his arms. "Did he call me? Oh, yeah. It's a wonder I don't look like you. Y'all have no respect. People can't even get married around here without drama, drama, drama."

I had to laugh then. "Shut up, boy. You are the one who started the drama, having babies and such. He shouldn't have called you, but I'm glad he did."

Jericho's face lost its humor. "I'm glad he did, too. Look, I know there's a lot more going on than what I know about, but don't be stupid, Mom. You can be a lot of things, but dumb you've never been. Now's not the time to start. The guy loves you…and he loves me, too. I know I'm not six years old or anything, but I'd be honored to have him be my father."

My son's face came into focus as his words registered in my mind. This wasn't the kid I'd known last year. Before me now stood a man. A man I was very proud of. "You've got your dad, honey."

He hung his socks over the back of the chair. "Right, I've got Dad. He's a good friend. Now I need a father. Shan is that for me. And he will be, whether you marry him or not. So I say, why torture yourself? Get the goods, too." That sent him racing down the hall with his hands over his head. I didn't bother to give chase or throw any more pillows. If someone had shocked me with a stun gun it might not have moved me.

The only thing keeping me from Shan was my own silly fears and not wanting to deny him the chance to be a father. How could I have missed that my son meant as much to him as Aida's, perhaps even as much to him as his own child. Hadn't he always called Moriah "our baby," too?

"So you and Shan are that tight, huh? What happened to you and brother Tad?"

Jericho shrugged. "Nothing. He's cool. Deep. A little too deep. I wouldn't feel comfortable talking to him about what I talk to Shan about. Don't sleep on Shan though. That brother knows the Word, too. He just comes to me on another level."

Tell me about it.

A horn blared from the street. "That's them," he said without checking. I, of course, jumped up to check all his stuff.

He tucked his shoes, socks and cummerbund into his suit bag and tossed it over his shoulder. "Don't worry, Mom. I've got everything. Mr. Tad will make sure I'm on point. Shan, too. And don't worry, I'll make sure he's not seated near you at the reception."

Shan at the wedding. Why hadn't I considered that until now? "He's coming?"

Jericho jumped over the landing and headed for the door. "Of course. This double-wedding thing was his idea in the first place. Don't worry. Take a nap and be pretty. She might be a supermodel, but you're prettier to hear them tell it. You're my mom so…"

"I know. That's weird. Thanks for the compliment. I think."

As the door slammed, a plan came to me, one that would require all my courage. All my love. I walked into my bedroom and set the alarm, preparing for the nap my son had suggested. I had a long afternoon ahead of me and I wouldn't be able to pull it off if I wasn't fresh.

Before turning back the covers, I walked to my closet and lifted the lid on the footlocker that contained my shoes. The pair I needed, made by my own hands and never worn, were at the very bottom. A few minutes of work unearthed the brown kraft box with two words scrawled on the top in my own hand.

Beautiful feet.

I could still hear Tad's voice that long-ago Sunday morning as I whispered the words to myself, then pulled off the top and pulled out the shoes—a multicolored pair of strappies, color blocked in purple and lime. I'd made those shoes for a day like today, one when Jordan's marriage would bring me joy, one when I could release my son to adulthood and one when I'd find myself ready for love seemed unthinkable.

Now it was time. Though in the past year I'd lost my son, I'd gained myself. It was time for all of us to grow up and get real, myself included. I didn't want a deacon or a basketball star. And though singleness had served me well for a very long time, I couldn't hide behind that anymore, either. What God had for me smelled of peppermint, mangoes and mechanical pencils. My good thing had sweet sauce on his fingers.

And supermodel or no, I meant to have him. I might not have three weeks to brew herb vinegar, but I had three hours—long enough to stir up *my* good stuff. My hands ran across a lime sari with the tag still on it. Amita, one of my Indian customers, had noticed me admiring the vibrant colors and generous fabric of her native clothing and gifted me with a sari of my own. Still not brave enough for the traditional short top, I'd go for a long silk shell tucked into the drawstring slip she'd given me. The shoes, held alongside, made a perfect match. All I needed was one more thing…

Across the room it hung, over the makeshift art station where I painted my scarves. Gold veined between the purple and lime blocks, stamped so meticulously last night during my bout of insomnia. Had I been planning for this in my subconcious all along? Trying to analyze Shan was hard enough. I'd leave that one for Austin. I walked to the scarf and touched a bright green square with my fingernail. Almost dry. By the time I woke up, it'd be good to go.

And go, I would.

There was just one more thing to do. My feet traveled quickly to the refrigerator, where a quick search yielded the prize I desired.

A bottle of olive oil. Extra virgin.

With a smile, I placed it on the counter and opened the

curtains so the sun could filter through it. By the time I woke up, it'd be warm to the touch…and ready for action.

When Jordan said they'd take care of things at the church, he meant it. I saw the flowers from a block away. They'd even paid off the surrounding neighbors to use their driveways and backyards for parking. I drove right up to the church as I was instructed and one of Jordan's NBA players, a kid not much older than Jericho, helped me from the car and took my keys.

He covered his mouth as he did so. "Are you getting married, too?"

"I hope so." I meant it, too. I pushed my hatbox purse up onto my wrist. On another day, the compliment would have stopped me, for a second or two at least. Today, the words didn't even break my stride.

In his own quiet way, Shan had told the world he loved me, by designing my store, through his response in that interview. If I was to have any chance with him, I'd have to show the world that I loved him, too. And I'd make it loud and clear.

The sea of churchgoers and long-lost cousins in front of me parted when I didn't slow down.

Their murmurs echoed behind me.

"Those shoes are bad enough to kill somebody."

"And that outfit? Why on earth would Jordan marry that tramp? Chelle has always kept herself up."

"She needs to get with youngblood. That other girl might model, but that sistah is doing damage today. Trust me on it. Trust. Me."

I almost stopped to nod on that one, but I didn't dare. Shan was never late to anything and the music was already playing. Putting on my game face and warming up my oil had taken a little longer than I'd anticipated. But it I was here now and that's all that mattered.

Inside the church, I slowed my steps, gripping the trellis of roses, each one pinker than the last. Smoothing the silk fabric pinned over my shoulder, I entered the double doors and spied Shan's growing locks on the second pew from the front. Aida turned first, latching her hands onto his forearm in a protective gesture.

Shan turned next and met my eyes. I moved faster then, passing Dana's outstretched hand without slapping it. I paused to take in Austin's approving eyes. She'd made it, after all. Short of my place on the front row, I stopped and turned to face Shan, waiting for him in the aisle. He stood slowly, shaking Miss Model's arm from his.

"Shan. Sit down," Aida said, loud enough for all to hear.

He climbed over Mother Holloway's cane. "Aida, you sit down. My wife is calling me…"

The pianist hit the wrong note. The sanctuary, one I'd entered in my choir robe on so many Sundays, fell silent. As he stepped into the aisle in front of me, I almost lost my nerve.

"Do it," a quiet voice said behind me.

Tad's voice. He sat at the end of the pew in front of us.

He was right. This was no time to be afraid, even with all eyes on us. Still, it didn't make me any less nervous…or less determined.

With trembling hands, I took the bottle of oil from my purse. I'd prepared something to say, but this was one more time with Shan when explanation wasn't needed. Shan leaned in closer, offering his freshly twisted locks.

The air echoed when I cracked the seal on the bottle before pouring a thin stream of oil onto his head.

"More," he said softly, head still bowed. "I want all of it."

Somebody, a deaconess I think, shoved a pile of baptismal towels under Shan's head and rubbed my back. I poured a little more, still trying not to make a mess of the church aisle. When I hesitated, he started unbuckling my shoes. I tipped the bottle forward until oil ribboned onto his collar, down his arms…

And into my shoes.

"That's it, sis. Do it right. None of that dabbing business. I've been meeting with that brother once a week to get ready for this. We'll clean the carpet later." My pastor, who'd entered without my knowledge, both startled me and put me at ease.

Terri, who should have been upset because we'd hijacked her wedding, agreed from the doorway where she was stalled. "Amen to that. I'll clean the carpet myself."

"I choose you, Shannon Inman," I said, as the oil oozed between my toes. "I choose you as my husband. For always."

Shan lifted his head. Oil trickled down his cheek. I smiled and mopped his brow with a towel, wondering who had cleaned up after Samuel anointed David. Surely there was more oil in that prophet's horn than in my little bottle, but this amount was just right. It was a beautiful mess, just like the both of us. "I choose you, Rochelle Gardner, as my wife, my mate, my partner."

My shoes were in his hand. To the tune of the crowd's applause, he lifted me off my feet and started for the door, pausing to speak to the pastor. "I would ask you if there was room up there for two more, but I'm not going to grease up your altar."

Pastor raised a hand. "Hold up now, don't let a little anointing oil trip you up. Sounds like y'all just did my job anyway. Go downstairs and grab a couple choir robes if you want, but I'd love to marry y'all."

Mother Holloway handed me a handkerchief. Deacon Rivers, being his spry self, sprinted downstairs for the choir robes, though our clothes were long past saving. I wiped at Shan's forehead as he walked toward the front of the church. The pianist, who'd long since stopped playing, started up "Here Comes the Bride." The crowd turned toward Terri in all her pinkness.

Shan's eyes stayed fixed on me as I slid back to the ground and knelt to put on my shoes. My feet squished right into them.

After fastening the second clasp, he stood and took my hand, touched my scarf. "I hope those shoes aren't ruined," he whispered.

I laughed, still out of breath and watching Terri's surprised smile as she joined us at the altar. "Forget the shoes," I whispered back. "I'll make another pair."

Shan squeezed my hand. "No, I'm going to save those. On our fiftieth anniversary, you're going to dance in them. I'll bring the oil."

QUESTIONS FOR DISCUSSION

1. As the book opens, Rochelle has a fit when Tad sees her feet. Do you have something about you (physically, emotionally or otherwise) that you try to hide? Have you ever had someone try to uncover it? How did you react?

2. Though Rochelle and Dana have been best friends for years, the transitions of their lives leave Rochelle to depend on a new girlfriend, Austin. Have you ever met someone and become fast friends with her? Or disliked someone at first who later became very close to you?

3. Jordan did some pretty hurtful things to Rochelle, but now he's trying to learn to live for Christ. Has someone who hurt you ever come back and asked for forgiveness? How did Rochelle handle Jordan? What could she have done differently?

4. Tad, Jordan, Shan and Jericho end up starting a prayer group together, The Keepers of the Door. How do you think this had an impact on each of their lives? How did it affect Rochelle's life? Do you have a group of friends that you pray with routinely? How has it affected your family?

5. Rochelle spends a lot of time thinking about the past with both Jordan and Tad. In the end, God gives her a new partner, a younger man she'd never met before. Have you ever had to let go of the past to receive a blessing from God? Did Rochelle make the right decision?

6. Rochelle's relationships with men haven't always been the best. She's used to taking care of herself and expecting to be let down by the guys around her. How does her perception of the men in her life—Jericho, Tad, Jordan and Shan—change through the story?

7. Though Rochelle makes wonderful, beautiful shoes with classic designs, it is the thrown-together pom-pom slippers that give her the boost she needs to move to a bigger store. Have you ever done something out of love and obedience, only to have God turn it into something bigger? How did you react?

8. Throughout the story Rochelle struggles with finding time to exercise and stay on her eating program. Still, she makes time to do workout videos and maintain her health even during a stressful time. When you are stressed, what are the first good habits to go? What are some ways to maintain health during a crisis?

9. Rochelle not only makes shoes, she also paints scarves and dabbles in interior decorating. Though now is the time God chooses to bring her a mate, she's spent the past seventeen years dedicated to the Lord, the church and many other creative interests. How important is it to learn new things and have creative outlets? Name one thing you're committed to learning more about or trying this year.

10. The verse at the front of this book is from Romans 10:15: "How beautiful are the feet of those who bring good news!" Though Rochelle helps other women look beautiful, she often sees her life like her feet—lumpy and broken. When Tad calls her feet beautiful, she's angry, not understanding that it is her ability to bring people to Jesus and her servant's heart that makes her (and her feet) beautiful. Have you ever truly seen your beauty through the eyes of God? Go in prayer and ask God to help you see yourself as He does.

Once, twice, ten times a bridesmaid!

Made of Honor

On sale January 2006

Dana Rose has a closetful of unflattering bridesmaid's dresses and a whole lot of stress! Between an ex who married someone else and opened a shop right across from her, and an unwelcome visit from her siblings, Dana has had it up to here. At least she's got the Sassy Sistahood to help her along.

Steeple
Hill®

Visit your local bookseller.

SHMG554TR